BABY
DUST

DEANNA ROY

casey shay press

BABY DUST

This is a work of fiction. All of the characters, organizations,
and events portrayed in this novel are either products of the
author's imagination or used fictitiously.

Casey Shay Press
PO Box 160116
Austin, TX 78716
www.caseyshaypress.com

ISBN 13: 978-0-9841-8792-8
ISBN 10: 0-9841879-2-8

Library of Congress Control Number: 2011906820

FOR MY ANGEL BABIES

Casey Shay
(December 1997 to April 1998 gestation)

Daniel
(June to July 2001 gestation)

Emma Hope
(August to October 2001 gestation)

ACKNOWLEDGEMENTS

The number of women who contributed their stories to me to help other grieving women is staggering. The online community at my website www.pregnancyloss.info truly shaped this book based on the things they wished they had known when they went through their losses. We wanted to help others feel less crazy, less afraid, and less alone. I could not have done this book without their insights, revelations, and willingness to say publicly what some people would hide.

At the same time, no single woman is truly represented in this story. Bits and pieces were sewn together, embroidered, and sometimes created purely from imagination. Because so many of our stories are similar, these women's tales will ring familiar to hundreds or thousands of others, some of whom may have posted to my website during the book's creation. But those who contributed know who they are—we talked about their stories over many months as I outlined the novel, and they knew some element of their personal experience would be included here. Take comfort when you read a story that sounds like yours that you indeed are not alone in the events you had to endure.

On the authorly side, I appreciate so much my beta readers and critique groups: Novel in Progress and the Austin Java Writing Company. This is tough material. You all did great. Several literary agents (they know who they are!) made amazing comments that helped this book grow and mature. I often feel the only credit I can take for the book is the typing!

I also wanted to mention my own doctors, perinatologist Dr. David Berry and obstetrician Dr. Marco Uribe, who were both supportive and so often answered questions about pregnancy conditions that were obviously not mine. And I can't forget the nurses: Kim, Michelle, and Julie. Unlike some of the women in this book, and many women out in the world, I was treated with absolute kindness and care. I was blessed.

PART ONE: *Melinda*

1

RAPUNZEL

The radishes called to her. Despite the hour and the warmth of her husband asleep beside her, Melinda slid from the covers, her bare feet arching against the cold floor.

She hurried down the stairs of the silent house, her lace nightgown billowing around her legs, and padded into the kitchen. The refrigerator's searing light forced her eyes closed, but she could not bear to hesitate and reached blindly into the vegetable bin.

Her fingers fumbled with lettuce, cucumbers, and finally, the radishes. Despite her mother's voice scolding her to wash them first, she crunched into an icy bulb. Her teeth throbbed, but the peppery bite eased her desperation to eat. She leaned against the counter, sated, running one hand over her stomach.

Ten weeks along and still no belly bump. Probably a good thing. Her Aunt Bea waited until thirty-five to have a baby too, ending up wider than the door of her travel trailer. Melinda had a closet full of custom-tailored suits to return to. Eventually.

"Quitter," she muttered. She'd been unemployed for six months and still hadn't stopped chastising herself for going domestic. She'd been out-argued, hoodwinked into stay-at-home-wifely submission by the lead attorney for Lindeman, Crum, and Finch. Her husband.

She tugged another radish from the stem, ignoring the dirt that clung to its wiry root.

Folic acid, a friend had told her. That's why she craved them so much. Melinda was glad for the reason, as ever since the need hit her, all she could think of was Rapunzel's father stealing radishes in the enchanted garden, and the deal he had struck to give up his first-born child to spare him punishment.

That man should have called her husband.

The third radish burned in her mouth, so she filled a glass with filtered water. Melinda glanced around the kitchen as she gulped. Only the scraggly vegetables broke the perfection of the sweeping marble countertops and inlaid tile, the gleam just visible in the light from the hall.

The cleanliness wasn't her doing. She had more help than a Louisiana plantation. Her mother would have had a conniption, never putting any stock in some other woman swiping your toilet. Melinda had no such prejudice. Too bad Mom died well before the onset of Jake. She would have thought he was a movie star.

Ajax whined from the utility room, so Melinda popped open the door to release the chocolate lab. "Hey puppy dog, love muffin."

His dark nose sniffed at her hands.

"Midnight snack for you too? Let me find some biscuits." She opened the cabinet beneath the sink and bent down to locate the box.

A strange pop low in her abdomen made her double over and clutch her stomach. A cramp began, like a fist in her belly, starting small and tight but rapidly rippling out. Her breathing shifted to huffs, like labor. Before she could consider what might be happening, fluid gushed between her legs, soaking her panties. Melinda froze, afraid to make it worse, trying to calm her breath wheezing in and out.

Ajax whined again, rubbing his nose on her thigh. Melinda grasped the hem of her nightgown and pressed the white lace between her legs.

Even in the dim light she could see it soak scarlet. The baby. God, the baby.

She walked in mincing steps across the floor toward the bathroom. A wet drop hit her ankle and she looked behind to see a red trail from the cabinet to her feet. She leaned against the wall, shivering and gasping to breathe.

Pull yourself together. Melinda reached for the phone to call an ambulance, her doctor, someone, then set it down again. Jake first. She could scream, perhaps, make enough noise to wake him upstairs. He was such a heavy sleeper.

Only one thing would get her husband up during the few hours he slept each night. She snatched her purse from the counter and tugged out her cell phone. She sent a text message to his work line, a ring tone he always answered unless he was in court. Her Hail Mary, one she never used. "Come downstairs. Emergency."

She heard his feet fall on the floor above, then his frantic steps crossed the room and down the stairs.

"What the hell?" Jake stumbled into the kitchen and stared at her as she leaned over the counter. Then he saw the floor, his eyes following the smear of blood on the tile. He flipped on the light.

Melinda could not meet his eyes. The chandelier blinded her, the room swirling white and hot.

He bent near her in his pajama bottoms, his bare chest tan and smooth. "Mel?"

"The baby," she said. "I lost the baby."

He picked her up, cradling her against his body, and carried her upstairs, away from the blood. "Let's get you changed and go to the hospital," he said. "They can do something."

Melinda could have argued with him, as she had read that first trimester miscarriages could not be saved. But she knew Jake, and he needed reliable testimony, expert witnesses, hard facts. They stopped in the bathroom, and he brought her a clean nightgown and panties. She searched through the cabinets for pads and cleaned herself, the bleeding now slowed to a trickle. Ajax had followed them, sitting quietly by the door, his pink tongue lolling out.

For once, Jake ignored her dog. "Ready?" he asked, handing her a blue pea coat. "Can you walk?"

Her arm caught inside the sleeve, and Jake tenderly tugged it on. "Would you rather have an ambulance?"

She shook her head for no, not trusting her voice. It seemed too much, the sirens, the uniformed paramedics. The baby, she knew, was gone.

They drove silently through their neighborhood, past mansions and perfect lawns, until he entered the freeway. "You going to tell me what happened now?" Headlights flashed into his face, chiseling his features with hard edges.

"I felt a pop, and the bleeding started."

"What were you doing in the kitchen?" Jake zipped across the freeway to the far left lane despite the lack of traffic. "Eating?"

Melinda gripped the door handle. "Yes, I wanted some radishes."

"And it just happened like that—pop."

"I was getting a dog biscuit."

"Did that dog jump on you? Jump on your belly?"

Melinda watched the signs whiz by. *Hospital, next right.* He was going to miss it. "That wouldn't hurt anything."

"You don't know that. Something caused this." He jerked the steering wheel to cut across lanes, just making the exit.

Her fingers tightened on the handle. "Not everything has to have a reason, Jake. Some things just happen."

"Not in my world."

"Then welcome to mine. Dead mom. Dead dad. Dead baby."

They coasted to the light. As the car idled in the red glow, Jake laid his hand on her arm. "Baby, I'm sorry. Let's see what the doctors say."

The bright cross marking the hospital beckoned across the intersection. Jake pulled into an emergency slot and pressed his palm to Melinda's back as he escorted her inside. "Sit here and rest." He directed her to an empty section of blue plastic chairs. "I'll check you in."

Melinda watched Jake stride to the large white desk, disconnected, as if he were some other man, and this was some other place. The cuffs of the coat scratched her bare wrists, so she pulled her hands up inside, shivering despite the wafts of heat coming from the ceiling. A dozen people waited in the long room, scattered among the seats lining the walls.

Jake returned to sit beside her. He crossed a foot over his knee and balanced the clipboard on his ankle. "I can't fill this out—date of last period and all that." He passed the paperwork to her and leaned forward, bracing on his elbows.

She stared at the words and lines, trying to decipher the questions. Date of birth. Allergies. Medical conditions.

Jake began tapping his leg with his thumb, a nervous habit he usually kept tightly controlled. Melinda hoped they would be called back soon, for his sake. She kept her head down, focusing on the white paper and its small checkboxes.

The nurse called for a mother carrying a sleeping child.

Jake stood. "What's the freaking holdup?" He strode back to the white desk and leaned on his arm, flashing a bright smile at the woman seated there. Melinda closed her eyes again, torn between chagrin and pride. Jake could get the job done. He always did.

Her eyes flew open when a hand cupped her knee. She felt a wave of embarrassment now at her nightgown covered in the blue coat. Everyone else in the waiting room was dressed despite the hour. Jake squatted beside her, taking her hand, eyes beaming concern. "They should call you soon. I explained things."

Melinda nodded, and the clipboard slid to the floor.

"Here, baby, let me get that." He scooped up the paperwork and stood, tapping the flat acrylic against his hip.

"Melinda Carmichael?" The nurse in scrubs standing by the entrance to the examining rooms looked right at her.

"Now that's more like it," Jake said, again touching the small of her back as the frosted doors hissed open.

The nurse slid back a section of blue curtain on a track and patted the examining table. "Up here."

Jake stood in the corner, his hands stuffed in the pockets of his jeans. He had ruffled his hair several times, and now the front section stood straight up like an exclamation.

The nurse asked about the amount of blood, and if she were cramping anymore. Melinda shook her head no.

"See?" Jake said when the woman left. "No indication whatsoever that this is the end. They can probably give you something, and it will all be fine."

Melinda could have told him that she just knew, some intuition, some internal warning system had sent out a flare, but he would not listen. "If you can't prove it, it ain't so," he liked to say both in court and out, paired with a thermonuclear smile and an almost-but-not-quite wink.

The curtain slipped aside, and a young doctor entered. "I'm Dr. Blais." He flipped through the chart. "Let's take a look. Have you had a sonogram yet?"

"Last week," Melinda said. "He measured out perfectly. Good solid heartbeat."

Jake stepped nearer to the table. "Any explanation for the bleeding and cramping? Does this happen often?"

Dr. Blais picked up the ultrasound wand. "About forty percent of all pregnancies have some sort of bleeding. Only ten percent of pregnancies miscarry overall. The odds are with you, especially at this point."

Jake turned back to Melinda, one eyebrow cocked.

The doctor sat by the sonogram machine and squeezed lubricant on the probe. "We'll do a transvaginal ultrasound, probably just like you had last week."

"I'm bleeding, though," she said.

"It's okay. It won't affect the image."

Melinda lay back and fitted her heels in the stirrups. Dr. Blais did not turn the machine's screen to them as her obstetrician had. The sound was on, however, its crackle and static puncturing the quiet.

The whomp whomp of a heartbeat filled the room, but before Melinda could relax, Dr. Blais said, "That's mom's heartbeat. A little fast at ninety but still nowhere near baby's speed."

He pushed the probe more firmly against her and she felt the pressure, the hardness of it. Her fists clenched until she couldn't feel her fingers. Jake's shoes scraped across the floor as he paced.

The pulse sounds skipped a beat as Dr. Blais shifted the probe. "I can see the sac and the baby now," he said. "I'm going to take some measurements."

He already knows. Melinda felt her heart race and waited for the echo of the machine to relay her anger to the men. He obviously wanted to hold off telling her the baby's fate until he'd done whatever the hell he was doing. Her pulse sped up another notch.

Their curtained space fell silent as he switched off the sound. Beeps and coughs and lowered voices penetrated from other parts of the ward. He grimaced as he worked, finally pulling away and switching off the machine. Melinda's face grew hot to the point of abject discomfort. *Just say it!*

He tugged off his gloves. "The baby doesn't have a heartbeat. It's measuring nine weeks now, so I am guessing it died shortly after your last doctor visit."

Melinda shot forward as if pulled up by a string. "I knew it."

"I'm very sorry." His mouth was set tight, firmly in a line, and his concern didn't meet his expression. He saw worse every day, she thought. This is small to him.

Jake waved his hands beside his temples. "Now, wait. Are you sure about this? What sort of equipment does this hospital carry?"

The doctor tossed the gloves into a lined can. "Good enough for this. With the combination of symptoms your wife is experiencing, it's really just a confirmation."

Jake turned to Melinda. "Did you strain yourself? Work on the baby's room?"

Melinda steeled herself with calm. "No, Jake."

Dr. Blais stepped forward. "Mr. Carmichael, your wife didn't do anything wrong. Most likely this was a genetic loss, something formed incorrectly inside the baby, and it just stopped growing. Sad and unfortunate, but common."

Jake turned to the doctor. "I already have two kids. We didn't have any problems."

Melinda gripped the paper cover of the examining table until it tore. "Stop it! Stop it now! You're acting like I caused this to happen!"

The ward silenced. She felt a small cramp and a gush of fluid or blood or maybe just the lubricant from the probe. She curled over her belly.

"Ms. Carmichael, are you okay?" The doctor bent over and touched her arm.

His eyes had softened. He'd lost his professional detachment.

She nodded.

He squeezed her lightly, then turned and picked up the clipboard. "You can call your regular doctor for a D&C if you don't want to wait it out."

"How long?"

"Could be today. Could be two weeks or more. Here's a prescription for some pain medication in case the cramps get very bad. Would you like something to help you sleep?"

"No, she doesn't," Jake said. "None of that."

Dr. Blais tore the paper off the pad and handed it to Melinda. "It's the Ambien. You can fill both or just one."

Melinda tucked the paper inside the sleeve of her nightgown. "What do I do if the baby comes out? Do I need to save it?"

"You can if you want—put it in a plastic bag and refrigerate it until you can take it to your doctor. But you don't need to. First miscarriages aren't generally tested and usually get contaminated at home."

The two men stared at each other, then at her, certainly picturing the grim scene to come. The doctor nodded, then rolled open the curtain and left her alone with her husband.

Melinda stood, holding the white liner in place until she could reach her underwear. Jake paced the length of the curtain.

Outside the room, Melinda halted, not sure where to go in the endless line of blue fabric on silver tracks. There seemed no escape.

A few feet away, a young man whipped open a curtain and dashed out. A teen girl, partially covered in a blue sheet, lay on the table, a machine strapped to her belly. Small feet sheathed in rainbow stockings peeked out the end. She was crying.

Jake came up behind her. "Is she pregnant? She can't be sixteen."

Melinda turned away, disarmed by the proximity of another pregnant person, the heartbeat on the machine, and the striped stockings. A nurse approached her, closing the open curtain as she walked by. "Ms. Carmichael? Here's some information for you. Instructions and a flier for the pregnancy loss support group the hospital recommends."

Melinda accepted the paper. "Thank you."

She glanced back at the examining table where she'd just been, empty and rumpled but otherwise unchanged by what had occurred there.

"The exit's over here," Jake said. "We should go." He strode away, strong and tall, glancing at the people he passed with curiosity and disdain.

What have I done? Who have I married? She struggled to keep up with him, each rapid step prompting another sticky gush from her body. The first crisis of their marriage, and he was failing miserably, unaware that he was losing her, rousing in her an anger she had forgotten she possessed. She was worth more than this.

Another cramp tightened in her abdomen. She froze, hand pressed to her belly, and decided *screw him*, and this time continued down the corridor at her own pace.

2

TRIPS

Jake came home from work the next day in good spirits, whistling as he pulled the duffel bag out of the closet. "Don't worry," he said as she watched. "I'll pack my own things."

Unbelievable. Clients expected them to attend a weekend at someone's lake house. Melinda pushed aside the pillow at the head of the bed and eased herself down. "I don't think I should go."

Jake set down the bag and rushed to her side, his expression changing instantly. Melinda prickled with apprehension. Emotional quick change, Jake's specialty.

He took her hand. "I could never leave you in this condition."

"So we'll cancel."

"Are you bleeding still? In pain?"

He wanted evidence, a compelling case file. The flow had slowed to a trickle, hardly worth the industrial-sized pads she'd stuffed into her underwear, but she didn't have to tell him that. "Yes, and yes."

He lifted her hand to his lips and held it there. "Patricia and Mike have been planning this weekend for months. It's crucial to the firm."

"So go."

"Not without you." He touched the tip of her nose then slid his fingertips across her cheek. "I'd be the odd man out."

Melinda closed her eyes to his disarming face, the absolute sincerity in his expression. He'd been so kind all day, checking up on her repeatedly. He had even called their part-time housekeeper over to deal with the blood. Melinda had planned to take care of it herself. Upon Connie's arrival, she'd madly scrubbed at the floor with wet paper towels, unable to stomach the idea that someone else would clean up the detritus of her body's betrayal.

But Connie had been patient, taking the towels from her and sending her back to bed. The maid had lost two babies herself, she'd said, shooing away any condolences with a wave. Melinda ascended the stairs, shamed that her miscarriage should be so public, and disheartened to think that she was not unique, even in her grief.

"Melinda?" His breath warmed the back of her hand.

She pulled away from him. "I'm not up for it, Jake."

"What will be different here than there? We could take your mind off it."

"I don't know what to expect. Things could happen. Hideous things that I can't deal with in front of pretend friends."

Jake jumped up then, lifted his briefcase to the bed, and tugged a sheaf of papers from the side pocket. "I had Mary get three doctors' assessment of your case. They all felt it would be a simple recovery."

God, he'd involved his assistant. "Jake…"

"I also spent my own lunch printing out instructions. You can read them in the car."

Melinda accepted the collection of printouts, almost wishing for the blood to flow so hard and so fast that it would soak her clothes. She'd known what she was getting into, marrying a high-powered lawyer with a staff of thirty and a penchant for obscene devotion to work. When she, too, had been an attorney, the mere idea of siding against Jake had scared her.

At her silence, Jake strode into the closet. He rummaged around, returning with a stack of clothes. Melinda frowned at the expensive leather bag. Such excess. Duffels should be nylon, with funny colors and industrial-strength handles. Everything about her life was out of sync with reality.

"I'll choose clothes for you." This was his concession to her condition, packing for her.

Melinda sat up. "I'll get my own things." She'd already chosen her outfits, yesterday, before the night of blood, the hospital, and the fear. But the pants were pale and might show any accidents. She entered the closet and pulled black ones instead. She'd wear all black, actually, despite the onset of spring. This was her only form of protest.

In the car, gliding through the neighborhood of gated lots and old money, Melinda realized she could have simply refused. Jake would not have picked her up and hauled her forcibly to the car. But she hadn't. She'd acquiesced, another of a thousand such acts of deference in their three years of marriage. How she wished for her father, his tender care, and his gentle manner when she was stricken by life's impossibilities. "You're too much like me," he'd always warned her. "Life would be so much easier if you were made of steel."

She'd married it instead.

Twilight had just tinged the sky a deep blue when they pulled up before a modern split-level near the outskirts of Houston. Malibu lights lined the walkway, revealing the pinks and reds of azaleas. Twenty grand in landscaping alone, Melinda figured. Probably what her parents had paid for the double-wide where she'd grown up.

"I don't see why they live in such rubble," Jake said, nudging a burned-out bulb with his foot. "He makes plenty."

Patricia opened the front door, her body in shadow in the backlight. "We're late," she called. "We need to get on the road."

Melinda took only a few steps when she felt another pop, a gush of fluid. She accepted a hug from Patricia, calculating how many pads she'd packed, and whether they'd get her through the weekend if the bleeding got bad. She shouldn't go. She should stop it right now. But Patricia didn't even know about the pregnancy. Melinda couldn't find the words to tell both things at once. She hadn't, she realized, even said the words aloud.

Mike stood just inside the door, a pile of bags at his feet. He had dressed near identically to Jake, his knit shirt too perfect to be casual, stretching easily across a well-honed chest. Patricia flicked her hair behind her shoulder and took his arm. They were magazine worthy, like all of Jake's acquaintances.

Melinda felt a second gush and panic bolted through her. "I need a quick stop in the bathroom."

"Just down this hall," Patricia said.

The bathroom walls were striped with salmon pink and powder blue, like a nursery. Melinda pulled down her black pants, grimacing at the blood in the pad. Nothing crazy, but enough to make the drive risky if she didn't change.

She fumbled through her purse, extracting another pillowed liner. She held it a moment, the heat of the row of bulbs above the sink warming her. She wished she could get out of this. She barely knew these people. No one should go through this surrounded by strangers.

A cramp seized her, much like the night before, rippling inside her abdomen. More blood trickled out in a thin stream, then stopped. The pain intensified, and Melinda found she was huffing, like movie actors in labor. She had never given birth and wasn't sure what a contraction felt like, but this had to be it.

She stifled the urge to call out as something opened up inside, like a potato coming out from between her legs. She reached for it, but found it was not that large at all, more peanut-sized. She clasped it in her hand, trying to avoid spilling any blood, and rested it on the pad.

Terror rose in her as she lifted the pad closer to the light. She couldn't stand up with the blood trickling down, but the searing light showed the baby, coiled on its pink bed like a small shrimp. It had eyes on either side of its hammer-like head and an engorged chest like a bubble.

Melinda touched it, carefully, fearing it would disintegrate beneath her fingers. But the baby was solid, all tissue and cartilage.

A knock on the door startled her so shockingly that she almost dropped the pad. "Melinda?" Jake asked. "You coming?"

She choked back an outcry, swallowed, and waveringly said, "Just a minute."

She heard his footsteps trail away and looked again at the baby—her baby—so small and perfectly formed. "I don't know what to do with you," she whispered and folded the pad in on itself. The trash can was empty, so she tugged out the liner and wrapped it securely around the pad, knotting the end. Like Connie, Patricia's maid kept a spare bag at the bottom, so Melinda pulled it out and relined the can, carefully placing the tied-up sack at the bottom.

A shadow appeared beneath the door. "You okay, honey?" Patricia called.

"Yes," Melinda squeaked, rapidly grabbing another pad to replace the soaked one.

As she washed her hands, Melinda stared into the trash bag, wondering if she should take it with her. What would Jake do if he found it?

Instead, she smoothed her hair and wiped away a smear of damp mascara on her cheek. She had no choice but to just keep going.

3

VISIONS

Jake slung the leather duffel jovially across his back as he led her through the garage. Melinda followed, relieved the trip was over, glad to have only endured a weekend sitting in a cottage by the lake, drinking wine, half-listening to conversation. It could have been much worse, a New York jaunt, or some crowded beach. Jake hadn't pushed her to go boating, and the quiet afternoons alone on the porch of Patricia's time-share had actually helped. Jake had been right to make her go. He was almost always right. It's what made his court record so impressive.

During the quietest moments, out on the dock in an Adirondack chair, she often closed her eyes and concentrated on her baby, cocooned in the white cotton, tied in a bag at a stranger's house. Patricia's maid came daily, Melinda had learned, so he had probably already been moved to a bin, cold in the chilly spring nights.

She shivered as Jake popped open the utility room door. Ajax beelined for her, nuzzling against her knees. She knelt to pet him. "Did Connie take good care of you?" The dog burrowed into her belly as though they had been long apart.

"Spoils him," Jake said, setting the bag on the washing machine. "At least he knows not to piss on any furniture, or I'd turn him out."

Melinda hugged the dog and whispered, "He'll do no such thing," into his furry muff. Jake's dislike of Ajax had been a thorn in the bramble of their marriage from the start. She had lost her dad only a month after their honeymoon, and Ajax had been his dog. Her father, in the last stages of pancreatic cancer, barely managed to walk her down the aisle.

"I'm going to check email," Jake said and strode away from her into the house.

Melinda walked with Ajax through the utility room and rounded the counter to the kitchen.

Then stifled a scream.

A trail of blood led from her feet to the sink, smudged with footprints and impressions of Ajax's paws.

Melinda collapsed to her knees, her hand covering her mouth. She'd cleaned this blood herself, and Connie had mopped and bleached.

Ajax whined, sliding his head into the crook of her arm. She covered her eyes. It wasn't real. She knew it wasn't real.

She could picture the trash bag and a pad, a baby surrounded by a chorion of pink. She wrapped her arms around Ajax and looked at the floor again. The blood remained.

She blinked, stared, and this time the footprints went away, then returned, as if the ghost of them were imprinted on the tile. Finally she reached down to touch it, to see if the vision would become wet on her fingers, but as she grazed the cold floor, it dissolved away, leaving only gleaming white squares.

"What's happening to me, Ajax?" She curled her hand into her chest. She couldn't stay on the floor. Jake might come back at any moment. He was on the computer, so she couldn't search for information, and if so, what would she type into the box? "Hallucinations"? "Post-traumatic stress"?

She stood and leaned against the counter, the rounded edge pressing against her empty belly. The paperwork from the hospital still lay in a neat pile, waiting for Jake to enter the charges into their accounts.

She shuffled through the stack, remembering the pink slip the nurse had handed her in the end. A support group.

She found it, a half-sheet with the name of a group and when it met. Six p.m. on Sundays at a church not too far away. She glanced at the clock. 5:45. She could make it. She thrust the paper into her bag and hurried to the study.

Jake sat in his enormous black leather chair, scrolling through messages.

"I'm going to stop at the store," Melinda said. "Be back in a bit."

He spun to face her. "Great. I'm glad to see you coming back around." He cocked a smile at her, the disarming one, an expression he used like a weapon. "You did great this weekend. Held up like a champ."

She nodded and turned away. He wouldn't like that she was heading to a support group. She passed back through the kitchen, the floor mercifully blank, and led Ajax into the utility room. "I'll be back soon," she whispered. "Don't bark and anger Jake." With a hug, she closed him in.

She took the Volvo instead of the showy Lexus and drove across town, hoping somebody, anybody, could help her.

4

CONFESSIONS

The red numbers of the clock read 6:04, but Melinda sat in her car. The meeting would be long, might run her a risk with Jake, and probably wouldn't even help. She couldn't imagine, now faced with the imposing entrance to the church, that she could go inside and confess the blood hallucination on the floor.

She should head to the epicurean market and buy some exotic vegetable for dinner. White asparagus perhaps, its pale fingers always reminding her of a slender phallus. "Skinny cocks," her friend Lailani had said when Melinda served them, "No use sugar-coating what they look like."

Lailani made Jake seethe, but she was Melinda's oldest friend, sharp and funny and uncouth.

"You won't talk that way when the children come tomorrow," Jake warned, pointing a silver fork at her.

Lailani aimed her fork right back at him. "You need to chill the hell out."

The Night of the Asparagus had been the last straw for Jake, and when Lailani had stabbed the asparagus and said, "Not sure this place needs any more dick," he'd left the table.

Melinda should call her. Lailani would help, make light of the hallucination, commiserate over the loss, get her drunk, and regale her with reveries of their mutual coming-of-age, when the two of them ruled their small-town Texas high school. Melinda was smart; Lailani was loud. Both wanted to get the hell out of there. Melinda had made it. Lailani's dreams had been deferred by pregnancy, a shotgun marriage at twenty, then a poker-hot divorce by age thirty. But she would make the drive from Odessa, where she owned a bar, to see her.

6:06. A car pulled up beside her. A slender black woman with perfect posture and a tailored Oscar de la Renta suit emerged, smoothing the navy skirt along her hips before she crossed the median. She looked completely together, an elegant chignon, crisp bag, sharp shoes, heading down the walkway in a clipped business-like walk.

Melinda slipped her key back into the ignition. When the woman entered the building, she'd start her car and go. No way could she admit anything before someone so poised, handling her loss without any outward sign.

But the woman paused before the door and bent her head. She seemed to collapse inwardly against the wall, a terrible shudder rippling through her body.

Melinda leapt from her car, her heels sinking into the damp grass as she rushed forward.

The woman popped her head up, startled. Melinda plunged on anyway. "Are you okay?" She stopped a few feet away, about to reach out, but clasped her bag instead. "I didn't mean to frighten you."

"You didn't. It's all right. I just have to compose myself each time." She pulled away from the wall, again smoothing her skirt. "Are you here for the miscarriage group?"

Melinda considered a lie so that she might escape, but instead, she simply said, "Yes."

"I'm Janet." The woman extended a hand, petite and angular, skin over bird bones.

"Melinda." Their grip was tight, smooth, firm, like two professionals.

"We should go in," Janet said.

"We are late." Melinda tugged on the cold iron handle.

"Oh no," Janet said. "Stella never starts on time."

The room was dim, overwarm, and stuffy, with lingering incense. Melinda stifled a sneeze.

A broad woman in a floral dress pushed two chairs into a small circle at the back of the chapel.

"That's Stella," Janet said, then called out, "We have a new one. This is Melinda."

Stella crossed the room with a gentle waddle. Melinda fixed a smile, already calculating minutes, worrying about a cross-examination by Jake.

"So glad you came." Stella clasped Melinda's hand between hers, warm and maternal.

Two other women already sat in chairs. One sat hunched over, crying, thin blond hair falling in her face. Stella turned and patted her sympathetically. "This is Raven. Just found out yesterday. Still waiting for…"

There weren't words. Melinda remembered the contractions, the pain, the potato feeling. She wanted to run, hurtle out the door, unable to face more loss, a story that might be worse than hers. Raven's tears made her feel stoic and cold. She had not cried herself, a self indulgence that never garnered sympathy from Jake.

"Look at your aunts," he'd whispered at her father's funeral, tilting his head toward her the middle-aged sisters, dressed in pale gray. "They're holding themselves together very well."

She would rather have been slapped. She had been sobbing into her handkerchief—her father's handkerchief—his initials faded and worn, embroidered by her mother a decade before. Melinda had her own handkerchief that read, "My miracle child," but she had never been able to bring herself to use it, the violet letters still vivid against the white.

She no longer cried, not even in private. The tears had evaporated in the glare of Jake's derision, and she no longer had the energy for both grieving and managing his moods.

"Melinda?" Stella had apparently been calling her name. The other women were seated now. She slid into a chair between Janet and a woman in sweats, this one leaning forward with her head down, hands in a death grip on an oversized silver cross hanging from her neck.

Stella opened a book. "I always begin with a reading, some inspiration to help us focus." She lifted eyeglasses from a gold chain and perched them on her nose, instantly aging ten years.

"Women are the conduit through which each successive generation learns patience, peace, and the receiving of joy." Stella read in a glossy monotone, smooth and rounded, like a verbal sedative. Melinda settled in.

She glanced at the others in the circle. Janet, sitting primly, knees together, ankles crossed. Raven, her sobbing abated, dabbing at her mascara smears with a soggy tissue. And crucifix woman, scraggly hair covering her face, sneakers hooked over the rail of her chair.

Stella droned on, but Melinda no longer heard the words. She imagined now these women's bellies and their shrimp babies, attached to the walls of their pink uterine balloons. They clung, swinging, then fell away, down into the bottom of the chamber to be squeezed out. She flooded with nausea, staring at the image of infant Jesus, lying on his mother's lap, holy beams coming from his head, and tried to picture him as a fetus, curled onto white linen, tied into a bag, then winging through the air toward an industrial sized garbage pail, dull green and marked "refuse."

"I threw my baby in the trash!" The words reverberated on the walls, skittering through the ceiling fans.

Stella closed her book. "It's okay. Just tell us what happened."

Melinda's panic whistled in her ears. "I had already started bleeding. Already went to the ER. They said it would come. I knew it would. I went over to my friend's house because we were going away for the weekend. We were all ready to drive down to the coast. I went to the bathroom…" Her stomach lurched so she bent over, arms crossed over her middle.

"Hang in there," Stella said. "Take your time."

She couldn't think. *Just talk, just talk. Don't think.* "The baby came out! I didn't know what to do! We were about to leave! I just put the baby in a plastic bag and left it in the trash!"

Her voice had reached a terrible pitch, almost a shriek, something she could not recognize as her own. "All I think about, all day long, all night, where is the baby? Is he still in her trash? In a dumpster? Will he get crushed in a garbage truck?"

She almost sobbed but stifled it. Stella walked over and knelt clumsily beside her chair. "It's all right. It's okay to worry about this. It's okay to think about it day and night."

Melinda accepted the hand Stella offered and squeezed it tight, too tight, but Stella did not flinch.

Crucifix woman sat up and cleared her throat. "I keep my baby's placenta in the freezer."

Everyone turned to her.

"I do." She pushed her hair back. "I don't think you're crazy. I often take it out and hold it. I keep it buried underneath a bag of peas."

"I plan to bury the baby in the back yard," Raven said. "I won't let her become medical waste in some hospital bag. I don't think you're crazy either."

Melinda loosened her grip on Stella. She was normal. This craziness was normal. "I'm having hallucinations. I keep seeing the blood on the floor."

Stella released Melinda, seamlessly passing her a tissue. "It's been mentioned before. Some things that happen to us leave a mark. It will get better. You won't always see the blood."

Melinda gripped the tissue. "I feel so out of control."

Stella settled back on her chair. "It's that way. Especially if you don't have good support at home."

Melinda clutched the tissue. "I have stepchildren. My husband blames me for the loss, since his ex-wife didn't have problems."

"We all need to feel control," Stella said. "Blame means that there was a reason, a cause and effect. But loss isn't like that. It's random, striking unevenly among all types of people."

Melinda clenched her jaw. It all has happened before, many times, to so many people. It was ordinary. She'd never known something so terrible could be ordinary.

"None of us are crazy," Stella said. "We're just surviving."

"I don't feel like I'm surviving," Raven said. "I feel like I'm drowning."

Melinda remembered suddenly a poem she'd read in college, "Not Waving, but Drowning." She understood exactly what that boy had felt—waving his arms because he was drowning, but no one understood. They just waved back.

Stella took off her glasses and laid them against her ample bosom. "That's why we're here. We live among those who cannot understand what we've been through, and this is the place you can say your piece without judgment or fear." She held the eyes of each woman in turn. "You're a survivor. Each one of you. And survivors don't have the luxury of acting like regular people. We do what we have to do to get by."

Melinda relaxed against the chair. She'd get through this. Knowing she wasn't any crazier than anyone else did help. But she knew the blood would remain on her floor until she undid her mistake.

She had to get her baby back.

5

REUNIONS

Melinda drove through the quiet streets of Patricia's neighborhood, hands tight on the steering wheel. She glanced at the clock. 7:30. She was stretching beyond credulity the time she might have spent shopping. She'd have to formulate a story for Jake, air tight. Corroborated, if possible.

Later.

She turned off the main street and pulled up several blocks before the cul de sac. Some of the families had already put their big green trash carts at the end of their driveways, preparing for the next day's pickup. Patricia had not.

She slipped from behind the wheel and jogged lightly down the street despite the high-heeled boots. She didn't care how crazy it seemed. She had to do it. Her baby would not get collected with this week's garbage.

She glanced up and down the sidewalk before cutting across the lawn to Patricia's back yard, praying it would be there and not in the garage. She wouldn't know how to get to it then, but she was not above breaking and entering.

The latch to the back gate stuck for a moment and she tugged wildly at it, snapping two fingernails. It finally worked free, and she inched it open. The squeak didn't penetrate far, so she eased through and crept across the lawn.

She should have brought a flashlight. The backyard was dark, protected from the street lamps by the house. Only a glow from the television in one of the rooms reached out into the yard. She'd never be able to see into the trash bin.

It had been two days since she had put the baby in the bag. No telling how much trash might be piled on top. She thought she would recognize the feel of the sack, the looped tie on top. She'd find it. She had to. She'd knock on the door and confess before she'd walk away without him.

The rolling garbage can sat next to the back door, like a guard post. Melinda crept up to it, intent on the goal.

The lid came up easily, resting against the brick wall with a light *thunk*. The can was tall, up to her chest, and she had to reach far down inside it to touch the pile.

She found one handle, tugged on it, and a large kitchen sack lifted free. She set it on the grass and reached again. Another large kitchen bag. She smelled orange peels and stale beer. Nothing she couldn't handle. Two bottles clinked as she set the second bag down, but the sound again was light, nothing that could be heard inside.

Now she couldn't reach. The rest was too far down. With a grunt, she grabbed the edge of the can and pulled it over.

The rest of the sacks tumbled out, white against the dark dead grass. Two large ones and then, there it was, one small sack. She snatched it and held it close. The contents gave a little as she squeezed it, so she took more care. She had him. Finally. She had him.

She set the baby aside and struggled to right the trashcan, quickly dropping the kitchen bags back in. She had just reached for the lid when the lock on the back door, not three feet away, began to turn.

Melinda snatched her bag and dashed toward the gate, but it was too far to risk. Light poured out onto the porch as Mike stepped out, cigarette in hand.

She dove behind the brick barbeque pit. The rattle of the bag seemed like fireworks popping in the stillness.

She tried to sit and calm her breathing, but with every sound, she flinched. Surely he had seen or heard her and would come to investigate.

A dog barked a few doors down. A dull thud piqued her curiosity too hard so she crawled to the corner of the pit and peered at the back door. Mike had closed the trash lid. "Pat? You leave this open?" he called into the house.

No answer. He shrugged and tossed the cigarette out into the lawn. He rolled the bin across the yard and through the gate, swallowed up by the dark. The cold seeped into Melinda's knees through her thin trousers. She'd be a mess when she got home, late and rumpled. Jake would think she was having an affair. Let him.

After a moment, Mike strolled back through the gate, whistling. He paused by a garden hose, loose and snaking across the dead lawn. He picked up one end as though he might roll it up, but a stream of water came out the end, wetting his shirt. "Damn it!" he shouted and dropped the hose.

The door still stood open, a hot rectangle of light illuminating the porch and a swath of yellow grass. Patricia's silhouette appeared. "You all right?"

Mike kicked the hose aside. "Yeah. Just wet."

Melinda settled back against the bricks. *Just go in. Let me escape.* Jake would interrogate her, no doubt. Maybe she should just never go home. Get a job again and be independent. Avoid the thought of having babies. Or failing at it.

The door closed, and Melinda peered around the corner again. The yard was dark. She scurried to her feet and raced through the gate. Time to get home.

During the drive, she wondered what to do with the baby. She could put it in the freezer, like that one woman had. Thank God for the group! But Jake might find it. He'd flip. No way.

She parked the car in the garage and wrapped the sack in her jacket. Jake was leaning against the cabinet in the kitchen, fixing himself a sandwich. "I gave up on you," he said. He glanced at her empty hands then resumed tugging meat from a butcher wrap. "Things in the car?"

Melinda realized with a panic that she hadn't done any sort of shopping, and that most things had been closed the whole time, after six on a

Sunday. Only grocery stores and restaurants would have been open, and she had no alibi.

"I got sidetracked."

The knife froze in the mustard jar. He didn't look at her but she could feel the machinations of his mind, turning over possibilities, considering angles, whether she might crack in cross-examination. His first wife had cheated on him. He caught her but didn't let on, gathering evidence, and prevented her from running away with his house and assets in the divorce. "Some sidetrack."

"I met Lailani. To talk about the baby." She'd say no more, letting it be understood that he wouldn't have wanted to see her friend or listen to their talk, but knowing mainly she didn't want to say something she couldn't prove later.

"She came all this way?"

"She was already in town."

He took a bite and chewed slowly, watching her. Melinda flashed a quick smile, then moved passed him toward the stairs, clutching her jacket to her belly.

Jake didn't press or follow her, so she bolted up to the second floor, dashing into the extra bathroom between the guest room and the nursery.

She unwrapped the sack and worked the tie loose. Would he come look for her in here? Maybe she should wait until he went to work.

But she didn't want to wait. She needed to see it. Friday seemed a lifetime ago.

She tugged the bag open and her stomach immediately lurched. A soup of thick blood with a watery tinge coated the plastic. She sat on the floor, unable to keep her legs stable, pulling the sack down with her.

She waited a moment or two to collect herself, letting her fingers test the thickness of the pad. She felt the heaviness of the lump of tissue and unfolded the pad with trembling hands. God, she'd have to be careful.

The smell of decay made her choke a moment. She'd rinse him off in the sink. Then she could see him.

She stood again, holding the bag out in front of her. Separated from the blood, it looked puffy, spongelike and small, less than two inches long. She turned on the water and rinsed away the strings of black, and then she could make out the fetus, miniscule and curled up, two dots for eyes.

She cleaned it all carefully and laid it on a hand towel. She folded the white cotton awkwardly around the tiny figure, then undid it again. "I'm sorry, baby. I don't know how to swaddle." She tried again, pulling up the bottom and sides, then rolling him in like a burrito. "That's better."

One part of her knew this was crazy. But most of her didn't care. She had her baby back. He was real. Not an idea, a hope, or even a conglomeration of white specs in a sonogram. Real flesh. Real blood. Eyes even. She left the bathroom for the nursery.

"Here's your room, baby boy," she said, even though there was no way to know if the baby was male or female. She knew. Mothers always knew.

She hadn't done much to the room yet, although they'd painted the walls a soft yellow and pulled her old wicker bassinet from the attic.

She laid the bundle in the small bed. The women in the group said nothing was crazy. She was fine. Just fine.

"I've got you," she said. "I'll never let you go."

6

BAGGAGE

Melinda sliced the potato in wild whacks, lifting the butcher knife high overhead and slamming it down against the marble cutting board. The effort felt good, so she raised the knife again, not even fearing the safety of her other hand as the metal whizzed through the air and connected with the vegetable. Ajax pressed his head against her thigh, whining lightly, as if he wished she wouldn't be so upset while holding cutlery.

Jake opened the door leading to the garage and passed through, blowing into his palms. "Chilly for this time of year," he said.

"Easter is a ways off still," Melinda said, slicing calmly now that she had an audience.

"I know where I can warm my hands," he said, coming up behind her and sliding his palms across her belly.

Melinda stiffened but disguised it with another hard cut against the board. "It's only been a week."

"You still bleeding?"

"No."

Jake shifted his hands to her breasts, and this time she didn't hide her reaction—the stiffening and recoil.

He didn't release her. "Hey. I know what will help. Come on." He took the knife away, then picked up a dish towel and wiped her hand clean before threading her fingers through his.

He led her out of the kitchen, past the dining room in its crystal coldness, across the formal living room in its modern black and silver gleam, and through the tiled foyer to the stairs.

She knew where he was headed. *You can do this. It's just sex. Just an act. You always liked it before.*

But every sentence of her pep talk burst into rebuttal. *You're not on birth control. What if you get pregnant again?*

She'd looked it up. Most women found that the few weeks after a miscarriage were extremely fertile, as if the body wanted to quickly rectify its mistake. She would ovulate at some random time, whenever the pregnancy hormone finally went away. This community of women revolved around inside terminology, as though it were a secret club. Aunt Flo was your period. BD was the baby dance, or sex. DH was the dear husband, whose sperm seemed more important than the man himself as women frantically tried to get back on the baby track.

And there was baby dust. Message posters liberally sprinkled each other with it on the forums, posting it in their signature lines and signing off, "Wish me baby dust!" Some had little animated icons with fairies tossing sparkles.

She couldn't manage it if she got pregnant right away. The wounds were too fresh. She was exhausted from trying to hide her sadness and angry at herself for yet again bending to Jake's will. She used to be so strong, so fearless, blowing out of Odessa and racing through college, then law school. She'd dazzled her professors and landed a great firm. She'd really made it.

Then there was Jake. And he stood there now, by the bed, cradling her into arms. "I love you so much," he said. "You are the best thing that's ever happened to me."

He stepped back and tugged off his shirt. The first salvo. He was so beautiful. She'd never known a man could look like this, a real man, a smart one.

Melinda's pulse throbbed in her throat. She could barely swallow, everything in her conflicted in the push-pull of desire and revulsion.

Jake sat on the bed and pulled her close to him. "You've been through so much. I'll be so careful. It will help. I know it will."

He kissed her neck and pushed aside the collar of her blouse. She closed her eyes to take away his offensive, to listen to her own body, test its willingness to do this, to trust him, to trust this act, the possibilities.

He worked her clothes loose and pulled her onto the bed. She thought of other things—the potatoes still downstairs, plans for dinner. And the baby, tucked carefully in the folds of the sheets of the bassinet with a lavender sachet.

He sensed her leaving him and pressed his fingers against her cheeks. "Anything you want. Anything."

But he already knew her, knew her body, the things that affected her. He plumbed that knowledge, worked it like a tough case, a hung jury, and she re-engaged, at first helpless, then needing him, the way she'd always needed him.

The room was black as she slid from beneath Jake's arm, but as she neared the bathroom, the motion sensor kicked on the light. The burst felt like a flash bulb close to the face. She blinked and her stomach lurched. Bloody footprints led from her bare feet to the toilet, red and wet, smeared like they had been in the kitchen.

She almost cried out but bit her hand, afraid to let Jake know that she was losing it so hard. She couldn't believe it. She'd gotten the baby. He was safely with her. Why was it back?

She reached for a towel and swished it along the floor. Surely if she acknowledged the blood, acted as though it were real, she'd make it go away.

The towel soaked through with red as though the tiles were hemorrhaging. She rubbed harder, eyes burning, her nose starting to run. The blood came faster and she realized it came from her, flowing out between her thighs onto the floor.

She did shriek then, high pitched but faint, and snatched at the silk robe hanging on the wall. She lay on the towel and dragged the cloth around her to stop her shivering, the sobs now echoing off the floor and walls.

"Mel?" Jake hovered in the doorway, shading his eyes. "What's wrong? Why are you on the floor?"

She couldn't answer just then, too frightened to open her eyes. She imagined his knees, drenched in blood, his hands disappearing into the flow.

"Mel, did I hurt you? Did something happen?"

She almost told him. She wanted to tell him. But his concern washed over her, calmed her. She really wasn't alone. He was here; he was trying. She pushed herself up to sitting and dared open her eyes.

The blood was gone, only the crumpled towel and pink silk broke the perfection of the gleaming floor. "I'm okay," she said. "Just a little sore. It surprised me."

"Oh, baby, I'm sorry." He tried gathering her up again, but she resisted. "I'll be fine. Just give me a minute."

But Jake didn't relent and moved into her again. She let him hold her, trying not to go stiff. He was doing what he could. Now she was the one acting distant and horrible.

The mirror reflected their embrace, his dark head buried in her frazzled hair. She looked gaunt and pale while his body gleamed tan and muscled from daily workouts with a trainer. No wonder women gravitated to him like moons.

But still she wished, now that she'd been too long a mere satellite in his orbit, that she'd kept some part of her universe for herself.

7

HIGH SOCIETY

The referee blew a whistle, signaling the start of play. Melinda shifted in the stands, trying to find a more comfortable angle on the hard bench. Her stepdaughter Anna waved from the court, then turned to watch the serve. Melinda didn't get a chance to wave back.

Where was Jake? He'd left her with a gaggle of society women, and the talk had turned to spring break ski destinations. Melinda had never been skiing but didn't let on. Jake didn't have time for vacations.

"We all know the current *thing*." Cynthia raised one waxed eyebrow at Melinda then glanced away. Her voice dripped with southern twang, half of which she faked. "Lesley was so insistent that nobody know she's pregnant. She even got on that lift and went down the black. I couldn't believe it."

Kay jingled a set of gold bracelets. "Jesus Christ. I don't ski blacks when I'm not pregnant. Something could happen."

"Let's not upset Melinda," Cynthia said.

"You brought it up," Kay said.

Melinda tried not to stiffen, concentrating hard on the volleyball game.

A slow lob crossed the net, heading straight for Anna. Melinda tensed, knowing Anna would be upset to miss. Her stepdaughter clasped her hands and held out her arms, cleanly knocking the ball back across the court.

A jostle to her arm forced her attention to the women.

"Have you given any thought to the Junior League ball?" Kay asked. "You're still going to chair the fundraising committee, right?"

Melinda returned her attention to the court. "I signed on for it, so I'll do it." Got roped in, was more like it. Jake had insisted she try to get along with the right moms so the baby would belong to the proper social circles, like Sarah had when they were married.

"Ah, good, good," Kay said. "We'll need all hands on deck."

The ball sailed over the net and the opposing team dove for it, jostling awkwardly. It pitched into the stands. Anna jumped up and down. They'd scored three successive points. Melinda gave her a high thumbs-up.

"I do hope they don't make it to the playoffs." Cynthia sat up and smoothed the perfectly tailored black cardigan against her petite torso. "I am ready for this season to be over."

Then why do you come? Melinda glanced at the painfully beautiful women a moment before turning back to the game. The lithe girls in shiny blue uniforms raced to save an errant hit, but the ball bounced into the net.

"Oh look, there's Lesley herself," Cynthia said, waving and plastering on a false bright smile. Her voice changed to a singsong. "I think she's coming this wa-ay."

Melinda's eyes dipped to Lesley's still flat belly, then popped back up to her face.

Lesley caught the look and pressed her hands self-consciously against her angora sweater. "Okay. I know everybody knows," Lesley said, and dropped to the bench in a huff. "Yes, I'm pregnant."

"Shhhh!" Kay hissed.

"What?" Lesley looked from one to another.

"It's okay," Melinda said. "It's fine, really." Her face burned, and she tried once again to focus on the girls on the court. Anna was waving furiously at the door, so Melinda followed her line of sight to spot Jake standing with his ex-wife Sarah.

They seemed to feel her watching because they turned to the stands and Jake pointed. He said something to Sarah. She nodded and began walking toward Melinda.

Great. A pregnant woman and the ex. Melinda glanced at the score board, hoping for a save. 3–4. No luck.

"Helloo, ladies," Sarah called, shifting a monstrous bag on her shoulder and tossing her waist-length blond hair behind her back. "Cynthia, Kay, Lesley." She paused deliberately. "Melinda."

She plunked down next to Lesley. "How's the wee one?" she asked patting Lesley's belly. "Percolating?"

"Never any secrets," Lesley said. "How did you all find out?"

"Oh, girl, you can't go to a fete like the Mardi Gras ball and only drink ginger ale," Sarah said. She dropped the heavy bag onto the floor. "People will talk."

"It's no big deal," Kay said, leaning between the women. "It's just a baby. You're acting like it's a scandal."

"I'm the queen of scandals," Sarah said. The others laughed. "Except, of course, with the babies. Those are legit. Jake had them tested."

They all glanced at Melinda. She shrugged back at them, even though she felt something uncoil inside.

"So, let's plan a shower," Sarah said. "Something decadent and full of booze so that we might torture the mother." She turned to Lesley. "So when are you due?"

"Mid-September."

Melinda stifled her gasp, a pain shooting through her ribs. She had been due in September. Sarah knew this too.

"You are taking good care of yourself, right?" Sarah said, her voice slipping into a coo. "You wouldn't want anything to happen."

Melinda clutched her thighs with tight fingers. She would not cry, not react, not do anything. She could curl into herself, retract, like a turtle under attack. Her focus on the game became frenetic, following each arc of the ball with hyper-intensity. The women prattled on, but Melinda did not let anything penetrate her perfect concentration.

She felt a push against her arm. "Wake up, Melinda! I asked, 'So what are you doing with yourself these days?'" Sarah was smirking.

The women all looked at her. She could see the turn of their heads in her periphery.

"I guess you are referring to the fact that I lost the baby and don't seem to have anything to occupy my time," Melinda said, hard and low, a voice she herself was not familiar with.

"She's chairing the upcoming Junior League ball," Cynthia said.

Melinda felt contempt rise in her, a furious bolt of anger and hate. They thought she was nothing—not one of them, all born into money, and not part of their society, as she didn't get into all their little causes, spend her time volunteering, making the world a better place.

"Actually," she said, "I'm going to start practicing law again."

Sarah examined her manicured fingernails. "Really, Melinda, that isn't necessary. Jake won't like it. He wants his woman at home, and it's not like you need to work. Jake can easily support both of us!" She broke into light laughter.

Kay leaned forward. "If you need to do some work, you can take on that Legal Aid group. They always need volunteers."

Melinda clamped down on her jaw and spoke with measured calm. "I liked being a lawyer before, and I'm going to do it again."

Lesley forced a laugh, trying to lighten the mood. "Oh Melinda, you don't need to do all that. The only thing you need to be happy is just to get pregnant again. Go tell Jake to take you home, and you can get started. We can bring the kids later."

"A few minutes later," Sarah quipped.

The women tittered at the joke. Melinda followed the ball's arc over the net, wishing an errant hit would smash Sarah's ten thousand dollar nose.

The game continued with dull roars and muted whistles. Melinda's thoughts were monopolized by law firms, people she still knew, who might take her on. The idea blossomed in her, gave her comfort. She really didn't have to sit at home, without even anything to clean, idly surfing the Internet and, admittedly, repeatedly visiting the online baby calendar to see what stage of growth the baby would have been in.

But there was Jake. He'd be livid. Maybe the girls were right, and he would divorce her. She wasn't sure she cared. This small-town girl had no patience for their big-city attitudes.

Sarah leaned back, her hair brushing against Melinda's knees. She stifled the urge to grab a handful and yank.

The final buzzer sounded and everyone around her cheered.

"Thank God that's over," Cynthia said.

Melinda still burned with indignation. "I actually LIKE attending these games."

Sarah turned and forced a laugh. "And she's not even your daughter!"

Melinda picked up her bag and wound her way along the row to melt into the crowd. She might like the beautiful house, the immaculate neighborhood, the good schools and secure futures, but she could not get around the fakery of these women. They had to be more than they let on around each other. People just weren't like that, deep down. Why the act, then? Why pretend everything was as wonderful inside as the beautiful, glitzy exterior? Everybody had problems.

Jake stood talking to a small group of men, so she sat on the corner of the bleachers to wait. Her stepson, Adam, had run onto the court with other boys his age, whooping and diving under the net.

She'd met Jake when they represented opposite clients in a corporate buyout. He'd been mid-divorce with Sarah. When he asked her out, colleagues warned her to stay far away, as he'd been burning out dozens of smart, well-connected women.

So she'd turned him down.

After his first phone call, she carefully opted out of the date.

After the second one, she'd tactfully told him she wasn't interested.

He became relentless, but she continued to spurn him. He sent her flowers, and she'd returned them with a note to kill the clichés. He'd emailed her, and she'd sent mock bounce notices as if he'd used the wrong address.

The tide began to turn when he wrote her an old fashioned letter. He admitted his hand at poetry was poor, but he'd torn verses from antique books and pasted them onto heavy parchment paper. She was charmed and intrigued by his choices, no love poems, but comic bits by Robert Browning, and odd lines from e.e. cummings. They revealed a depth to him, a romantic streak she hadn't seen in their business interactions.

On the day of the poems, he'd called, his name glowing green in the dim light of her living room on the caller ID—Jake Carmichael. She let it ring, transfixed by the bright dot by his number that signaled he had called before. The voice mail would take over the call in a moment. She hesitated another second, then snatched the phone off the base.

"I didn't think you'd answer. I really didn't." His smile was visible even in his voice.

"I didn't either."

"Have I begun to swing your vote?"

"I'm listening. That's as good as it gets for the moment." Melinda gripped the receiver with both hands, trying to shut out all the warnings and let him plead his case.

"Dinner at the Americas?"

One of the fanciest restaurants in town. Of course he'd choose that. Power date. Show-off. She'd never been there. "Maybe."

"I'll pick you up?"

"I'll meet you there."

Their first dinner had been too smooth—glossy and sexual. They were constantly interrupted by people Jake knew, and the introductions felt more like bragging than an authentic collision of friends. When he'd followed all that with a press to get a drink in her condo after dinner, running his hands down her waist and hips before he'd even kissed her, she'd put him off and decided not to go out with him again.

The corporate buyout had proven a lengthy ordeal where she encountered him repeatedly. Jake's firm represented the buyers. Negotiations were painstakingly slow as the seller wanted dozens of nonstandard provisions.

Melinda was not lead counsel on this, but assisted Harvey, one of the principals. She mostly sat during the meetings, eyeing Jake with a mixture of curiosity and revulsion.

At the end of a meeting a few weeks after the Americas dinner, Melinda got delayed packing their paperwork. He waited for her in the parking garage at the base of the elevators.

"Melinda." His tone had softened from the hard edges it had carried in the boardroom.

"Don't put on another glossy show of sexual prowess with me," she said. "You've got plenty others to choose from—pretty little attorneys in pinstripes abound in this town."

He'd held out his arms as if helpless, the handle of his briefcase balancing on three fingers. "I've run through a lot of women, I know this," he said. "But don't think I'm the one doing all the playing. Some of them are sharks."

"And you're what, the bait?" she asked, exasperated, grasping her own briefcase in both hands before her like a shield.

"I feel totally out of my element with you. I can't do anything right. You aren't like the others with their rich daddies and entitlement issues. They come at me like vultures on road kill."

"Jake, spare me. You're the power player. You should see yourself in there. The tide of concession flows entirely based on the quirk of your eyebrow."

"But the quirk of my eyebrow has no affect on you. You make me humble. I need humble."

"You do not need humble."

He took a step forward. No one else came down and Melinda wondered wildly if he'd somehow rigged it so they would not be interrupted. Nothing seemed to get in this man's way.

"You can set every pace, be in charge in every way," he said.

"What if I don't even want to get involved?"

"I think you do. I sense you do."

She could not stop looking at him. He was so beautiful, so charismatic, so strong. His broad shoulders in the navy suit were practically Exhibit A in ideal man. His jaw Exhibit B. She might have pretended that first night not to wish she could see that body of his, to possess it, but she knew better. "I don't think it will work for us. You're just too slick for me."

He set down his briefcase. "I don't feel smooth around you. I feel like an awkward jock who thinks because he can play football, that means the girls will adore him, but then the one girl he's doing it all for doesn't even notice."

"Jake."

He took her briefcase from her clenched fingers and set it next to his.

His nearness to her was totally unlike the dinner. Not smooth, not overbearing, not oozing confidence. He touched her face lightly, near the ear. "I didn't even get to kiss you that night. You were impenetrable."

"You made me uncomfortable."

"Do I now?"

"Yes."

"Is it worse?"

"Yes. No. Maybe."

Melinda wished for the ding of the elevator, a car to go by. But it was late, the garage mostly empty. She couldn't handle this.

"Can I kiss you, Melinda? I could scarcely listen to old man Beaks from thinking about it."

Panic broke out over her in a way she hadn't felt since junior high, when Arty Mora passed her a note asking to kiss her after school, adding little check boxes at the end for yes or no.

She opened her mouth to answer, but he was already there, pressing his lips against her, kissing her softly, a subtle mix of hesitancy and desire. Exhibit C, she thought, but didn't feel like fighting it. What was the worst that could happen? She'd go on some high-end dates, maybe even—okay, highly likely—take him on as a brief lover. She didn't find it possible they would fall in love.

A volleyball thudded at her feet, startling her. Adam ran up. "Sorry, Melinda!"

She glanced over at the door. Anna had come out, dressed and excited about the win. Jake looked out at her expectantly.

She had fallen in love with him, and him her. In their way. It wasn't a gushy emotional thing, but a blend of their strengths. He was faithful, completely and utterly loyal to his team when attacked by outsiders. He would never cheat, considering it a lack of discipline and integrity. Looking at Sarah, she could see why he'd be unforgiving. Both were relentless fighters, but she'd attacked from the inside. Melinda understood this.

"I'm turning them over to you!" Sarah said, passing Anna's gym bag on to Melinda. "I'll be over tomorrow to fetch them." She turned to hug the kids and sauntered off, flashing a wave.

"Okay, everybody, to the car," Jake said, spinning his keys on a finger. "I'll order a pizza on the way, and it'll be delivered about the time we get there." He took the gym bag from Melinda and squeezed her fingers.

Melinda followed behind her husband and his buoyant kids. Anna jumped and shouted about the other players and highs of the game. Adam ran in crazy circles around the other cars as they cut through the parking lot.

Jake opened the hatch to their Lexus and tossed the bag inside. "Load 'em up!" he said.

The kids scrambled in the back, and Melinda turned around in the passenger seat to make sure everyone was buckled in.

"Mom said Lesley's going to have a baby," Anna said, watching Melinda. "Same time we were supposed to have one."

Melinda's throat tightened. She glanced at Jake, who was adjusting the mirror.

"That's about right," he said. "September."

"Do you think she'll lose her baby too?"

Melinda faced front, snatching at her seat belt. Jake dropped the gear into reverse and backed out of the slot. "Not likely. Doesn't happen too often."

"But it happened to Melinda."

"Not going to happen again," he said. "New subject."

They drove in silence a moment, then got stuck in the line of cars trying to pull out of the parking lot.

Anna sat forward. "But mom said it's always the mother's fault when a baby dies. If you take care of yourself, it wouldn't happen."

Melinda's vision flashed red. "Anna Carmichael, sit back and get that seat belt on properly. And don't talk about things you don't know anything about."

"The girl's just curious," Jake said.

"Don't tell me what to do!" Anna shouted. "You're not my mother. You're not anybody's mother!"

Melinda felt punched. Her stomach contracted.

"Is this the sort of children you've raised?" she asked him.

"Don't overreact. Anna—apologize to your stepmother."

"You can't make me!"

"I can take away your iPod and your DVD player."

Anna flung herself back in her seat. "Sorry, Melinda. Didn't mean to speak the truth and upset you."

Jake's jaw clenched. "That's it, Anna. No movies tomorrow night."

"Dad!"

"Now hush!"

In the angry silence of the car Melinda realized she indeed had a lot more to lose than she first thought. Getting involved with Jake had meant more than a few high-end dinners and taking on a lover.

She'd settled for too little. She had fidelity, security, and loyalty. But they came at the cost of understanding, compassion, and unconditional love, things showered upon her when she was a girl and therefore had completely taken for granted until now.

8

COMPETITION

She shouldn't do it.

Melinda stared at the email, an evil glee washing over her. She'd sent out a round of inquiries to attorney friends in town, getting a feel for what might be opening up. And lo, she'd found it.

Markson and Associates, arguably the biggest business firm in town, fifty years old.

And Jake's company's main rival.

The position was sound, nothing grand, but then Melinda had only practiced eight years and wasn't expecting a partnership. This was a lateral move from where she'd been six months ago, and with a better firm.

And one of her study partners from UT Law School was on the committee.

He wanted her to come immediately, the next day if possible, to meet the others. She fired off a quick email and raced to the bedroom, hoping one of her suits would still fit. Ajax barked at her, bouncing up the stairs on her heels.

She tugged a half-dozen outfits from her closet and tossed them on the bed. They were all, unfortunately, custom altered to her former size four. The first three wouldn't snap at the waist. Ten weeks of pregnancy had changed her middle just enough. It wasn't doughy, just soft. Enough, anyway, to screw up the tailored lines of her suits.

Melinda flung her favorite burgundy Anne Taylor across the room and took up a dark gray Ralph Lauren with a bit of stretch. She slipped the knee-length skirt on with apprehension. If this one didn't work, she'd have to go shopping, risking a credit card charge Jake might notice. Why had she consented to consolidating their credit? Jake had made it sound like such a great idea at the time, doubling their ability to get frequent flier miles.

Like it mattered. Jake could afford to fly to the moon and back.

She zipped the skirt. The lycra in the knit was just enough to keep it taut over her belly but not bubble out. She sighed relief. Now to locate her resume.

The lobby to Markson and Associates bristled with activity. Even the Ozarka man, shouldering two giant bottles of spring water, strode through the atrium with purpose.

Melinda did not have to wait even a moment, but as soon as the receptionist buzzed upstairs, an aid in a Jos. A. Bank suit materialized to escort her to the conference room.

"How long have you been with the firm?" Melinda asked. When she had clerked, she couldn't afford clothes like that. But he may have come from money to start with.

"Six months," he said. "I take the bar in May." He held open a heavy wood door for her. Inside, three men and one woman chatted amicably around an oval table.

"Good luck," she whispered, her nerves jangling slightly at the sight of the well-connected group. She'd worked on opposing cases with two of them during her tenure. Hopefully any memory they had of her would be favorable.

The woman stood first. "Melinda, how good to see you again. We worked together on the Fairbank case."

The men stood then as well, each shaking Melinda's hand with firm grips. She noted each name carefully, repeating them three times to herself, holding them long enough so that they would not shake loose in her memory. Among them was Anton Jeffries, a senior partner, a rare sit-in on a first interview. They were taking her very seriously. Jake would be proud. And angry.

When they were seated, Jeffries lifted a copy of her resume from the table. The others had stacks. He had only the one.

"I came down here when Henry forwarded your name. You both went to UT Law?"

"We did," Melinda said. "I graduated in 2000." She left out the honors. Those were listed in front of him, and she did not want to be arrogant or redundant.

"Both of my colleagues here recalled your name as well. You were underutilized at Chase Bigham, in many estimations."

They'd checked on her. It was true, her old firm had kept her as secondary on almost every case, although her research and briefs were often what brought results. "I have a background in case law. My argument skills were strong in school but were not well tested in that particular position."

"A situation that seems necessary to correct. Is that why you left? You have a gap here."

Melinda had prepared for that question. The truth was less important than her ability to convert a negative mark on her employment history to a positive.

"I opted to pull out when the timing was right in my case load rather than when an offer came along. I have concentrated solely on locating a more established firm since then, and merely waited on the right opportunity." For twenty-four hours, anyway.

"You're aware this is just another junior position?" Jeffries asked. The other members of the committee sat in patient silence, deferring to him.

"Yes, but the potential here is much greater." Time to turn the tables. "Are you going to also keep me in the corner, all research and no face time?" This was not a risky move with someone like Jeffries, who would expect a touch of aggression.

"I have clerks for research."

"Exactly."

Jeffries tapped the edge of her resume pages against the polished table with a click. "I'm done here." He glanced around at the committee. "Try to scare her off."

He winked at her as he rounded the table, stabilizing his stride with a black walking cane. "It was a pleasure, Ms. Carmichael. Tell Jake to say hello to everyone at the hell pot where he works."

So they knew. Of course they knew. Melinda didn't know how that rivalry might come into play. Would they expect her to share inside information? Suddenly she worried about what she had done. But that was John Grisham, not reality. "I will."

Jeffries chuckled. "We won't put you two against each other, you know. Conflict of interest and all that."

"Of course. Besides, I'd kick him to the curb."

This drew a booming laugh. "You know, I think you might."

Melinda fought the urge to skip as she left the elevator to cut back through the lobby. She looked up through the millions of glass panes, creating a greenhouse effect in the lush, plant-filled atrium. This might be her new home, very soon.

The rest of the meeting had felt like a formality, although they said many were applying. Unless Jeffries appeared to have more pull than he did in truth, she should be meeting the other partners soon, which was generally the next stage.

She tugged her keys from her bag as she crossed the parking lot. A man in a hat headed in her direction, and she smiled at the old-fashioned look of it. The only person she'd known to wear a fedora to work was—

"Harrison?" She stopped cold. He'd gone to school with Jake, and they kept a bitter rivalry on case wins, meeting once a year for a beer-drinking tally. Both were considered hotshots, although Harrison had not made his way to partner as Jake had. He wouldn't love Melinda coming in at his level, although he was a quirky jovial person outside of work.

"Melinda!" He hurried forward and enveloped her in a hug. "What are you doing at the evil empire? Jake would crap his pants if he saw you."

"Just. Visiting." So much for her mental acuity. God. He'd mention it to Jake in an instant.

"Right-e-o." He glanced at her suit, the briefcase, the Prada bag. "Quite a visitor's getup. Not angling for that open slot, recently vacated by dearly departed Whitney, are you?"

Melinda swallowed. "Whitney—did what?"

"Departed. For the outback. Lured to Australia by her hubby. True love." He cocked his head, examining her face. "Makes for quite an opportunity."

"It … it does."

He tipped his hat. "Well, good day, visitor. 'Twill be interesting to see how this shakes out."

It would indeed. "Bye, Harrison." She almost pleaded for discretion, to give her time to break the news to Jake herself, but did not.

If she got the job, he'd find out anyway.

Unless he found a way to stop her.

9

CLOSING ARGUMENTS

The kitchen clock ticked at twice its usual decibels, each movement of the hand like an ax falling. Melinda stood by the sink, washing carrots. She felt jittery, glancing back and forth between the door, which would open any minute, and the white tile. Blood free, so far today.

Ajax lay at her feet, napping, his ears perking every time she turned. Poor boy couldn't get any sleep with her like this.

She didn't know what Jake would do if Harrison had told him. Call her immediately? Send an angry text? Normally she knew he'd wait until he got home, but he was bringing Adam and Anna with him. Surely he wouldn't fight in front of them.

She reached into the vegetable bin of the refrigerator, lifting out a forgotten bag of rotting lettuce. Then she saw it.

Lying on the bottom, somewhat shriveled but still intact, was one last radish.

Her legs gave out. She landed on the floor, and the cold air made her shiver. She leaned her head against a shelf and stared at the faded red bulb, finally reaching for it.

Ajax began to bark. Melinda turned to him and her heart squeezed. He was surrounded by a pool of blood. She leapt up, dropping the radish, and searched through his fur. "Are you hurt? What happened? Baby!"

Ajax rolled onto his back, but his coat was clean. The blood remained on the floor, but none of it stuck to him. It wasn't actually there.

She touched the floor to make it go away. At first her finger swirled through it, revealing a trail of white tile. Then she wiped faster. Ajax jumped up, barking again at her fervently. Her hair fell out of its French twist and caught in her mouth as she frantically pushed her palms along the tiles. After several minutes of great effort, the tiles were white again and her hands had never turned the least bit red.

She sat on her heels, breathing steadily. Freudian. Had to be. A projection of her memories and intentions combined with a brain chemistry shift, probably due to hormones. That's all she could remember from her scant studies from an introductory psychology course in college over a decade ago. She should see a doctor. Do something.

A baby cried upstairs. She jumped to her feet and dashed to the nursery. The bassinet was empty. She paused, listening. Nothing.

She sat in the rocking chair, her hand to her chest. She might be going crazy.

She didn't have time to be crazy. Jake would be back in less than fifteen minutes.

She looked longingly at the mini-fridge, originally intended to store formula and breast milk. She had time for that. Remembering what Dot had said about the placenta, Melinda began keeping the baby in the tiny freezer compartment. She'd carefully packed the small white square with clean linens, lace, and stuffed animals.

The baby was wrapped in a blue receiving blanket meant for preemies. She sat in the rocking chair, laying the bundle on her shoulder.

She recalled what Stella had said at the end of the meeting about survivors. She knew she was not acting within the range of normal here, but she didn't care. This was the only moment that was truly hers.

She hummed lightly in the dark. A peace washed over her, stillness and calm. When she felt in control again, no longer plagued by the blood on the floor, what would happen when Jake came home, or if he had found out about the interview, she returned the bundle to its freezer, carefully tucking it away behind a soft white poodle with a blue ribbon, stiff from the cold.

The garage door hummed upward, a gentle sound vibrating through the kitchen. Ajax lifted his head and whined. Melinda dried her hands on a dish towel, feeling thoroughly composed now. She petted Ajax's soft head. "I know, boy. You don't want to have to go back to the utility room. But I'll spring you again after dinner."

Doors slammed and quick footsteps preceded the bursting open of the door.

Adam thrust a mouse cage at her. "Look, Melinda! I got to bring the school pet home for a sleepover!"

"Oh, wow! That's quite an honor, isn't it?" Ajax sniffed at the cage, and Adam pulled it away.

"Don't eat Suzie!" Adam shouted.

Anna kneeled on the floor, burying her face into Ajax's coat. He licked her ear, setting her into giggles.

Jake pushed through the door, lugging both kids' bags. "Anna, you can put the dog away and wash up. I assume dinner's close?" He hadn't even looked at her yet.

"It's close," Melinda said, assessing him. He didn't seem agitated. She relaxed against the counter. "Who's going to help me set the table?"

"Not me!" Adam said.

"Not me!" Anna said.

"Then I'm the only one who gets dessert!" Melinda lifted the cake plate lid to reveal a chocolate cake.

Adam set down the cage. "Where's the plates?"

"I'll get them!" Anna ditched the dog and hustled across the room.

"Miracle worker, as always," Jake said and leaned in to kiss her.

"Chocolate is the glue that holds this family together," she said. "Run those bags up, and we'll take care of things down here."

Ajax sniffed at the cage again, and Adam lifted it from the floor. "Where can I put Suzie?"

"Set it up here on the counter. Ajax won't jump."

"I'll get him," Anna said, grabbing the dog by the collar. "You want a biscuit boy? Come on! Come on!" She began dragging him toward the utility room.

Jake's cell phone rang. Melinda hoped the call wouldn't keep him from dinner, although he generally avoided that when the kids were with them. He'd grown up in a fractured family, parents who remained married but never saw each other, often in separate cities either working or taking power vacations. He did his best to have together time, one of his best qualities.

He looked at the name, muttered, "Look at that," and headed through the back door.

"Go wash up," she told Anna and Adam. "We want to be ready when your dad gets off the phone."

They scurried away, knowing that if they dallied, they could get out of helping without consequences. It was okay. Melinda could do it faster herself.

She'd just taken the plates out of the cabinet when Jake came back in, slamming the door so hard that the fern hanging in the breakfast nook showered potting soil onto the floor.

He knew. She moved away from him and bent over to sweep the dirt into her hand. She didn't even want to look up.

He hovered in the door, watching as she brushed her fingers off in the sink. He stood in a wide-legged stance, arms crossed, like a linebacker about to be charged.

"Something wrong?" she asked. Time to get it out.

"You know exactly what's wrong."

Melinda's stomach contracted and she swallowed. "So, you've heard then."

Jake slammed his hand on the counter. "You not only snuck behind my back and started asking about openings at firms where people I know are partners—you interviewed at Markson!"

Melinda relaxed her own posture and tilted her head in calm assessment. "We were on opposite sides of the table when we met. I don't see why it matters now."

"You are my WIFE!"

"And an attorney."

"We were starting a FAMILY!"

"No need to give up my career completely."

"You lied to me!"

"Nope, not once. You never asked me about my plans after we lost the baby."

"That's a lie of omission!"

"Then so would be my failure to tell you we've run out of milk."

"You can't take a job with Markson. I won't allow it."

"You have no power over me." Her poise surprised even her. She'd quailed before Jake since they married, even worse in the last six months after she quit to get pregnant. But she was back. No matter what Jake might be, power lawyer or snake charmer, she would no longer let him intimidate her.

He set the phone on the counter. "Do you not want a baby anymore?"

"I'm not totally sure you're the father I had in mind."

He took a step back. "Is our marriage over?"

"Possibly." The answer surprised her even as she said it.

"Damn it, Melinda."

"That's all you've got to say?"

Jake brushed past her to peer down the hall. "Where are the kids?"

"Probably hiding behind the door."

"I thought you cared about them."

"I do."

He turned back to her. "But you're going to leave us?"

"Possibly," she said again. "Sex doesn't fix everything. No matter how good it is."

"The kids could be listening to this."

With that Adam dashed into the room and crashed into Melinda. She grabbed the counter to absorb the impact, then moved back into him and held his head against her belly. "Adam, sweet boy. You okay?"

He looked up at her with earnest wide brown eyes. "Are you really going to leave us, Melinda?"

"Of course she is," Anna said from the doorway. "They're fighting just like mom and dad did before they divorced. It's what grownups do."

"This isn't good for them," Jake said. "Please reconsider."

She ruffled Adam's hair. He had only been four when she and Jake first dated. He was attached. So was she. "I never said I was going anywhere. But it's been a long few weeks, and I've been very sad about the baby and not having anything to do."

"But you take care of us!" Adam said. "Mom never played War with me before. And you do it all the way to the end!"

"Don't beg," Anna said. "It's useless. She'll go anyway."

"Let's stop this right now," Jake said. "Melinda's not going anywhere. She and I will have to talk." He picked up his phone. "I'm calling your mother to come get you. This is more than you two should be hearing."

Melinda sank into a chair, Adam still clinging to her. Anna glared at her from the doorway, angry and defiant. Another divorce might damage her even more, and Melinda would have to live with that.

10

DETRITUS

Melinda lay across the bed, waiting for Jake to come upstairs. Sarah had been unreachable. Jake insisted dinner go on normally. Melinda had walked out. They could eat without her.

Maybe she should just leave. Anna was not her problem. The girl seemed to hate her anyway. She'd been fine when she was younger, but now, at fourteen, they couldn't get along at all. She seemed to love making Melinda mad or upset. It was too much.

In fact, she should pack. Get away from all this and figure out what she wanted for herself. She opened the closet and pulled out the ridiculous leather duffel. In any case, it was important to know when to settle. Cut your losses. It wasn't exactly admitting defeat, but just an acknowledgment that to continue the fight would create more casualties.

Anna popped her head in the door. "Packing?"

Melinda set the bag on the floor. "I am."

"Figures." She flopped on the bed. "I'm supposed to apologize."

"I don't think you have anything to apologize for."

"That's what I said! But Dad said I had to."

"Your dad was wrong."

She sat up. "Nobody says that about my dad."

"I just did."

She smiled and lay back down. "That's why he likes you. You fight him."

Melinda returned to the closet and surveyed the racks, tugging several hangers of clothes from the rod. She didn't know what to say to Anna or what Jake expected from the conversation. She dallied, trying to figure out what should happen next.

But when she walked back into the room, Anna was crying.

She dropped the clothes across an armchair and sat on the edge of the bed. "You want to talk about it?"

"Mom said Dad was hard to live with. Not to like you because he'd make you want to leave too."

Whew. "I think your mom is still pretty sad things didn't work out."

"My mom doesn't get sad."

"Maybe she just doesn't show it."

Anna turned on her side, wiping her face with her fingers. "That's why I knew you were going to pack. We never did feel like a family."

This was not the conversation she could have ever imagined. "Why do you think that was?"

"Mom calls him a snake charmer. He lures you in; then he bites you."

She hated that Sarah talked like that to Anna. No wonder the girl was jaded. "I don't think so. He thinks family is very important."

Anna fingered the loops and lace on the bedspread. "We're not a family."

"I think families come in every shape. The baby would have been your brother or sister, just like Adam."

Anna covered her eyes with her arm. "I was going to teach her how to wear lipstick!"

"The baby?"

Anna rolled over, racked with sobs. "I told everyone I was going to have a baby sister."

God. "Anna." Melinda reached out to touch her fingers lightly on the girl's arm. "I didn't know you cared about the baby."

"She was going to be a girl. I just knew it. And I could pick out her clothes and play with her toys and show her how to dress her dolls." She shifted and Melinda saw her eyes were red and wet, her cheeks blotchy. "Nobody played dolls with me. I'd make sure she had dolls."

Good God. "You never said anything."

"I don't talk to you."

That was true. "I'm sorry we haven't really gotten to be friends."

"You're not supposed to be my friend."

"True. But I can't be your mom either."

"I wish I didn't have a mom or a dad. No one is nice to me."

Melinda brushed the hair away from Anna's face. She wasn't sure which thing to tackle, the grief or the selfishness. "Things can be hard. Things are hard right now."

She noticed the tall figure of Jake in the doorway but didn't acknowledge him, not yet. "It's going to be okay, Anna. Families fight, and families mess up. But we figure it out. We work it out together."

"Mom and dad didn't."

Melinda had no answer to that. She looked up at Jake, to see if he would step in. His arms were crossed over his chest, his eyes angry.

Anna saw him and sat up. "But you're already packing. Aren't you and Daddy going to divorce?"

Melinda looked at the duffel. "I don't know. We might. We might not. I don't know anything right now."

Jake moved through the doorway, and Adam dashed into the room. He flung himself onto the bed, grabbing his sister hard around the waist.

What should she do now? The children clung to each other, looking far younger than their ages, as though they had nothing else in the world to comfort them.

Her chest hurt. She had some responsibility for them, she realized. She had accepted that when she married, and certainly she was the best buffer between Jake and their mother.

Jake sat with them. "Melinda's going to get a job for now. She needs to get a little stronger again, and then maybe later we will plan on another baby."

Anna wiped her nose with the back of her hand. "You're not going to divorce?" she asked Melinda.

What else could she say? "Not right now, no."

"And you'll have another baby?" Adam asked.

She hesitated. "Maybe. It's hard to know what will happen."

Anna pushed at her brother. "It won't be the same as this baby."

"No, but there's no reason we have to forget her." Melinda snagged a tissue from the box by the bed and handed it to Anna.

Anna blew her nose. "I wanted to name her Kelsey."

"Okay then, Kelsey is what we'll call her. Would you like to make a scrapbook for Kelsey? We can write about her and how we felt and put the pictures from my sonogram in it."

Anna nodded.

"We'll go this weekend to pick it out. You'll help me decide?"

"Okay."

She glanced at Jake. He swallowed hard, his neck bulging with the effort. He nodded at her and picked up Adam, hoisting him onto his shoulders. "Time for bed, little man," he said. "Anna, go finish your reading."

Anna jumped off the bed. She gave Melinda a furtive hug and ran out. The room emptied, leaving Melinda alone again with her bag. Slowly she rose and picked it up, neatly sliding it into the space inside the custom shelving of her closet.

11

CONFLAGRATION

Her email had been silent. Melinda hadn't even written her friend at the firm, afraid to hear the post was filled, that they wouldn't be scheduling her meeting with the partners after all. Everything had happened so fast, and now nothing. Definitely suspicious. She dialed Lailani's number.

"So what did the asshole do this time?

"And hello to you, Lailani!"

"You only call me when he's been an asshole."

Melinda gripped the edge of the desk. "I think he may have made some calls after I applied for a job."

Melinda held the phone an inch away from her head as Lailani's indignation flashed through the cell towers in a lightning bolt of curse words ending in, "I'll come down there and cut off his wanker."

Melinda sighed. She was so happy to talk to someone totally on her side. But Lailani had voiced her fear, that Jake would pull strings to prevent her from working. "Surely not."

"Surely nothing!"

"Look, Jeffries knows there's a rivalry. These are not stupid people."

"They won't want to get involved in a domestic dispute."

Melinda found herself reaching for the phone cord to twist around her finger, like she had in so many heated conversations with Lailani when they were teens. This cordless business was no good for the anxious.

Lailani sighed. "When do you expect to hear?"

"By now."

"Shit."

"I know."

The grandfather clock that had been in Jake's family for eighty years chimed 5:30. "Lailani, I gotta go. I want to go to the miscarriage group." She hadn't confessed the hallucinations to her friend. They had too much else to talk about. But the group would ask.

Lailani sighed heavily into the phone. "You let me know, you hear?"

"I will."

Melinda closed the phone. Jake was out on a business dinner, even though it was a Sunday. Some client who had flown in. Melinda was relieved not to have to lie about the support group, although at this point, she'd just tell him. She didn't feel like hiding anything anymore.

She slid into the Volvo to head to the church. She and Jake had been circling each other warily since the night of the suitcase. He asked her daily if she'd taken a job from Markson, as if he didn't have a dozen people checking up on her now.

When she entered the building, Stella and Raven were setting up the chairs.

"Good to see you again, Melinda," Stella said.

"Did you get your baby back?" Raven asked.

Melinda had hoped no one would ask that. But she was an attorney and therefore could deflect any question with an ambiguously worded answer. "I have dealt with what happened."

"Good," Stella said. "Pull another chair up, will you?"

Janet arrived next, neatly dressed in a Chanel suit, her chignon traded out for an updo arrangement of dozens of tight braids.

"Lovely hair," Melinda said.

Janet smiled her thanks and sat down, hands pressed against her belly.

"How's the bleeding?" Stella asked. "You should be through this by now."

"Still strange," Janet said. "Black. Awful. It comes and goes."

Stella settled on her chair. "You call your doctor?"

"I've bothered them so many times."

"That's what they're there for."

Dot shuffled in, crucifix tight in her hands. Her sweats were gray today, the letters "WWJD" printed across the front. Melinda wanted to thank her for the information about the placenta and the freezer, but Dot bowed forward, whispering a prayer as she clutched the cross.

Melinda sat in the chair next to Dot. Stella tugged out her book of meditations and began to read again in her methodical voice. Raven sighed and shifted in her seat, looking around the room. Janet sat primly, still as a stone, attentive to the message.

Dot stopped murmuring but kept her head down. Melinda wondered about her story, imagining the freezer with the placenta in a Ziploc, wondering how far along she had been. She'd have to see if Stella would give her Dot's number.

"That's enough of that drivel." Stella closed the book with a snap. "We're all here anyway. How are you, Melinda? Are you feeling better?"

"Yes, no. God." What to say? "I might be getting a divorce. I applied for a job." She looked around. "I stopped working six months ago. I'm an attorney."

"You got canned?" Raven asked. "I didn't think lawyers got canned."

"No. My husband asked me to quit."

Dot's head snapped up. "And you just quit? Just like that? Because he asked?"

She made it sound so terrible. "I did."

Stella nodded. "Any more visions?"

Melinda stared at her nails, tattered now she'd stopped going to the salon. "I've had more."

Stella slid the glasses off her nose and let them dangle from the chain. "Are they getting more frequent?"

"Maybe."

"Have you thought about going to a therapist?"

"Oh no. Jake would…" What would Jake do? "I might."

Stella set the book on the floor. "Something to think about."

Melinda glanced at Dot, who had her head down again. "Thank you, Dot, for talking about … about your freezer."

"Did you put your baby in the freezer too?" Raven's eyes were large and round.

Stella cleared her throat. "Perhaps one more reading would do us a bit of good."

Melinda settled back. Maybe a therapist would be a good thing. Her phone beeped through with a text. She glanced at the screen. Jake.

Check your email.

12

SONOGRAMS AND ANGELS

Melinda didn't wait to get home, but pulled up her mail on her phone in the parking lot of the church. She had no idea what to expect. Divorce paperwork? Had he been downloading her mail and knew about something she had received but hadn't checked herself?

Two were spam, one was a Junior League meeting notice. But the fourth was a forward from Jake's secretary. It read, "Markson announces its new attorney: Leah Walker."

Melinda's stomach clenched. So it had happened. Jake was probably pleased. Just as she was about to close the window, she noticed something else about the email. It had an attachment.

She opened it. A list of law firms in town. And positions.

Jake had sent her all the openings for attorneys in Houston.

~ ❧ ~

Bellies of all sizes filled the waiting room. Melinda was sure these women all had heads, arms, and legs, but she could only see the bellies.

Striped ones. Flowered ones. Lots of big ones.

Jake put his phone away and clasped her hand. "I think we should lobby for a bill to make it illegal for pregnant and non-pregnant women to be in the same doctor's office," he said.

"Some doctor's offices schedule us with the annual exams so we don't have to sit with them. This practice is just too big for that, with six obstetricians." Melinda glanced through the stack of magazines on the table. *Fit Pregnancy. Parenthood. Baby!* "Nevermind. Let's do it and outlaw these too."

"Now we're on the same team."

Melinda smiled and pressed her hand against her stomach, already flat again, although not quite the same as before, softer somehow, less muscle and more cushion.

"Melinda Carmichael?" Dr. Valenza's nurse waited by the hallway.

For a moment Melinda stiffened, the moment aligning too closely with the night in the hospital. The room shifted, making her lightheaded. She glanced at the floor, expecting blood. The words "post-traumatic stress" shuttered forward. This had to be her problem.

Jake stood and held her arm. If he hadn't come, she might have asked the doctor about the hallucinations. But she couldn't now.

The nurse led them down the hall and stopped by the scale. Melinda stepped on it, not wanting to look.

"Very good," the nurse said, typing the numbers into her electronic pad.

Still five extra pounds. It didn't matter. She wouldn't let it matter.

"You look great," Jake said. "Perfect as always."

He was trying. Really trying. She'd never seen him go to so much effort.

Jake looked over baby pictures in the examining room as she undressed and slipped into the gown. "Some ugly kids here," he said.

Melinda sat on the examining table. "All babies are beautiful."

"No. Not this one. It looks like a squashed bug."

She had to laugh. "What about Adam and Anna?"

He leaned against the examination table and took her hand. "The most beautiful squashed bugs ever created."

"Well, there you go."

Dr. Valenza entered with a knock.

Melinda calmed at seeing his friendly eyes and overgrown mustache, accepting his hug with a sigh. He always listened to everything she had to say.

"Let's take a look-see," he said, moving a light closer.

Melinda lay back. Jake stood by her head, holding her hand. The resemblance to the moment at the hospital had ended. No pacing. No blame.

A few pinches and a bit of pressure, then Dr. Valenza rolled back and held out his hand to help her sit up.

"Looks good. Nice and tight. I don't see any reason why you can't try again as soon as you get your next period."

Melinda exhaled suddenly. "Okay."

"We'll probably wait a bit," Jake said. "It's been a hard few weeks."

Dr. Valenza noted a few things on his clipboard. "Sounds like a sensible plan."

"Is there anything we should do differently?" Melinda asked.

"We just have to have faith," Dr. Valenza said. "It's not likely to happen again."

"But what are the odds?" Jake asked.

Dr. Valenza sat the clipboard on the counter. "You are thirty-five. In good shape. So it's just the condition of the eggs we have to worry about. Some of them will have sticky chromosomes and will create genetic errors. So twenty percent."

"One in five?" Jake was incredulous.

Dr. Valenza nodded grimly. "One in five."

Jake took Melinda's hand again, as though he needed her more than she did.

"Then it's four out of five for us," she said. "Overwhelmingly on our side."

"It is," Dr. Valenza said. "It really is."

"Pass me the glue stick?" Anna held out her hand, eyes still on the scrapbook. Debris littered the table, bits of colored paper, baby stickers, and glitter.

A few days after the exam, Melinda had gone shopping with the kids to pick out supplies for Kelsey's memorial book. She'd made her choice. No pregnancy right now. But no rash decisions either. Jake had been conscientious and careful, as if seeing her with the duffel bag had changed him. Maybe Sarah had done the same thing, taken the same duffel out of the closet. This was his post-trauma.

Melinda glanced at Jake as she dug through the box. He sat at the end of the table, surrounded with papers. "You need the photo safe one?" she asked Anna.

"Yes. For the sonogram," Anna said.

Melinda handed her the glue. "Which one will you put on top?"

Anna had lined up the photographic copies of the sonograms in front of her. Melinda had the originals stored in air- and light-tight boxes, but they would still fade within ten years. Sonogram paper was not permanent. The prints would be.

"I think ..." Anna reached across the row of glossy black prints. "... this one." It was a full-body shot, the little lima-bean body in silhouette.

"Good choice," Melinda said.

Anna pasted it into the book and carefully wrote, "Kelsey, 8 weeks," above it.

Jake rifled through a file folder. "You're worth more than this offer. You should be in the position to make junior partner in three years." The light from a desk lamp shone hot on his forehead. Between them, Adam drew pictures of the baby as an angel.

"Which one is that?"

"Valdez. He's lowballing."

"Hmm. Maybe. What about the Rhinefield one?"

"That contract is crap. Didn't they think you'd read it? We're lawyers, after all." He flipped to another page.

"What is wrong with it?"

"Oh, the clauses about taking clients with you if you leave. Some of them are standard, but others suggest some stiff penalties, and an opening for a suit."

"I don't think I'm going to take either of those anyway," she said. "I'm not sure full-time is right for me."

Jake set down the papers. "You never said that before."

"I just decided. I don't want to be working late, and you know they drown you with grunt work when you first start. Who'd be here when Sarah brought over the kids?"

"Okay then." He clipped the contracts together and threw them over his shoulder. The kids giggled.

"Now what?"

"I heard there might be something at Fenner's."

"He hasn't keeled over yet?"

"Nope."

"You aiming for partner before he pops off?"

Melinda smiled, shaking her head. "No. Just a half-time position."

"There is no half-time in law."

"You're probably right. I'm just going to check into it, that's all."

"It's a good firm."

Adam held up his drawing. "Look, Melinda, it's Kelsey." A stick figure in a dress flew across a blue sky with big yellow sunrays and two puffy clouds.

"That's beautiful."

She helped the kids put away the scrapbook supplies and watched Jake lead them to bed. She followed them up the stairs, then turned into the nursery, opening the refrigerator to retrieve the small blue blanket.

She hugged the cold material to her to warm it as she headed through the house and into the utility room. She paused in the garage to collect a trowel and a small wooden box she'd bought along with the scrapbook, inlaid with three types of wood, with a small lock and key. She hadn't told the kids what it was for.

Ajax followed her into the back yard. The landscaper had recently planted new bulbs along the fence. She walked to the corner, past the recently turned beds, and over to where a dwarf crepe myrtle tree had stood since long before she and Jake had bought the house. The ground there remained untouched, just sprinkled with new mulch.

She knelt and cleared a spot, digging deeply with the trowel until she had a hole wide enough for the box, about a foot deep. She opened the box with the key and unwrapped the blanket. The baby lay inside, soft and warm again from the heat of her body. She held him in her palm, pink and small against her skin, then set him inside the box. She memorized how he looked, the curl of his back, the tiny dot eyes. She tugged from her pocket an extra bit of Anna's scrapbook work, a piece of pink paper that simply read, "Kelsey." She placed this on top of the baby and closed the lid, snapping the lock closed.

Ajax sat beside her, panting lightly, as she covered the box with dirt and spread it with mulch again. The dog sniffed the spot for a moment, then sat up stiffly, like a guard. She hugged him, and he rested his nose on her shoulder. Perhaps he had done the same with her father in his last hours. He'd died at home, and the hospice worker found him in his bed, Ajax at his feet.

She wrapped the blanket around the key and stood. The night was starry, bright, and clear. The light in Adam's room popped out, then Anna's.

"Time to go back in, Ajax," she said. "Let's go."

She knew life still had its problems. Jake still hated her dog. Sarah would still connive to set her children against her. Anna would still be a teenager and prone to outbursts. Her new job, if she took one, might not work out.

And another baby could die.

But she had talent, she had friends, and a place to go to spill her secrets when she wasn't up for being judged. She hadn't seen any blood in several days. Maybe she was on her way to being well.

Her baby had changed her, changed all of them, if only a little. And now, upstairs, Jake waited for her. Driven, snake-charming, controlling, but faithful, loyal, and able to adapt. And, like Kelsey, all hers.

PART TWO: *Dot*

1

PENANCE

Dot clutched the cross on her necklace as she squinted through the streaky windshield at the general store. The lights were off. She'd run by later and make sure the girl locked everything. She had a time finding someone to close up for her, plus someone else to watch the kids, but she always tried to make the meetings. God couldn't take exception to her being there, right in His own house, even if it was protestant.

The van lurched down the rutted road between lines of trailers. Dot had been nursing the old thing for years, and she certainly couldn't afford a new car with Buster not even sending money anymore. She had to drive something big enough for all the car seats.

She rolled to a stop by the rickety wood steps of her double-wide and jammed the gearshift into park. As usual, the van chugged several seconds before settling down. Dot ran her hand along the dash. "Just a bit longer, Bessie. Don't fail on me now."

She kicked the door open and wondered why she fooled herself by acting like a little longer would help. Buster had been gone two years without a word. It wasn't like he'd suddenly show up with car money.

He'd never stayed away more than six months before. He must've found some other woman. A keeper this time. She knew there'd been others.

When they were first married, she confronted him about his ten-day drive to Colorado Springs that ended up taking three weeks. He grabbed her and said he loved only her and not to worry about anything, he'd take right good care of her. After that he straightened up for a couple years, but then the gigs got longer and longer, with more and more distance between the drive and when he'd show up again. Still, she always took him back. They had three kids by then and she had to make do. Then she ended up with two more.

Dot unlocked the door and waved to Martha watching television on the sofa. "Hey. Kids act all right?"

"Oh yeah. No trouble at all. They're all down, but only little Lottie's actually asleep."

"I figure they'll be out again in a sec, if they heard me come in."

Sure enough, Ben peeked through the door that led to the hall. "Mama?"

Dot set her bag on the floor. "Hey Bennie boy. You're supposed to be in bed."

"Kiss?"

Dot picked him up. "When you go to kindergarten you won't want me to kiss you anymore." She pressed her mouth against his cushy cheek. Heaven.

"Oh no, mama. I'll always kiss you."

Dot set him down and squeezed his shoulder. "You go on to bed now."

She waited until he was gone and turned to Martha. "Thanks for sitting for me again."

"Of course, Dot. I got something for you, though."

Something in her tone made Dot's stomach flutter. She sank into the recliner and brushed cracker crumbs off the arm. "Oh yeah?"

Martha picked up a shiny envelope with a big FedEx logo. "They delivered it to the wrong trailer yesterday. Helen walked it over. But I don't want to give it to you."

"Is it bad? Can you tell?"

"Don't matter. It's the who, not the what."

Dot leaned forward and snatched the envelope.

Martha sat back against the sofa with her arms crossed over her skinny chest. "Maybe he's dead," she said. "That would make it a good thing."

"What are you talking about?" Dot examined the typed address. She didn't know anybody in Nebraska, but certainly knew the name. Buster Miller. Her husband. She ran her fingers across the type.

"Open it, why don't you. I'm dying to know what it is." Martha pressed on her gray poof of hair, agitated.

But Dot took her time. What if he was dead? Or maybe they were divorce papers. She wasn't sure what she hoped for. She yanked on the pull tab.

Inside was a cashier's check for $2,000.

Martha scooted in close. "Wowee. That's four months' rent."

They stared at the check a moment, more money than they usually saw at one time. Martha held it up to the light. "You think it's good?"

"I'll find out when I cash it, I guess."

"Wonder how he got so much at once. Did he send a note?"

Dot opened the envelope wide to see inside. "Yeah." She wasn't sure she wanted to read it. They didn't tell you people were dead or divorcing on a hot pink sticky.

Martha snatched the envelope and pulled out the note. "Good God."

Dot's heart hammered. "What is it?"

"He says, 'See you Sunday.' That's today."

Dot released the breath she'd been holding. He was coming home after all this time? And sending money to butter her up.

Martha scooted closer. "Now, listen here. I don't think you should see him. He's a rat, banging every truck stop floozy on his route, and obviously shacking up with who knows what kind of tramp all this time. Tell me you aren't going to take him back."

A Felix the Cat clock ticked in the silence, the tail swinging back and forth just over Martha's head. Dot sucked in a breath. "I can't keep him out of his own house. I owe him."

"That's exactly why you shouldn't see him. You'll feel all this guilt over Gary, and the baby, and it's not right. He's the one who probably has little bastard kids from here to Wyoming."

"Yeah, and God justly took my bastard child from my own belly."

"I don't believe that."

Dot laid her head back against the towel covering the top of the recliner. "I did this, brought the wrath of God upon this house."

"Dot, please. Gary is a good guy. He's torn to pieces you won't see him anymore."

Dot glanced out the front window as if she could see right through the curtains to Gary's trailer. She could picture his face, friendly and gentle with a scruff of beard on his chin. Her heart clenched, and she automatically reached for the cross at her neck to burn out the memory.

Martha sighed. "Did you talk to anyone in your support group this time?"

Dot shook her head.

Martha slapped her knees. "I think you should. You won't listen to me or your friends. You deserve better than all this. We all think Gary is better."

Dot sat still in the big brown chair, cheek pressed to the towel spread across the back. "I am going to burn in the fires of hell for cheating on my husband and getting pregnant."

"You weren't thinking that when Buster'd been gone over a year and you were broke and lonely and Gary came to help you out. And you didn't think of it when you fell in love and Gary asked you to be his, to get divorced from that awful man. You were happy then."

"I was misled."

"Dot, you didn't do anything wrong." Martha picked up her purse and pushed open the door. "I'm not giving up on you. We've been friends too long. Let me know when you need me, and tell me when Buster's coming 'round. I'll avoid him like ten-day-old stink bait." She walked out with a wave.

Dot reached down to kick off her sneakers. That Martha. Her oldest friend, from back when Aurora was born. They'd both lived in this trailer park for ten years. But she was wrong. And Buster was coming back. Any minute, maybe, unless he meant next week.

She pushed on the arms of the chair and stood back up to check on the kids. He couldn't ever know about Gary. Buster was a jealous man, prone to temper.

She paused by baby Lottie's room, the toddler's halo of blond hair just visible in the haze from the nightlight. This one had never known her own father. Buster had taken off on this long stretch when the baby was only six weeks old.

She closed the door and popped on the hall light. Thank goodness she had a double-wide. No way to fit five kids in anything else.

Bennie and Matthew shared the second bedroom. "Off with that flashlight!" she warned the glowing lump under the blanket on Matthew's bed. The light clicked off.

She cocked that door most of the way closed and passed on to the last room. The girls were huddled on the floor by the portable stereo, listening to the radio.

"Hey mama," they both called.

"Hi girls." Dot squatted down beside them. Aurora, the oldest, was ten and the reason she and Buster'd had to get hitched when Dot was seventeen. She didn't feel spite about it, though. The girl was an angel, and smart too.

"It's too early for sleeping," Aurora said.

"Not on a school night." Dot scooped up Sunny, who was petite at seven, and popped her onto her bed. "You got to get your rest."

"Guess what, mama," Sunny said. "I get to be the line leader."

"I bet you'll be a good one."

"I will. I been practicing opening doors."

"That's real good, honey."

Dot kissed the girl and backed out of the room. Buster was still around a lot when Sunny was conceived. The first three came hard and fast; then he started taking longer trucking gigs and staying away more. At least with him gone she had stopped popping out a new kid every year. That boy had an appetite. She blushed just thinking of all the things he liked to do.

Dot checked to make sure no lights were back on in the boys' room then dropped by the kitchen. She pressed her hands against her belly. She could squeeze a good inch all the way around. He wouldn't like that, would tell her to quit eating so much. She'd gained with each kid but had started out so skinny with Aurora it hadn't mattered till Bennie. But now.

She thought of Gary, who'd run his hand along her body and said he loved her however she came. They'd always joke, "As long as you do come!"

She caught herself almost smiling. She snatched a catechism from the counter and clutched it against her chest. Make your heart cold to him. You have to be strong.

Then, as if God Almighty Himself wanted to send her a sign, the phone rang.

Only one person ever called her this late. Two years apart didn't make a difference at all, when a man had a habit.

She almost reached for the beat-up handset, hooked on the wall with a tangled cord like a noose. But she didn't. Without an answering machine, it would just keep going until he quit trying. He knew this. He also knew he'd wake the kids.

It cut off mid ring.

Dot relaxed her hands where she'd left them in mid-air. Now, why hadn't she answered it? Wasn't it just going to rile him? She couldn't stop him from coming home. He was her husband.

The phone rang again.

She lunged for it this time. "Buster?"

"Yeah, hon. It's me."

"You coming home?"

"I'm outside Lake Charles right now. Be there in a couple hours."

"No shittin'?"

"No shittin'. See in you in a few, darling."

So close. Practically home.

Dot set the phone back on its base and quickly surveyed the trailer. A few dishes in the sink, but she could take care of those quickly.

She wanted the place clean, but she also had to make extra sure nothing was left of Gary. She couldn't have even the smallest clue around. Buster might've been on the road two years. He might've not seen his youngest since she was an infant. She had no doubt he'd been shacking up with dozens of women. But he would have expected her to wait for him.

She sat on the living room sofa, going over in her mind yet again any possible thing she might have forgotten. She jumped up suddenly and went to the freezer, digging through the box dinners until she found a slender Ziploc bag, icy and blackish-red. No one knew the contents but her. She held it close to her chest. She should get rid of it. She couldn't spare any risk. Buster would know she couldn't have been pregnant by him. He hadn't even called in all that time.

The cold seeped through her sweatshirt. She could make out the shape of it still, like a section of a popped balloon. It didn't give when she pushed on it, surrounded with iced-over blood.

She opened the junk drawer and sifted through the box tops, rubber bands, and broken pencils to find a permanent marker. She wrote "raw livers" across the top of the Ziploc and shoved it under a bag of frozen peas. Buster wouldn't question it now.

She had to change clothes. She couldn't greet her husband in sloppy jeans and a sweatshirt. Thank goodness the kids were in bed. She could see him, at least for his first night, alone.

She fingered the cross as she flipped through her closet. She ran her palms over his shirts, all short-sleeved in solid colors. The hangers shifted, and a dress fluttered to the floor.

Dot bent to retrieve it, her throat catching when she realized which one it was. How often did a new dress change your life?

The day she'd bought it, Buster had been gone a year with no word. Dot had run out of sitters and started taking baby Lottie with her to work at the store. She had finally gotten her belly mostly back down again and picked up the dress at Goodwill for $4.

"I always notice when a lady has a pretty dress," the man said. He'd been coming into the convenience store every day for a week or so. New to the trailer park. He was kind and courteous. Always got the same thing. And always smiled at her.

Dot rang up his pack of smokes and single bottle of Dos Equis.

"The lady can't talk?" He handed her ten neatly folded dollar bills, then leaned his arm on the counter and grinned. His teeth were white and straight beneath the blond-red moustache. His beard was clipped close and his eyes were bright blue, like lake water in summer.

Lottie tossed a toy outside her playpen. Dot stepped back to pick it up and flushed hot when she realized the man was watching her closely, catching the drop of her neckline as she bent over.

She glanced up and he smiled. He obviously didn't even care if he got caught.

"Nice dress," he said. "You look mighty fine in it. But I best be on my way." He touched his ball cap as a salute.

She still didn't answer, just grinned like a damn fool. He picked up his cigarettes and his beer and strode out.

Dot leaned against the closet door as she fingered the crinkly blue fabric of the dress. Not something she'd ever wear to work, ordinarily, as she had to haul cases of stock around the back most days, but that day she'd felt happy and good. Not having to pay the sitter had allowed her to catch up on a few bills, and the owner of the trailer park had actually given her a bit of a raise by way of letting her have $20 in food each week from the store.

And Gary had noticed her. A beautiful, courteous man.

Dot sat on the bed, still holding the dress. She hadn't had to wait long to see him again. The next day the boys were acting like fools and tried to swing off the front door into the yard. Dot heard a crunch and a scream and ran though the trailer to the living room.

"I didn't do it!" Ben screeched and tried to dash past her.

She snatched him by the collar and hauled him with her. Matthew clung to the knob, knees clenched around the front door, which now hung at a crazy angle past the end of the porch.

"Matthew Jason Miller!"

"I didn't mean to, Mama!"

"Get down right now!"

"I'm tryin'!"

She released Ben and wrapped her arms around Matthew, pulling him off the door. She tried to shut it, but the hinges were bent and it wouldn't fit into place.

"Now what am I going to do?" She turned to the boys and they took off through the house. "That's right—get to your room!"

Dot snatched a toolbox from under the sink and returned to the door. "Good God almighty," she said. "Those boys."

She took a hammer to the hinge, trying to bang it back into place. The plaintive clank of metal striking metal echoed through the trailer park, quiet on a Sunday morning.

When she tried to close the door, it wouldn't budge. She dropped the hammer in the toolbox. "Well, hell," she muttered. "Now what?" She certainly couldn't afford any handyman. Maybe somebody's husband could help.

"You want me to take a look-see?"

She knew the voice. The new man. Mr. Dos Equis and charm. She turned. He was pale in the summer sun. He must not do outside work.

"It's a lot of trouble."

"Not a bit." He examined the damage, then used a screwdriver to wedge open the hinge. "I think I'll just take it off for a bit, to repair these." He knocked the pins out, lifted up on the door, and pulled it away.

Dot saw Lottie toddling awkwardly toward the door and hustled back in to grab her. "Let me know if I can help you," she called from inside.

"Will do."

Dot ran to the bathroom, smoothing her hair and tugging at her sweatshirt. Dang it, if she wasn't dressed all to hell that morning. She set Lottie on the sink and swiped at a streak of jelly near her shoulder. She really ought not be in a twitter. She hadn't even looked at another man in all the times Buster had left her before.

But he'd never been gone so long. Usually he came back just in time for a new one to be born and left when she was growing the next.

A hot ball of resentment burned in her belly, but she'd felt it plenty times. She'd picked Buster knowing good and well he'd be gone a lot, driving that truck. She just didn't think he'd leave for a year. She picked up Lottie to go take another peek.

"Yoo hoo! Where are you, Dot-girl?" Martha leaned through the empty door frame.

Dot disentangled Lottie's fingers from her hair. More jelly. "What you doing here?"

"I heard all the banging and peered out my window to see a young Greek god outside your door, working like he belonged here!"

"Matthew broke the door."

"And Gary's fixing it."

"That's his name?"

"You mean you don't know? Every female over the age of ten has been checking him out since he drove in with his trailer two weeks ago. You work right there at the store! How could you not know?"

"I've seen him around. I just hadn't met him proper."

Martha pushed on the bottom curls of her own mass of gray-streaked hair and peeked between the front blinds. "If I were twenty years younger," she said. "Look at that butt!"

"Shhh! The door is off!" Dot gestured toward the bright rectangle. "Now scoot over and lemme see." Dot squeezed in beside her and watched

Gary bend over the door. The clink of metal echoed with every rise and fall of his arm.

Martha stood up, hands on her hips, and tilted her head. They were both acting like damn fool schoolgirls.

"I'm going to the kitchen," Dot said, shifting Lottie more securely against her.

Martha nodded knowingly. "Gonna fix him some lemonade? I would."

"Actually … I might."

Dot set the baby in a highchair with a pile of Cheerios and searched through the cabinets for the powdered mix.

"I think it's time," Martha said, plopping in a chair and waving a plastic puppy at Lottie.

"For what?" Dot focused on measuring the lemonade into a clear pitcher, her face reddening. She knew what.

"It ain't right the way Buster carries on, running off with truck stop floozies and leaving you to raise these kids. Not even sending you any money. If you divorced him, at least he'd have to pay."

Dot added water and stirred. Martha never did know when to shut up.

"You know, he's probably shacking up with them and not paying a dime to anybody. You ever figure out where his paychecks go? I bet he's got a pretty penny stored up somewhere."

Dot poured a glass of lemonade and set it in front of Martha. "I checked into that once, when I thought I was going to lose the trailer. Called the company he worked for."

"You never told me that!"

"He'd been moonlighting and that wasn't allowed, so they let him go. I never did know which company he switched to."

"Did you ask him next time he came?"

Dot bent to scoop up fallen Cheerios and drop them in the sink. "Nah, you know how it is. He's so…" She couldn't explain. He paid attention to her when he was there, and everything was real good as long as she didn't rile him and didn't make a fuss when he left.

"He's nothing. And he treats you like nothing." Martha handed Lottie the puppy toy. "Now you get on out there and smile at the boy and see if you don't feel a little different. All you need is a real man and you'll see what you've been missing. You'll be ready to sign on the dotted line in no time."

Dot poured another glass. Martha didn't know squat about Gary. He could be another Buster or worse. She shook her head. "I'm going to take this out there, to be polite. But I'm a married woman and nothing is going to make me think any different."

She'd no more handed him the glass of lemonade and everything had slipped into slow motion, the sun on his hair, his broad smile, the smooth bit of cheek above his beard. And then those eyes. Crystal blue, merry, honest.

Her demise had come around quick after he'd fixed the door. She couldn't get him out of her mind. To compensate, she'd tried to track down Buster, calling every trucking company she could find to see if he worked for them. She turned up nothing, so she tried calling truck stops along routes she knew he sometimes took.

The waitress who answered the phone at the Palace Truck Stop outside New Orleans knew exactly who she was asking about.

"Yeah, I seen your Buster," the woman said in an accent so strong, Dot could barely understand her. "That boy got a whale of a dick, waving it like a fat flag at anything in a skirt. Two-Chump Charlie done thrown his sorry ass out. He won't be coming back here. You his wife or some-thin'? He mentioned he had a wife one time. You one kinky girl, he told us. I heard all about that time you got your legs up over the—"

Dot hung up the phone and right then and there stopped looking for him. It was one thing to think he was cheating. It was another to know it. But to know he was spouting his mouth. Dot snatched the phone up again and threw it across the kitchen.

That very night she made a casserole and took it over to Gary's trailer after dark when all the kids were down, but before it got too late. Knowing she had to dash back after just a few minutes made her feel better about doing it.

He opened the door, wearing a thin white undershirt and loose jeans.

"I wanted to thank you for fixing my door," she said, holding up the tin. "I was in a mighty fine mess otherwise."

He accepted the casserole and turned to set it on a cabinet by the door. His trailer was small—travel-sized, really. She assumed he had to live there alone.

"That's right kind of you, Mrs. Miller," he said. She realized they never had actually introduced themselves.

"Dot, please. My husband…"

"Dot then. I reckon you know I'm Gary."

"Yes … Gary. You're the talk of the trailer park."

He blushed and Dot blushed right back. Good Lord, twenty-seven and acting like a teen.

"I'm not much to talk about. Just a welder doing regular work like anybody else."

"Do you have any family?"

"My ma lives back in Oklahoma. I go see her when I can get up in those parts. My brother is in Tallahassee, but we don't speak much."

"But no…"

He made what her daddy would have called a shit-eatin' grin. "No wife, no. Had one for a spell, but she ran off. Wanted a white collar fellow, I think. She was educated. Real smart gal."

"Oh, I'm sorry."

"Yeah, I was too. Thought we'd signed up for something good."

"No kids?"

"Nope. Always wanted some. Reckon they'll come along. You've got a passel. I've seen Matthew around. He's a real corker."

"Yes. My oldest boy. And, I should get back. Kids are in bed, but you never know who's going to get up and make trouble."

"Here, I'll walk you back." He stepped down, his feet bare against the gravel.

"You don't have shoes!"

He chuckled. "Never found much use for shoes. My mama beat me black and blue at how many pairs I lost leaving them by riverbeds or in fields."

"Sounds like you were a bit of a corker yourself."

They crossed the short distance between his trailer and hers. It felt like a date, somehow, and when he opened the door for her, she wondered, crazily, if he would kiss her.

But he just nodded his head. "Goodnight, Dot."

She watched him walk back, hidden behind the thick curtains of the front window, her belly filled with longing.

2

FALLEN WOMEN

Dot turned away from the dresser when headlights flashed outside the bedroom window. They grew closer, so she rushed to peer out. Just a neighbor. She relaxed again and pulled the big silver chain with the cross over her head.

Thank God her mama wasn't around to see her fall from grace. She made the sign of the cross then blew a kiss at the picture on the wall. Mama in a gray dress, surrounded by Dot and her sisters. Good thing Mama didn't know anything. She'd roll over in her grave.

But after the casserole, Gary had still been real careful, real good. He hadn't tried to kiss her, hadn't asked her out. He came over for dinner at times. Played ball with the boys. Once Sunny'd even gotten him to sit with her dolls.

He recognized she had some turmoil about it all, though Martha said she'd told the man herself all about Buster and his disappearances and meanderings.

Things changed rapidly the night Lottie caught the croup. Dot had been up all night with her, running the shower to steam up the room, but the baby was turning blue and her coughing was getting weaker.

She called Martha to watch the kids so she could take Lottie to the hospital. She got in the lumbering old van and the damn thing wouldn't start. She'd been crying, Lottie on her lap, turning the engine over and over when Gary opened the door, took the baby, and loaded them both in his truck. He stayed with her in the long wait in the ER, while they put Lottie in an oxygen tent, and when the doctors asked if this was the baby's dad, as no other visitors were allowed, she just said, "Yes."

They slept curled together on a cot in the room Lottie was moved to once they got her breathing better. Dot woke, Gary's arms around her, the morning light on his face, and realized she felt safe. Somehow, without so much as kissing the man, she'd fallen in love.

He felt her shift against him and woke up. She looked at him, into those crystal eyes, and even though the baby slept nearby and the nurses hustled past the partially closed door, she kissed him.

Once Dot let in the water, the dam burst. She saw him every day, dashing over to his trailer with food or news or just to look at him. She'd never felt anything like it—he was a rush, a hope, a white-gilded glory. Like Christmas. Like birthday candles. Like weddings.

As the months passed and still no word from Buster, Gary settled into their lives. Nobody seemed to think anything of it. Half the park was shacked up and unmarried.

But they weren't anywhere close to careful with the birth control. The first time she woke up to the quease in her stomach, she knew she should have gotten on the pill, or done something serious. This random condoms or pulling out or timing it close to her period was risky and they both knew it. She wondered, as she held on to the knowledge, the only one in the world who knew she had a bastard child in her belly, how much she'd almost hoped it would happen.

Gary paid for things—doctor visits, vitamins. He seemed unfazed by it, and they continued on the way they had. He kept his trailer but stayed in hers, though he never moved so much as a toothbrush over. "It's still yours and his place until you get divorced," he said. "But it might be time to locate your husband."

Dot tried again. She called the government this time, acting like she thought he was dead. He must have filed taxes or something. They had to have a paper trail on him somewhere.

She called about his truck driving license renewal. He'd kept it up, but his home address was still their trailer. By then she figured he must be running cash under the table for some outfit. No W-2, no taxes, no Social Security.

In January they had their big sonogram to see if the baby was a boy or a girl, and to check on things. They went to a clinic, happy and excited.

The radiologist was chipper, animated like a Saturday morning cartoon.

"Hallo Mom! Hallo Dad!" he said, shaking each of their hands. "I'm Enrique, your radiologist. I'll be peeking at your insides today." He flipped a hank of dyed blond hair away from his square glasses.

Enrique's skin shone lily white and his accent was fake, but Dot liked him. She lay back on the table and pulled her big shirt up to expose her belly.

"You've done this before!" he said, laughing. "I see from your chart you are a serial mama!"

Dot wasn't sure what he meant, but said, "I have five kids already."

"Boys, girls, both?"

"Two boys, three girls."

"Oh!" he said, pushing down the elastic to her pants. "Then the sex does not matter, or do you want to even things out? More testosterone like your big guy here." He winked at Gary.

"We'll take either flavor," Gary said, smiling.

"Okay now, girls and boys. I warmed up the gel for you," Enrique said, squeezing the bottle over her exposed belly. "Nobody wants to be covered in cold goo. Very amateur."

Gary and Dot looked at each other and laughed. She imagined the scene with Buster instead, who would have certainly said something nasty to the man about his clothes, his hair, the funny accent. She couldn't be more glad to be with Gary.

He took her hand as they watched the black screen. Dot remembered her other sonograms, lying there alone or with Martha, kids usually running amok in the room. She really didn't have to worry about her husband being mean to someone like Enrique, as Buster had never been to a single appointment and only showed up for two of the kids' births.

"Can we find out what it is?" Gary asked. They'd agreed they wanted to know.

"If junior cooperates," the tech said. His hair flopped over his eyeglasses. "We'll try to see parts!"

He pressed the paddle to her belly. Dot watched the screen even though she couldn't make out much of anything, just white blips on black.

"How can you tell what's what?" Gary asked.

The radiologist did not answer and Dot looked at him. He was biting his lower lip. All humor had fled.

She grasped Gary's hand more tightly. He had not noticed, still peering at the confusion of curves and blotches on the screen.

"Is this your first sonogram for this one?" Enrique asked. He'd dropped the act, the accent, the happy lilt.

"Yes. We don't have insurance, so we just do this one," Dot said, fear already making her shake inside.

"What's wrong?" Gary asked.

"I will have to forward this to your doctor."

"I go to a clinic," Dot said. "I don't really have one designated doctor. You're probably the nicest person I have to talk to."

Enrique set the paddle down for a second and took off his glasses, wiping his eyes. "Let me take a few more measurements. But I can't make a prognosis."

"Can you point out anything for us? On the baby?" Dot asked. Her voice wasn't steady.

"Yes." He picked up the paddle again. "Here is baby," he pointed to the screen. "Here are legs, and belly, and … head," he quickly moved the paddle down.

"Can you tell what it is?" Gary asked.

Enrique shifted the paddle around, circling Dot's belly. "Not easily. This one, he's shy. And also moving a lot, really bouncing around. You feel him move?"

"Yes," Dot said. "Though he's small yet. It's more like bubbles than kicks."

"That is normal," he said.

"But he's alive right? He's moving all over." Gary had a death grip on Dot.

"Oh yes. See, here is the heartbeat," he centered on a rhythmic pulse of tissue. A number came on screen. 170. 182. 164. "That's his heart rate. Very normal."

"So what's wrong with him?" Dot asked.

"Wait, let me measure." A cross appeared on the screen and he moved it. "He is normal length for twenty weeks." He moved and clicked a few more times. "Femur fine size. All dates seem right." He typed in a few things and a printout came from below. "I'll do that one again, for you." Another print rolled out. "It was a good angle."

He rolled the paddle more. "Ah, see. It is a boy, look, there are parts." He held the cross on a moving section that still looked like nothing to Dot.

"A boy, Dot." Gary squeezed her hand again. "Our own little Bubba."

"He hasn't measured the head," Dot said. She remembered the drill, after doing it so many times. "I have pictures of all the kids' sonograms, and there's always a full body, a belly, a leg, and a head."

She turned back to the sonogram and could now make out a curve of the baby's face, nose, ears, chin. "What's wrong with his head?"

Another number flashed on screen, but Enrique quickly printed it and turned the machine off. He set the paddle down. "Technically, I can only refer you to the doctor," he said, reaching down to tear the strip of printouts from the bottom of the machine.

He bent the curl of paper over the edge of the keyboard and tore the bottom print away. "Here is one for you." He handed it to Gary.

"Is he going to die?" Gary blurted.

"I'd really rather you talk to your doctor."

Gary leaned forward. "Just tell us. Is he going to die?"

Enrique hesitated, his lips tight. "Yes."

Gary pushed his ball cap up, wiped his forehead, then pushed it back down. "It's not right. We ought to know what is wrong."

Enrique sat on a short stool, his back bent. "Your doctor will explain it better to you, but the baby has a condition called anencephaly. His brain is not growing."

"It won't ever grow?" Gary asked.

Enrique took off his glasses again, his face strained. "No."

Dot lay back, looking up into the white circle of light above her, and at that moment she saw God. He loomed over her bed, suffused in the hot cone from the lamp. He was angry, arms crossed, robes flaring out below flowing hair.

She rolled on her side, sobbed once, and threw up.

3

WAVES

At the memory, Dot felt the nausea flood her again and immediately rose from the bed. She opened the door of the bottom cabinet built into one wall. Inside she had a large crucifix, a painted Virgin Mary, and a cluster of candles.

She dropped to her knees and picked up the rosary beads lying on the bottom of the cabinet. "Hail Mary full of grace, the Lord is with thee, blessed art thou among women, and blessed is the fruit of thy womb, Jesus. Holy Mary, Mother of God, pray for us sinners now, and at the hour of our death. Amen."

She began another, but headlights flashed through the window. She quickly closed the door and peered out. Gary.

Her breath caught. She watched his truck bounce down the dirt road between the trailers and turn the corner. She turned away, unwilling to see him step out, to watch his jaunty walk, and the way his shoulders drooped a little more than they used to.

When the bad news came, Gary's concern was for her. He held her hand when the doctors insisted she terminate the pregnancy.

They sent her to an abortion clinic, as the regular clinic couldn't perform the surgery that far into the pregnancy. Gary shielded her from the others in the waiting room, mostly teens, anxious with their parents.

"They're getting rid of their babies, when we've lost ours," she said to him as the nurse called back another young woman, this one hanging on to her teenage boyfriend.

He squeezed her arm. "They've got their stories, their hardships too."

Dot nodded and leaned on his shoulder. The baby was moving. "Hey, feel him," she said. "We won't get to much longer."

He put his hand on her belly. "Hey Bubba," he said, leaning close to her distended stomach. "You probably can't hear us, but we're here. We're right here."

Dot pushed his hand hard against her belly. "Please tell me you can feel him. I know he doesn't kick very hard as small as he is, but tell me you can feel him."

"Here, let's try this." He ran his hand beneath her shirt, oblivious to the people around them, the clerk at the desk, the ding of the elevator outside in the hall.

"There it is again," she said, and shifted his hand. "Please tell me you can feel him, this once."

Gary closed his eyes and held firm, his hand warm on her skin. "Is it small, like bubbles?"

"Yes." Dot turned her face into his shoulder. She had told herself she could be strong in this, but she didn't feel strong. She was afraid to start crying, afraid she couldn't stop.

"I feel it, Dot. I do. It's Bubba."

The nurse called her name. She stood as if in a dream, the scene had gone liquid around her. They couldn't do this. Bubba was alive, and they were going to kill him. Her knees gave out and she stumbled. Gary caught her and wrapped an arm hard around her waist. "Here, I'll help you," he said.

The nurse opened the door and light poured from overhead. Her wet eyes magnified its intensity, and she was momentarily blinded. She held up her arm like a shield. "I see God."

"He's here to watch over you and the baby," Gary whispered.

"He's here to carry out his punishment," she said. "My child is dying for my sins."

The nurse approached, so Gary led her into a room and seemed to concentrate on the instructions. Dot quit listening. She could not follow the stream of words. She looked around the room—a table with stirrups on the end, not little ones for feet like in the doctor's office, but big ones for your knees, like the ones in the hospital where she'd had her babies.

The room had a large closet, and inside it she could see crates of glass bottles with big open mouths. Did they put the babies in those jars? Surely not. Surely they wouldn't be clear. Surely they couldn't do that—look at the babies in jars.

The nurse left, and Gary helped her undress and settle on the table. "Why won't they let us just have him?" she said. "Why do we have to do this?"

"The doctors, I guess they just know. They said it's dangerous, that you could die. You got all those kids, Dot, and they ain't got no dad. You can't risk it."

"This is too much. Too much." Dot rolled away from him. This was not to be borne. She had to set things right. "I can't see you after today, Gary. I may not risk dying to see this baby, but seeing you another day means I might not get to see them in heaven either."

"Dot, you've been talking this way every since we found out. I love you. I want to take care of you. We're going to get you divorced and get this all straight. You'll get right with God."

She couldn't see him, facing the closet and the jars. "You think those jars are for the babies?" she asked.

He expelled a rush of air. "I don't know. I don't think I want to know."

The nurse returned and set up a little tent with a drape over her knees. "Let's get you on your back."

The door opened. "Hello, Dot," the doctor said.

Dot fitted her head on the pillow. "Are we sure I have to do this?"

"Your doctors sent you to me. That means they were sure. We're going to attach two monitors while we do this—blood pressure, heart rate. You should have taken some medications this morning. Did you get those?"

Dot nodded.

"I'm going to check your laminaria," he said. "Make sure you're well dilated. They went in okay yesterday?"

"I didn't feel it once they were done."

The doctor helped lift her feet in the stirrups. "You might want to lose a little weight before getting pregnant again," he said. "Not healthy."

Dot washed cold. They were taking her baby before her eyes, and he wanted to talk about her weight? She turned to look at Gary, who sat stiffly in the side chair, his knuckles white with his grip on the arm rests. He wants to punch that doctor, she thought. But he won't. He's too good a guy. Buster would've punched him.

"It all looks good," the doctor said. "I'll be back in just a few minutes. The nurse will start the gas."

A large woman in pink scrubs fitted her with an arm cuff and checked her blood pressure. Then she placed a monitor over her belly. Bubba's heartbeat flooded the room, a rapid whomp whomp. The nurse flicked off the sound. The screen still silently showed the pulse of it, a small corresponding number blinking in the corner.

184. 178. 192.

Dot closed her eyes until she felt the nurse touching her face. "Try not to cry," she said. "It will interfere with the gas." The woman fitted a rubbery mask over her nose and mouth.

Gary took her hand and she concentrated on that one touch, every callus, each rough spot in his skin. Had she just told him she couldn't see him anymore? It seemed the right thing at that moment. But his being here felt right in this one.

The door opened and the doctor sat on a stool between her knees. She felt the cool slide of metal inside her and the opening of the instrument. She looked over at Gary, who sat on the edge of the chair, leaning forward to hold her hand.

"Does she have to be awake for this?" Gary asked. "I didn't know she would be awake."

"There's no need for a general for this procedure," the doctor said.

Gary looked at her and drew his eyebrows together in concern. She shrugged.

"Here we go, Dot," the doctor said. "You're going to feel a little pressure, but no pain."

"Is the baby going to come out alive?" Gary asked.

The doctor paused a moment. "No," he said. "We are not dilating her to get it out whole. That would require labor and delivery."

"It's going to be in pieces?" Gary turned ashen.

"Yes." The doctor sat back on the stool. "If you think you'd rather not be here, you can wait outside."

Gary bent over and stared at the floor, still holding her hand. "No, I'll be here."

The doctor leaned forward, and Dot struggled with the rubber pieces on her face. She felt claustrophobic, but the air was hot and sweet. She felt mirth rising, a bubble of funny, and stifled a giggle.

How could they do this? Make her want to laugh when she should cry? She looked over at the nurse, who scowled slightly, as a warning. She looked past her at the monitor.

186. 178. 182.

The doctor reached beside him for a long tube. She couldn't see much more, as the blue panel blocked her view. She turned back to the monitor and felt Bubba moving within her, slowly, like a wave.

The pressure began low between her legs and pushed up, as if she were swelling, then reached higher and higher until she could feel it near her belly button, then by her ribs. The graph on the monitor began spiking and she couldn't tear her eyes from the screen.

196.

186.

0.

4

BIBLE BEATING

Dot lay on the bed at home, fingering the cross while she waited for Buster. She hadn't cut Gary off totally after the surgery. She needed him too much. She had the kids. Work. Bills. Dinners. She couldn't manage it alone. He and Martha helped out during the long hours she lay in the bed, curled around her rosary beads and unable to move.

Dot could still recall standing in the kitchen a week later, feeling a bit better that the bleeding had finally stopped, when a horrible cramp took hold.

Gary was there, spooning cereal into Lottie. She'd dropped the cookie jar, the pieces shattering across the floor. He had dashed to her despite his bare feet and held her as she bent over. The pain was tremendous. When it eased a moment later she knew something was coming out.

They took tiny steps to the bathroom, Gary's feet bleeding on the linoleum. She yanked down her pants just as something passed out of her. It fell into her hands.

She felt hysterical, blood spilling everywhere, sorting through the clots until she had cleared it enough to see. Her heart clamored as she held her breath. What would it be? A little foot? A finger? A bone?

It looked like a piece of popped balloon. She opened the cabinet with her elbow and grabbed an empty Wal-Mart bag from under the sink. She dropped the piece in it. This might be all she'd ever have of Bubba. Later she'd transferred it to a Ziploc and placed it in her freezer.

After that day, no more Gary. She took his key ring and removed the spare to her trailer. He stood just inside the doorway, his bare feet in bandages, and waited for her to finish.

He quit coming into the store for Dos Equis. Sometimes she caught a glimpse of him driving by from work to his trailer, but she always closed the curtains.

A key jingled by the front door. She jumped up and shoved the cross in a drawer.

The door opened with a squeak. "Baby Dot?" Buster called.

She walked down the hall and peered through the gloom of the living room. He stood, big as a bear, wearing a ball cap and blue overalls.

"Baby Dot, my Baby Dot," he repeated, scooping her up in a full body hug. "I'm home."

Buster lay sleeping. Dot slid from the sheets and snatched a robe from the hook on the door. He wasted no time getting her into bed the first night and seemed to want to do nothing but drag her back into it since he'd been back. They probably hadn't said ten words to each other that wasn't about the kids. But with him seeming intent on knocking her up again, she could barely keep up with the kids and meals and her work at the store.

She padded down the hall to the kitchen. To hell with not eating. Buster was obviously going to rut into her no matter what she looked like. She sat by the open refrigerator door, staring into the light.

She closed the door and opened the freezer. Buster cared nothing about what she felt or if she even liked what he was doing. He hadn't been that way before. She flashed to Gary, the way he'd been so tender with her, tucking her head against his shoulder, stroking her hair. A sob caught in her throat and she shoved boxes aside to find the peas and her hidden bag below.

She clutched it to her chest, the gesture now familiar and comforting, and gave herself just the briefest moment to think of Gary, and her life before she lost the baby. Life was hard now, and she prayed less, too tired even for God.

But in these moments alone, away from Buster and the endless sex and kids and food and cleanup, she thought of Gary, rubbing her belly. Gary, concerned when she worried what everyone would say about her pregnancy. Gary, spooning cereal into Lottie while scooting a soccer ball across the floor to Ben with his foot. Gary. Gary. Gary.

She was sinning. Her rightful husband had come home. She couldn't do this. She held the bag in her hands and knew the hour had come to let it all go. It hadn't been right.

She opened the cabinet under the sink and dropped the bag in the trash. The mere act of letting it go—her only link to Gary and her baby—set her to sobbing. The pain in her stomach was so fierce she had to sit on the floor.

She reached automatically to her chest for the cross but it wasn't there. Buster didn't like it, said it banged him on the head while she straddled him.

She slid across the floor, trying to find a catechism, or a rosary or her Portals of Prayer. Anything.

Lottie's crayons bumped her knee—the big fat kind she could hold in her fist without breaking. She snatched one and wrote, "Hail Mary full of grace" across the smiling face of a puppy in the coloring book.

It wasn't enough, so she wrote, "The Lord is with thee, blessed art thou among women." The page wasn't large enough, so the words carried over to the floor.

The crayon was orange and did not show up on the linoleum in the dim light so she switched to purple. "Blessed is the fruit of thy womb, Jesus." How could she write this when the fruit of her own womb had been anything but blessed? She kept going. "Holy Mary, Mother of God, pray for us sinners." That was better.

The floor ended abruptly at the wall so she continued the words up the wallpaper, stopping at a picture hanging in the way and taking up the rest above it. "Now, and at the hour of our death." She wrote hastily, the scrawl growing into enormous loops and lines. She returned to cross the "t" in "death" and swung her arm so far that she knocked a plaster mold of Sunny's hand off the wall. It crashed to the floor and shattered. She stared at it, little pieces spread in a starburst of her daughter's broken handprint.

Buster stumbled into the kitchen. "Woman? What are you doing?" He flipped on the light and blinked.

Dot fell back, bracing her arms on the cabinet. "Petitioning the Virgin," she said.

He shielded his eyes for a moment, then saw the words across the floor. "What the—"

He read the sentences as they traveled up and across the wall. "What the hell has gotten into you?"

She peered between the strands of hair that fell into her eyes and stared at the mottled red of his face. "Finding my place with God."

"You better find your place to clean up this mess!"

"I must pay for my sins."

Buster froze. "Now, what sins would that be?" His voice came slowly with measured calm.

She had gone so far. Too far. "I have killed my child."

Buster grabbed the edge of the cabinet on either side of her. "My God. Which one? Lottie? The baby? Aurora? My God. What have you done?" He turned to the door as if trying to decide which way to run.

"The one to be born this Easter." She sank to the floor, hands clutching her head.

"What baby this Easter?" he roared and hauled her back up. "There couldn't have been no baby this Easter!"

Dot had never felt his rage this way. He'd never hit her or thrown her around. She ran for the back door, but he caught her around the waist and yanked her against him. She grasped the back door and wrenched it open, kicking against his legs.

"Tell me who you were fucking!"

His voice echoed through the night, reverberating off the walls of other trailers in the park. "Tell me who it was! I'll send him straight to hell!"

The light popped on in the windows across the gravel road. Dogs began to bark.

"I'm already going to hell!" she screamed and tried to claw her way through the door.

He held her tight, moving to kick the door closed. She blocked it with her wrist, shrieking with pain.

"I'm going to kill both of you! Tell me who the fuck it was!"

She couldn't see Buster, but he still held her firmly, trying to wrench her away from the door.

"Mama?"

One of the babies. Oh God.

Buster turned for a moment. "Get your ass back to bed right now!"

Dot used the moment to kick harder, lurching toward the door. She caught a movement along the road and saw Gary running toward the trailer, baseball bat in hand.

"Is that the one?" Buster roared, letting her go and lunging toward the door.

"No! He's a security guard!" She called out the door, "Everything's fine here! No need for help!"

She grabbed the door and slammed it shut. "We'll just quiet down now, and he'll pass on by!"

Buster grabbed her by the collar of her robe and dragged her through the kitchen. "Clean up this mess and don't ever talk about God in front of me again, you little whore." He flung her down. "I don't strike a woman, but I'll beat you senseless next time. And I'll find out who your little dick was. I have friends around here."

Dot nodded and rubbed the frayed corner of her robe against the crayon words on the floor. Her thought flickered to Gary, him arriving with the bat to save her, but no one knocked on the door, nothing else happened.

Buster left the room and headed back to bed. As soon as she heard the squeak of the springs she scrambled to the kitchen window. Gary was still out there, sitting on a picnic bench by her neighbor's deck.

He saw her in the window and stood. Her heart lurched again, but she just closed the curtain.

The pain in her gut remained. She swiped at the writing on the floor, then crawled on her hands and knees to the bookcase just outside the door in the hall. She tugged a Bible from the bottom shelf and lay on the floor. Growing up, they'd never really read directly from the Bible, only the Catechism. But God had to have a message for her. She was still his child, sinner though she was. She opened to a random page and stuck her finger blindly on a verse.

> *I have eaten my honeycomb and my honey;*
> *I have drunk my wine and my milk*
> *Eat, friends;*
> *Drink and imbibe deeply, O lovers.*

She closed the book, confused and lost. She'd never heard anything like that in church. It didn't sound like the word of God. Her whole world felt foreign. She'd been forsaken, and even God could not help her now.

5

WOUNDS

She was late to the meeting again even though this time Buster was there to watch the kids. One of the boys had jumped off the sofa and crashed the lamp, leaving broken glass everywhere. She had to sweep it up before the baby got into it.

The van took six tries to start. Buster even came out and messed with it a spell. He'd wanted to know exactly where she was going. She couldn't say church, as he was still in a piss about the Hail Mary on the wall. He'd thrown out all her crucifixes. Luckily she had a bunch hidden, including her mama's rosary beads.

Finally she said she was going to take care of some ladies. It was the truth, and he saw that when she said it. She was able to tell all about Melinda and her trash can baby, and Janet's oozing black tar out her privates, and Buster said no more, no more.

So she was off, relieved to be away from the trailer and the mess her life was in, if just for a couple hours.

Stella and Janet had already arrived, dragging chairs into place.

"Hello Dot," Stella said. She was breathing hard just from the effort of moving the furniture. Dot could see she had once been a real looker—still was in her way, but the pretty in her face was weighted down now. Sort of like her own. "You been doing all right?"

Dot didn't think she should answer, afraid to start the torrent of explaining life with Buster back. She just nodded, grabbing chairs and moving them into the circle.

"We have a new one coming today," Stella said. "A young girl, seventeen."

"Good Lord," Janet said. "What happened to her?"

"I expect if she makes it, she'll tell her story." Stella pinched her lips into a firm line, and Dot knew there was more to it, but Stella couldn't say. Couldn't be anything much freakier than the society girl coming in to say she'd trashed her baby.

Melinda herself walked in, taking a seat next to Janet. Skinny little sticks, both of them. Showed what money could do. Funny that the people who afford the most had to eat the least.

"Raven won't be with us today," Stella said. "She called and said she was ovulating, so they couldn't waste any time."

"Good for her," Melinda said. She sat all proper, ankles crossed, like Dot's mama had forever tried to get her and her sisters to do. She was dressed up even more than before, a fancy knit suit with black buttons covered in the same fabric as the skirt. Dot had never seen anything like that, buttons made up to look like the cloth. She was glad the woman hadn't called her. Must be too busy shopping.

She reached for her crucifix by habit and frowned when she realized it was gone. Damn Buster. If only she'd held it together that night. She remembered Gary again, bat on his shoulder, gray in the dim light.

Stella started reading that same old boring book. She only did it to kill time so everyone could get there and not miss anything.

She'd barely gotten started when the door opened.

"Is this the pregnancy loss group?" The girl stood in the doorway, skinny with black hair in tiny ponytails sticking straight out from her head. Her long legs stood out in rainbow tights leading to denim jeans cut off above the knee.

Stella heaved herself from her chair. "It is! Come on in. We've got chairs. Are you Tina?"

"The one and only." She ambled toward them, and Dot noticed right off the bulges beneath the fitted sleeves of her DayGlo orange top. Her wrists were all bandaged up. This girl had problems. Maybe bigger than any of them.

Tina slouched into a chair. She looked around, noticed Melinda, and abruptly sat up. "I saw you."

Melinda peered at the girl, raising her eyebrows when she got to the stockings. "Yes, you were at the hospital the same night as me. I saw you too, strapped to a fetal monitor."

"Weird." Tina slid down in the chair and pulled her striped knees up to her chest.

Stella set the book on the floor. "Since we have some new folks, we can do introductions. I'm Stella. I'm the leader of this group and first joined in 1996. I've had two miscarriages. Both happened at eight weeks, one natural, one D&C. After that, I couldn't get pregnant. Did six rounds of IVF before funds ran out. Wiped us out, I should say. So now we have cats."

She stopped, then gestured to Janet.

Janet smiled beneath a pile of perfect hair. Dot couldn't even imagine how she did that every day.

"I'm Janet. I lost my first pregnancy seven weeks ago. I'm still going through the missed miscarriage. I would like it all to happen naturally. I'm not much for surgery..." She trailed off, eyes downcast, her hand pressed against her beige suit. Dot figured she had to be constantly in pain. That woman was no wimp.

"I guess I'm up next," Melinda said. "I lost my baby a few weeks ago." She turned to Tina. "Apparently the same night as Tina. I did worry about you. Jake has a teenager, Anna. Fourteen. And a boy, Adam. Everyone seems to think that makes it easier, but it seems, well, harder, actually. She could do that for him, and I didn't."

"You'll be all right," Stella said. "There will be more chances, I think. Has your recovery been easy?"

"Easier than it seems it should have been."

Stella nodded. "I understand what you mean. All that hope we put into them, seems like it would come out in screams and pain."

"Like labor," Tina said quietly and everyone turned to her. "I had that, but it wasn't too hard either." She looked around the circle. "I guess it's my turn." She tucked her knees even tighter to her chest, the orange sleeves wrapped around the striped leggings. "I got pregnant in November. Told my parents as a Christmas present." She forced a laugh. "Arnie—the baby's dad—he's a senior. I'm a junior. We fixed up a little place over the garage behind my parents' house. Didn't get married though." She rested her chin on her knees.

"I haven't seen him since I had Peanut. He took off. He's probably back at school, but I mostly cut class." She held out her hand. "The baby only weighted thirteen ounces. His little butt fit right here in my palm, his head against my fingers. He had the tiniest legs; they sorta dangled on my wrist." She glanced at the bulge beneath her sleeve and Dot held her breath, waiting for her to mention it, but Tina just wrapped her arm around her tights again.

"He lived for three hours. Arnie never saw him." She cocked her head to the side and closed her eyes. "I miss my Peanut. That's all I have to say now."

"You just let us know if you need anything, Tina," Stella said. "We know how it is."

"This group really will help you." Melinda looked at Dot. "We have no secrets here, and the willingness of everyone to share is … it's a real blessing. I wouldn't have made it without Dot."

Dot shifted in her chair. "It was nothing."

"But it wasn't," Melinda said. "You telling us about the placenta meant a lot."

Not that again. Dot sunk down a bit in her chair.

"I thought I was crazy, and you showed me I wasn't," Melinda said. "It was the turning point to everything for me." She leaned over to clasp Dot's wrist, her bony fingers chilly. "You matter to me."

Dot tried to swallow around the lump in her throat. She never knew why she came here, other than to get some time away from the kids to think about Bubba. But maybe it was a good thing, helpful to somebody else.

"I'm a lawyer, you know," Melinda said. "If you ever need some help, you call me. I will help you."

Dot nodded, and Melinda moved away.

Stella nodded, the chain on her glasses swinging against her cheeks. "That's mighty fine of all of you. We have to take care of each other, especially young Tina here."

Dot watched the girl from under a curtain of hair. Poor little mite, all curled up on that chair. The rest of them all had men, were grown, and none of them wanted to end it all. For the first time in a long while, she thanked God for what blessings she did have.

6

BETRAYAL

Dot lugged the crate of dog food cans from the back to the front aisle of the store. She knelt down in her jeans and sweatshirt, her hair sticking to her neck, and unloaded the cans. She'd be off tomorrow for Easter Sunday. Last night she'd spit-shined the kids and taken them to Good Friday services but Buster hadn't wanted to go. "You watch that religion stuff," he'd warned.

She'd cleaned all the Bible verses off the walls and life was settling in a bit. Buster was no dream husband but at least he kept the kids out of her hair while she worked. She couldn't ask for much more.

"Dot?"

At Gary's voice, she dropped two cans, and they started rolling across the floor with a clatter.

She could see his blue-jeaned knee as he bent down to pick them up. She couldn't turn her head even a fraction or she'd see too much—a foot, maybe, probably bare—or a thigh. That would be too much. A foot or a thigh, either one.

She breathed in measured increments and kept her eyes on the floor, stacking cans with razor precision. Each label got turned out just so; every canine face level, creating a perfect line of eyes and collars.

"Can I talk to you, Dot?"

Even his voice was more than she could manage. In all these weeks of avoiding him, and him politely not coming in the store, she'd forgotten how he affected her.

"It's best not. You better go. Buster might come in any moment."

"He's tied up right now, I promise."

She looked up. "What do you mean?"

He knelt close to her, those crystal eyes holding her steady. "Are you okay? Is everything okay with Buster?"

She stood. "He's home now, seems to intend to stay for a bit. Kids took right to him again. We're doing okay."

"But the other night—"

"Just a disagreement, that's all. Every couple has them."

Lucy, one of the park housewives, cut through the door with a bang. "Helloooo! Anyone here?"

Dot stood suddenly, her head popping over the aisle.

"I'm here! You need something!"

"I need change for a dollar! Dang Laundromat machine stuck again. OH!"

At her exclamation, Dot realized Gary had also stood.

Lucy fluttered the dollar bill by her neck. "I didn't know I was interrupting!"

"No, no, I was just stocking shelves."

"I can see that!" Lucy's wispy white hair ruffled around her pale sweaty face. Dot felt a wave of panic, then cold fear. Lucy was no friend of hers. No telling what she might say to Buster.

Dot took the money. "Let me get you your change. Gary was just leaving, right?"

"No, ma'am, I'm not done here."

Lucy coughed and hid her laugh behind hot pink nails.

Dot clanged the cash register shut. "Here's your quarters," she said and dropped the money into Lucy's outstretched palm.

"Too-da-loo!" Lucy said, waggling her bright fingers as she banged back through the door. "Don't do anything I wouldn't do!"

When she was gone, Gary said, "I bet that ain't much."

"That woman is trouble." Dot held tight to the register.

Gary moved closer. "I'm worried about you. It's my right. You carried my child. We went through hell."

"And everything's back to how it was. I got my husband and you're free to find a woman."

"I don't feel free. I feel all knotted up inside. I love you and I miss our baby and the plans we made. You just shut me out. It's not right or fair."

"Then hate me and go on," Dot said. "It hasn't been a picnic for me neither."

Gary rounded the back of the counter to stand next to her. "Dot, you looked so frightened the other night. I wish I could believe you're okay." He took her hand.

Dot pulled away. "It can't ever be like it was. It shouldn't have ever been. I was wrong."

"I wasn't. I loved you. I loved that baby and that passel of kids you have. You think I don't miss them?"

She dared to look at him again. His hair flopped on his forehead and his eyes were so earnest. If only she'd been free. What a life they could have had.

"What the fuck is this!" Buster roared through the screen door, his long hair flying behind him. "I knew this was him! You're still cuckolding me!"

"I am not!" Dot cried. "He's just in here getting some beer!"

"Beer my ass! I'm going to finish this one right here and now!" Buster's face was mottled red, wild and angry with its mane of shaggy hair.

"You best get on out of here," Dot said to Gary, not taking her eyes from Buster.

But Gary casually leaned on the counter. "He don't scare me," he said. "And you're a fine one to talk of cuckolding after the parade of trailer trash going in and out your door since you got back."

"You lie!" Buster growled and snatched at the man's collar.

"I believe there's a little floozy named Arlene Summer there right now."

"What!" Dot skipped past Gary and rounded the register. She'd almost made it to the door when Buster grabbed her shirt.

"Baby Dot, don't be believing that damn fool boy. You stay right here."

"Like hell I will!" She yanked free of Buster's fingers and dashed out the door. She ran full tilt to her trailer and hurled herself inside.

Kids were scattered on the floor of the living room. The boys were playing with boats. "Where's Aurora?" Dot asked, looking wildly around. Her oldest girl would tell her.

"Out back."

Dot dashed through the kitchen and opened the back door. Aurora sat on the picnic table, getting her fingernails painted by Arlene.

She paused on the cinderblock steps. Maybe Gary was wrong. Maybe she was just here to help out.

But suddenly some things started to make sense. Buster, willing to stay home with the kids and keep even Lottie, who had new girlie hairdos. Little tins of leftovers randomly sitting in the fridge. Buster couldn't have done all that.

The older kids were normally at school and Buster could probably count on the little ones not talking.

"You got a fine bit of mettle being here on a Saturday," Dot said.

"Mama!" Aurora jumped up and showed Dot her hands. "Look, Arlene's putting daisies on the ends!"

The woman closed the bottle. "Now, Dot. You're one to talk."

So it was true.

"There's at least a dozen others," Dot said.

"Fine by me! I ain't in it to get married!"

A shot of hysteria surged through Dot again, only this time she didn't see Jesus. She saw fire. "Get out of my yard!" she screamed. "Get out and don't come back or I'll shoot you!"

Arlene scrambled out of the picnic table. "Ain't like you should care. You got Gary on the side, and Buster says you don't got no interest in his bed anyway! That man's got skills."

"GO!"

"Mama, she didn't finish my nails!"

"Get inside!"

Aurora's face pulled in fear. She almost protested, but instead she ran in the house just as Buster rounded the corner of the trailer.

"Ah, Dot, don't go chasing off my help," he said as Arlene packed her purse.

"That's a fine way to put it," Arlene said. She looked old in the sun, the black roots showing through her brassy red hair.

Dot raced up to Buster. "You son of a bitch!" She beat her hands on his chest. "I give up the only thing that's ever mattered to me and you run around while I work! In my own house that you don't even pay for! With our kids around!"

Buster grabbed her hands. "Now see, that's why I don't hang around here much. You're just too uptight. Damn Jesus freak no less."

Dot sat on the cinderblocks. "I tried to keep us a family. All this time while you were running around banging truck stop floozies."

"I figured you didn't care much."

"I don't anymore. And I don't want you around at all."

"You can't kick me out of my own house."

"It ain't yours. I done paid for it all these years. One of my friends is a lawyer. We're going after you."

Buster laughed. "Dot, you're all talk. I'm going inside." He stepped past her and up into the trailer.

Dot sat a long time, not crying or angry or anything, just thinking. She would kick Buster out or else just move the kids and leave him to it. She could find some other job, surely. She'd figured it out all this time. She'd figure it out again. "You got to help me," she said to the sky. "I can't do this on my own."

"I'll help, you know. I want to help."

Dot jumped and turned to see Gary walking toward her. "You want me to haul him out of your house, I'll haul him out. You want to cram the kids into my place, we'll make them fit." He pulled her in close. "It's our time, it really is. Will you come with me now?"

Dot didn't answer, just leaned her head into his chest. "I don't deserve you," she said. "I'm all messed up."

"We'll be all right. Will you come with me now?"

She nodded against his chest, and he spread his fingers out in her hair.

"It's about time you figured it out," he said.

"I guess I'm lucky you're patient with dull-witted trailer trash."

He grasped her jaw and pulled her away from his chest to look at her. "I got a thing for dull-witted trailer trash."

PART THREE: *Tina*

1

DEVELOPMENT

The paper slid underwater in the tray, ghostly beneath the dim red glow of the darkroom's safety light. Tina pushed the wet corners with her tongs, agitating the chemicals as they drifted over the surface of exposed emulsion. When the image began to emerge on the page, her premature baby in his final hour, Peanut appeared to float in his rosy sea, materializing as if from a dream.

The portrait grew in density and contrast, the edges more distinct, his pencil-nub nose, heart-shaped mouth, and closed eyes. This was the last picture she had taken, after they'd removed the wires, when the doctor said he was ready to go, his heartbeat barely discernable anymore. He had been too early to save; only half the pregnancy months had passed when he was born.

His body had fit in her palm. He weighed no more than a handful of feathers, fragile and warm, each feature perfectly formed. Her mother had reached out her arms, and Tina passed the baby to her. She picked up the camera, adjusting the settings for the shot. His face showed only in profile against her mom's white sweater, his tiny hand curled beneath his chin.

The image was ready. Tina wiped her nose and lifted the paper from the chemicals, letting it drip for a moment before sliding it into the stop bath to neutralize the developer. Peanut rocked lightly as she tipped the tray to wash the print, his face blurring with the gentle motion of the liquid. After thirty seconds, she tugged the paper out and submerged it in the fixer, where the silver-halide crystals, now stained in shades of gray, would become permanent, no longer vulnerable to the glare of outside light.

A small buzzer sounded, the signal someone was turning the light-proof door to enter the room. Tina wiped her nose again and pushed the picture around, watching the clock. Two minutes until the fixer would be complete. She tensed as she waited to see who might intrude. Pretty much every choice was bad.

Mrs. Smits, the photography teacher, would admonish her for using school facilities to make private prints, probably guessing Tina had only joined her staff to gain access to the darkroom. Jeremy, the newspaper editor, would ask about the photos for the sports pages, as if she cared a rat's ass about baseball. She hadn't bothered to go to the game.

Any of the insipid girls in Intro to Photography would giggle, whispering to each other about the slutty junior who got knocked up by Arnie, the art freak.

She dunked the image deeper into the tray, trying to retain the feeling of peace she'd felt at first seeing it. But the circular door groaned on its track, and her quiet was about to be interrupted.

The noise stopped. Whoever it was would have to adjust to the red light before stepping forward. She stole a peek with a sidelong glance.

A tall lanky boy stood by the entry. Simon, a page designer on staff. She didn't know him too well, but he was probably the least of many evils.

He crossed the long narrow room and passed her from behind. "Just getting some prints to scan," he said, unclipping photographs from the drying line in the corner.

One minute to fix, then she could rinse and get out. She clenched her jaw, daring Simon to look at her photograph, to make a comment. She might deck him if he did. Getting suspended from this godforsaken school would be fine by her, especially now that she possessed the only thing it offered her—this last critical print.

"You're one of the last holdouts, you know," Simon said. "Most everyone switches to the digital camera once they pass Smits' archaic black and white exam."

Tina pushed the print around again. Thirty seconds.

She heard the shuffle of his feet as he turned. Don't look at my picture, she silently warned.

He passed by, prints in hand, and paused by the door. "I agree with you, though. Your work is way better than the digital stuff—more like art."

She didn't want conversation. She wanted him to leave. After a moment, the low rumble of metal bumped along the track. She released a long-held breath, grasped the corner of her portrait of Peanut, and began to rinse it in the final tray.

She wouldn't stay at this school any longer than she had to. Now that she had all the prints, she'd quit worrying about what anyone thought about her, the teachers, the principal, her parents, everybody. Her baby had died. Her boyfriend had ditched her. She'd been kicked out of the High School for Pregnant Teens and sent back to this hellhole of public school. She didn't have anything else to lose.

Tina stepped off the bus to a chorus of hoots. She should have taken her Jeep, if she could have afforded the gas. Her parents quit giving her money. Said she wasn't responsible and could ride the bus. She'd been responsible enough to have a kid and watch it die. Gas money would not be a stretch.

She skirted the lawn and headed straight to her garage apartment in the back. Her parents, in one of their better moments, had set it up for her and Arnie a couple weeks after she'd told them she was keeping the baby. They'd only gotten to live together there a month. Best month ever, too.

The screen door slammed as her mother hurried out the back to intercept her. Damn. She'd have to start getting off the bus a stop early, see if she could fake her out.

"Tina! Oh, Tina!" her mother called, drying her hands on a dish-towel as she careened across the grass. She looked like some sort of fifties mom with her big hair and a ruffled apron.

Tina kept her head down, barreling toward the stairs leading up to her apartment. She did not want a mother-daughter chat today.

"Tina!"

The strident note in her mother's tone made Tina halt on the third step. She turned slowly to look at her mom, who pressed a hand against her chest as she held on to the rail.

"Whew! I need to get in shape!" She huffed lightly. "I thought you could come in the house today, tell me how things are going. I made ginger cookies, your favorite."

That was so totally like her mother. As if cookies could save the world.

"Nah, I've got homework." Of course, she'd ditched class, other than Newspaper, but no one seemed to report her. Life was undoubtedly easier for her teachers when she wasn't there, fighting catcalls and dirty notes that sparked her rage. Tina continued up the steps, now several feet above her mother.

"I could help you! I know you've got a lot of catching up to do."

Tina stared down at her mother's black roots, visible against the mixed blond highlights. She might try to force Tina back into the main house. Better to avoid all conversation.

"No thanks. I just need to get to it." She climbed the rest of the way, wondering if this would be the day her mother would finally get the guts to follow her up, to insist her daughter do what she said.

"Well, call if you need anything!"

Apparently not.

Tina unlocked the door and bumped it open with her hip. Another day salvaged. She dropped her bag on the kitchen bar. The handle caught on her sleeve, stripping the tape off one of her bandages.

"Holy crap!" she shouted, pressing her hand against the fiery burn of her wrist. "Don't ever slice yourself!" she called to the ceiling. "It hurts like a mother!" Then she clapped her hand over her mouth, edging over to the window to see if her mom had heard.

The screen door at the back of the house banged closed.

She headed back to the sink, bracing her arm over the edge as if blood might come pouring out any second. Part of the adhesive had worked loose.

She tugged at the bandage, revealing the pale swollen skin marred by three distinct lines, now crisscrossed with a mending tape. Steri strips, or something, they had called them. Better than black stitches and Frankenstein arms.

Down in the bathroom where the light was better, she opened the mirrored cabinet and pulled out a roll of white adhesive. She tore a strip with her teeth and flattened it against the bandage, grimacing at the pressure. What a stupid thing to have done, really. But she couldn't help herself. That day had been too much, too awful.

She opened the cabinet again to return the tape, noting the empty shelves. All the razors were gone, of course, her parents had certainly scoured the apartment for anything sharp. She sat on the toilet lid, still holding her arm, and leaned her head against the shower stall. A chalk drawing of Peanut hung opposite her, all soft colors and striated tones.

Just a few weeks ago, her life had been all right, a little messed up, pregnant and pissed-off parents, but Arnie was being cool, moved in and treating her decent.

She had applied to the School for Pregnant Teens and got in, focusing on photography as art, and the teachers there were way better. Yes, everything had been going pretty grand until the night the contractions started.

Back pain had plagued her all that day, but that was par. The school nurse wasn't worried, reminding her this was a rapid-growth period of the pregnancy. Then at dinner, one minute she was shoveling Chinese noodles in her mouth, the next she was doubled over, huffing. She let the first cramp go, and then a second, but when the third one came, she called out to Arnie, who was working in the back.

"We gotta go!" she shouted. "Hospital."

He wandered into the room, a brush in his hand. The metallic sheen of his red paint glittered in the light. More Goth stuff, probably. He liked gold angels with ruby eyes. He didn't quite believe she was in trouble, but when the fourth contraction came, he stuck his brush in the sink and helped her out the door.

He was great at first, nervously pacing the waiting room, phoning her parents, waiting to be called back. But for some reason, when Tina leaned back on the examination table inside her blue-curtained room, the nurse fitting her feet into the stirrups, Arnie took off like a startled deer, leaving the curtain open so random people could peer in.

She didn't have her cell phone to call him. After sticking an IV in Tina's arm and strapping some box on her belly, the nurse excused herself. Suddenly she lay alone with the machine measuring her contractions and the rapid heartbeat of the baby. Well, not entirely alone. She had Peanut still. She turned her head to the paper rolling out of the printer. Thin levers ran along the page, drawing the spikes of its measurements on a never-ending scroll.

A tear ran into her ear. She stuck a finger in to wipe it out, supremely pissed off that she was crying. She idly watched the monitor, a little heart icon beating in sync with the baby. The pulse flashed on screen. 172. 164. 170.

Another contraction began, and her breath came out in huffs. She knew she was in labor. Her birth coach had told them the signs. There was some drug they could give you. Figures Arnie wouldn't be here to hold her hand or anything. Not that she needed it. Really.

The curtain slid aside, and she popped her head around.

"Tina!" Her mother rushed forward and pressed into her shoulder with a hard hug. "My baby! Are you okay?" She pulled away, her face wet, eyes red, and stroked Tina's hair away from her forehead.

Tina swallowed hard, coughing until her throat cleared. Parents didn't seem like a bad thing at the moment. "No one has said anything."

A nurse led her father inside the partition, where he stood tall and gray-haired in the white light. "What is happening?" he asked.

The nurse checked the long roll of paper. "She's having premature labor. We've paged an OB to assess her. He'll be here any minute."

"Why isn't she on the labor ward?" her mother asked. "It's horrible down here."

The woman shifted the box on Tina's stomach. "We'll move her when we get the doctor's okay. Maternity may not be the best option."

"What do you mean?" Her mother faced the nurse, her eyes wide. Tina held her breath. This was more than anyone had told her.

"We need to stop her labor. We don't want Tina delivering the baby at nineteen weeks."

"Of course," said her father. "Let us know when the doctor can come."

Her parents crowded in the tiny space near Tina's head, maneuvering around the equipment.

Her mother bumped into the machine. "I don't think we can stay here long, Frank. There simply isn't room."

"I'll see about moving this along. I don't think Tina's paperwork is in order anyway." He shoved aside the curtain and stepped through.

Tina relaxed her head again, feeling the trickle of fear now. "Mom?"

"Yes, baby."

"Is Peanut going to die?"

"Of course not. We won't let that happen." She gripped Tina's hand. "We're here now."

Her dad returned with the doctor in dismal gray-blue scrubs that matched the curtains. "This is Dr. Blais," he said.

"Doctor, what's happening?" her mom asked.

He looked over the printout. "Your daughter came in with contractions, but they should respond to the medication and stop." The doctor smiled at Tina and pushed aside part of the paper sheet, slipping a finger inside her as he pressed on her belly. He frowned.

"Speculum," he said to the nurse.

Tina laid her head back, feeling the pressure of the instrument inside her. The nurse snapped on a light.

Dr. Blais turned to the nurse. "Call surgery. We need a room."

Fear washed over her. She clenched her mom's hand, forcing herself not to wish for Arnie.

"What's happening? What is it?" Her mom's voice squeaked. Tina was glad she could ask the question. Her own throat was too dry and tight.

Dr. Blais removed the speculum.

"The baby's foot has already begun to descend through the cervix. She's six millimeters dilated. The baby's going to be born. Probably within the hour."

Her mom gasped. "What? Can't you push it back up?"

"No. The likelihood of infection is very high. That puts baby and mother at risk."

"But the baby can't survive this early."

"No. It needs a few more weeks at least."

"What will happen?" Her mom's face was ashen.

He flipped through the chart. "Let me get the room arranged. It is best to get out of the ER for this. And I'll send someone with the paperwork." He stopped and turned to Tina. "You'll need to think about what you want to do if the baby is alive when born."

"Save it, of course!" her mom said.

Dr. Blais held Tina's eyes. "Just what measures you want to take."

Tina watched him, his face set, eyes blue behind small frameless glasses. He wanted to know what she wanted, nobody else, not her parents, not Arnie. Just her.

She'd taken the childbirth classes. She knew the deal. No miracle was going to happen here today. "I don't want Peanut to hurt. Don't let him hurt."

Dr. Blais squeezed her forearm. "We won't let him hurt."

The baby had been so tiny, so feathery light. They'd wrapped him in a white blanket with a blue stripe, a small white disk with a wire attached to his chest, and laid him under a heat lamp.

He had slid out of her without incident, as he was tiny and the pain of labor had mostly already passed before her arrival at the hospital. After they cleaned her, she sat up in her bed, leaning over the plastic wall of the crib, hand resting lightly on her baby's back, warm under the lamp. She'd touched his tiny cheek, but not stroked, as the doctors said his skin was very sensitive and to over-stimulate him would cause pain.

The nurses took some Polaroids of the baby, but Tina knew she wanted something better, so her father left to get her camera. He returned to find them in the same positions, Tina leaning over the crib, her mother sitting on a chair in the corner. Tina took a few close-ups of the baby, then returned to her position, vowing not to sleep as long as Peanut was alive. Then the monitor had beeped a warning.

A nurse walked in, checked the monitor, and called in a doctor. Peanut still occasionally moved, but his arms no longer flung out with the energy they had before. The baby doc came in and removed the disk and handed Peanut to her. "It won't be long now," he said. "You can hold him until his heart stops. He won't feel any pain."

Tina pulled him very close, then gave him to her mom while she took a picture of him without the wire. But her mother had begun sobbing, handing Peanut back to Tina and fleeing the room, followed by her father. Tina ended up alone on the bed with her baby. She pressed him into her neck, her hand on his back. She nestled onto the pillow, and after a while realized he no longer moved at all.

She tucked him next to her on the bed then, the stressful hours now past, labor, delivery, panic and fear, her overbearing parents and Arnie dashing out—all behind her. Peanut was still warm against her cheek as she dozed off. Sometime later a nurse woke her and said she would have to take him away.

The next day she had come home from the hospital, clutching the Polaroids, something to hold on to until she could develop her own film. She wasn't sure how she would do it, if she was allowed to return to her classes at the school for pregnant teens. They would let her in the darkroom now that she wasn't pregnant.

Her parents wanted her back in her room at home, but she felt certain Arnie would be waiting for her in their apartment, and she wanted to show him the pictures.

The apartment was dark and silent. When she flipped on the light, his paint brush was still in the sink, the red paint dry against the white enamel.

She turned around and gasped. The walls were empty, bits of wire hanging in places, big blank spots where his art had been. She walked through the two small rooms. He'd taken everything that had been his, his paintings, the white canvases, the brushes and oils, clothes and the funny cheeseburger alarm clock.

She stumbled to the bathroom and saw he'd left one drawing on the wall, his vision of what he thought their baby might look like. This image was so different from his others. He'd outlined Peanut in pencil based on the sonograms, then colored in the delicate skin and features with soft chalk.

The one work he hadn't taken with him was their baby.

The world rushed at her too hard. She felt completely out of control, her future whizzing forward—back to her old classes, the mountain of problems, bad attitudes, teachers who didn't like her, mean kids. She'd been so happy at the alternative school, accepted and unique. She and Arnie were artists and revered over there. Girls without supportive boyfriends were so jealous. She couldn't face any of them now.

She washed her face and hands and the gleam of water on her white wrists seemed too pristine, too pearl. The razors lay neatly on the shelves, and she stopped thinking, stopped rationalizing anything at all. The act wasn't about killing herself, not in that moment, or about escaping, it was about marring the perfection of her arms. She was tainted, her baby had died, she was unloved and unwanted. She felt she should be marked by this—that her physical body should bear the scars.

She leaned her pale arm against the sink and didn't hesitate once. Three sharp lines straight down from mid arm to wrist. Before she could feel weak or frightened, she switched the blade to the left hand and made three more on the right.

The blood didn't pour like she thought it would. The lines rose to the surface, first white, then pink, then a thin red etching lifted up. She hadn't been consistent in the pressure, so some parts bled before others, creating beads that slid down her skin. Then one of the cuts opened wide and pulsed out blood with every heartbeat.

She sat amazed by the color, red on white, so bright and harsh. She'd thought she would feel woozy, but the only effect was the light sting of the cuts. She stepped back from the sink and that movement made the blood really come forth, and now it flowed down her palm and off the tips of her fingers.

She realized then she might die. She sat on the toilet lid and tried to decide. Did she call an ambulance and save herself, or did she lie in warm water and let the blood flow sweetly out? She pictured her face beneath the red water, her own amniotic bath. She could wake up with Peanut. No one could take him away from her then.

Her arms hurt something awful now, and she began to see pinpricks of light. The color was draining out of her vision. Some instinct took over, and she stumbled into the living room. She bent to snatch her cell phone out of her bag, almost fainting, leaving streaks of red everywhere. She dialed 911 and managed to tell them what she'd done and where she lived. When the paramedics arrived, she lay on the floor, still lightly conscious as they loaded her into the ambulance. Then her memory ran out.

Back in the bathroom, Tina exhaled in an elongated rush and fingered a bandage. She wouldn't do it again, no way. The ordeal had been entirely too much trouble—parent freak-outs, another visit to the same hospital, then the sophomoric case workers who insisted she go to therapy and the pregnancy loss support group. They, at least, seemed sort of cool, even if they were all old. She felt like a real mother in there with them.

The baby's drawing hung over the towel rack, protected behind glass. It shouldn't be in the bathroom. Tina lifted it off its hook and hugged it close to her. Peanut had been a real person. He'd actually lived. She had pictures to prove it, and he'd even had a dad for a while—a dad who'd been interested enough in him to draw him before he was born.

If only Arnie had stuck around to actually see him. He'd regret it one day. Tina could live with the fact that he'd ditched her. Boys in high school were a drag like that. But to miss your kid's entire life. That's the kind of thing you always end up wishing you'd done different.

2

FATHERS

Nabbed.

In the two weeks she'd been back at school, she'd completely cut Life Skills class. Every day she hung out in the girls' bathroom by the cafeteria, mingling with the kids who had first lunch. Until today.

"Tina Schwartz, you are in serious trouble," said Ms. Deen, the guidance counselor. She was the one who'd stuck Tina in the insipid class, figuring she wouldn't get knocked up again if she were forced to take care of some stupid crying doll. Dumbest. Idea. Ever.

The woman personally escorted Tina to class. "This is going on your record. And if you cut once more, we'll have you suspended."

Sounded like bliss. She crossed the room, head down, and flung herself into a chair while Ms. Deen spoke to the teacher out in the hall.

"Look who returns," Megan had said, flipping her blond hair behind her shoulder and gesturing toward Tina. "The knocked up fuck up."

The other girls on her row tittered.

"I'm not sure why you'd take THIS class," Megan said. "You already know all about makin' da babies!"

Tina's face burned, but she kept her head down.

A tall jock-type sat on the other side of Megan. "Is that the pregnant chick?" he asked her.

"Yeah," said Megan. "Though she must have had the kid."

"I thought she'd have a big rack," the boy said, eyeing Tina's shirt. "Not seeing anything there."

Megan turned and slugged the boy on the shoulder.

"I'm just saying!" he said. "They're like milk duds."

Tina sank lower in her chair. This was not to be endured.

The boy turned back to her. "So where's your kid?"

Tina stared at her desk.

"Hey, I SAID, where's your kid?"

"She probably offed it," Megan said. "Threw it in a dumpster or something."

"We gonna see you on *Cops*?" the boy asked. "Hey, we could get some money out of the deal. Turn her in to the feds."

"Not on *Cops*, you dolt," Megan said. "They only give rewards on *America's Most Wanted.*"

"I don't think so," the boy said. "I distinctly remember a bit at the end about tips leading to the arrest of someone."

"Hardly!" another boy called from behind Tina. "*Cops* just shows them taking the perps down."

"Nah," the jock said. "They do re-enactments too."

Tina let out a breath, glad they had stopped talking about her.

The teacher returned and pulled a life-sized baby from a desk drawer. The class hushed.

"I assume you've all seen this sort of doll on television shows by now and know what's about to happen to you," she said.

"Oh yeah," said the jock. "We're going to be cleaning up fake piss and stay up all night."

"Actually, I can set the levels on the babies and choose to give you an easy happy child or a holy terror. I wouldn't make me mad, Mr. Ellis."

Tina smiled behind her hand, her sweater sleeves tugged down low over her bandages. At least no one here knew about that.

The teacher prattled on about the rules for the babies. Tina had argued with Ms. Deen about this class when she re-enrolled. "An ounce of prevention," the old woman had said, tapping on her keyboard to set Tina's new schedule.

"But I took far more advanced classes on this at the alternative school," Tina had argued. None of this fake baby crap there. They had worked shifts during the day in the infant room, a place for the newborns since the moms were allowed to stay at the school until they graduated.

Megan held a sheet of paper near her shoulder, high enough for Tina to read.

Tina tried to look away and avoid seeing what she knew would be some awful insult, but she caught the words in her peripheral vision anyway. The paper read "Baby killer."

Tina got up and stalked straight out of class. Screw them.

The school bell intoned its horrid modernized bleat. Tina stared up at the red box near the ceiling of the senior hall. She'd like to take a sledgehammer to it.

"Aren't you on the wrong hall, misfit?" a girl said, pushing past her into the room.

It was true. She shouldn't be on the senior hall. She didn't have any classes here, and all the lockers belonged to students older than her. But she wanted to see Arnie. Had to. She was desperate to get back into the good school, even though it meant another pregnancy. He was her solution.

She leaned against the door to Arnie's class. She'd be late to math, but she might just skip. No part of the solution involved doing well in school. And old man Clacker had it out for her. She would probably fail trig anyway even though her grades had always been okay in all the subjects before. But it all seemed so pointless now. Nobody used trig. It wouldn't help her have a baby, or raise it, or be an artist.

She scanned the halls for Arnie. He must have been watching out and deliberately avoided her. No way she could have gone so long back in this hellhole without running into him at least once.

She walked from the end of the hall to the stairwell, keeping her chin down but eyes up. At the corner she paused. He used to have senior English with Mrs. Ashton second period. Surely his schedule hadn't changed.

She peered over the short wall to see if he was on the stairs. The final bell would follow the warning by only ninety seconds. He was either skipping, absent, or late. She turned and strode back to his classroom door. She'd wait.

Fortunately nobody else dashing through Ashton's door knew her, so she did not have to endure any more nasty comments. Just as the bell sounded, Arnie barreled up the stairs and careened down the hall.

"Hey," she said.

He stopped immediately when he saw her. "Shit. Tina."

"You've avoided me."

"I'm late."

"You never cared about that before."

"Well I do now."

"Putz."

"Whatever." He started to circle her for the door. She stepped in the way. Behind her, she heard the teacher calling roll.

"Tina. This is uncool."

"So was moving all your stuff out while I watched our premature baby die."

He exhaled in a long gush. "Shit."

"Yeah. You ran out."

He shifted his books against his hip. "Tina, that was a rough scene."

"Yeah, even rougher when you have to do it by yourself."

"Your parents were coming. Why do you think I blew?"

"It was wrong. You never even got to see Peanut. You left me alone. Everyone left me alone." Her voice cracked, which angered her. No way was she going to show him an ounce of weakness.

Mrs. Ashton came to the door. "Mr. Carrollton, are you going to come to class or shall I mark you absent?"

He stared at Tina and she glowered right back. "Lunch. Okay? I'll meet you then. Looks like you're skipping anyway. So come to third lunch."

She'd have to ditch another class to meet him, but that was fine by her. "I'll be there. By the big tree, like we used to?"

"Yeah."

Tina paced inside the bathroom by the auditorium where she wouldn't be seen by anyone. Trig passed. She'd fail it, but big deal.

The bell rang for second lunch, then finally third. She ducked out of the bathroom after checking her hair sprigs and walked with confident nonchalance to the oak tree behind the cafeteria.

He sat alone under the low branches, an occasional leaf dropping from a limb overhead and landing near his knees. Stupid confused trees, shedding in spring instead of fall. But it would make a good picture. Isolation. A slow disintegration. She wished she had a camera on her.

She hesitated, remembering why she'd fallen for him in the first place and wondering how she might seduce him again. She HAD to get out of this hellhole. Everyone had it out for her.

It hadn't always been that way. She and Arnie were pseudo-popular in the alternative crowd. She'd selected him during a pottery class her sophomore year after Will Price had taken all the sexy stuff she'd taught him and applied it to Bonnie Broom.

She hid in the shadow of the building and watched his hair ruffle in the wind. He checked his watch and scanned the clumps of students hanging out to talk.

Heat rose in her just thinking of Arnie. He made her wait a whole month of dating before he'd sleep with her, which normally would have been a deal breaker, but the way he worked his mouth and fingers kept her going.

He'd been worth the wait. She'd never felt love before, but when his dark head hovered over her face, his eyes smiling, the strength of his body pressing against her, it expanded through her like a mushroom cloud. He'd cooled her jadedness with honest-to-God emotion.

Right till he disappeared the night Peanut arrived.

She was glad for the anger that displaced the sentiment. She couldn't walk up to him all love-smitten again. Control. It was all about control. She touched her hair and strode across the brown lawn just starting to sprout with feeble shoots of new grass.

"Hey," she said.

He tried to unfold his legs with panache and but lost his balance and fell back on his hands. Papers scattered across the dirt.

"Shit," he said. "Look at me. A mess already."

"You were a mess before. I kinda dug that about you."

He stood and brushed dirt off his jeans.

She wanted to close her eyes to the sight of him. His hair was so dark as to sheen blue in the sun. His skin glowed olive and smooth—a rarity among adolescents, including herself with the ever-present smattering of acne. He had the barest hint of a goatee on his chin. She'd never loved anybody before him. The pain in her chest cracked through her. She'd loved him and he'd ditched her anyway. Did she really want this again?

She'd never let herself think the words before, not even the night she'd slashed her wrists. Out here, with springtime shouting in the birdsong and sunshine and fresh blades of grass, the recognition of his betrayal seemed painfully large and out of place, like a splatter of black paint on a Monet.

"So, what did you want to talk about?"

His casual tone made her anger froth over. She swung her backpack at him, aiming right for his fat face.

He ducked and grabbed at her wrists. Pain shot through her where the wounds were still tender, and she collapsed to the ground with a scream.

"What? Tina? What?" He knelt next to her and held her arms loosely, peeling back her sleeve to reveal the angry scars. "Oh my God."

She cried then, from pain and from embarrassment. "I didn't mean anything by it," she said. "I just got home from the hospital and your stuff was all gone and I really thought you'd be there. I thought you'd just freaked at the hospital but you'd wait for me. I wanted to show you pictures of our baby, our Peanut."

She would throw up; she just knew it.

"Tina. God. Damn."

They sat there a little longer as the lunch crowd filed past, and when some of them stared, she dropped her head to her knees so she couldn't see.

"I don't know what to say. Is that what you wanted to tell me? How mad you were?"

She shrugged.

"I'm sorry I was such a fuck-up," he said. "I had no idea so much shit went down."

Tina raised her head and gulped a breath of air. "You didn't exactly stick around."

"I know. I suck. Hey. I'm gonna go. All I do is upset you."

His shadow covered her, leaving a chill where the sun had been. He was going to leave. He hadn't even apologized. She hadn't gotten him back.

He crossed the courtyard where a tall black-haired girl waited for him. She'd been watching the whole time. He had someone new.

Humiliation washed over her, and once again she thought she'd throw up. She put her head back to her knees and hiccupped to swallow any errant sobs. Her wrists throbbed and now her lungs ached. Arnie wasn't her way out after all.

The walk back to her garage apartment made her feel better, the chilly air and hint of spring. She ran along the back hedges to make sure her mom didn't spot her. The school might have already called to say she'd cut class now that she'd been outed by the counselor.

Tina didn't want to flunk out, to never graduate. She wasn't stupid. If she wanted to go to art school, she'd have to get a diploma. The school for pregnant teens had been perfect. She was the top of her class, a shoo-in for scholarship. This was totally wrong. She was screwed in every way a person could be screwed.

She had to get back in.

Tina flung her backpack on the floor and searched through the books in the flimsy shelves she'd bought when she first moved to the apartment. The one she wanted had to be here somewhere.

She ran her finger along the titles, skipping over the small paperbacks and staring hard at the glossy oversized art books. Then she spotted it. Her high school yearbook. She hadn't wanted one last year, but her parents ordered it anyway. She and Arnie had actually had great fun with it over the summer, drawing elaborate additions to their classmates' faces. That was before everything happened.

Now she had another purpose for the book. She needed a man.

Sperm donor, more like it. No, not true. The baby should have a dad. Surely there had to be some potential in here somewhere.

She flipped through the section of juniors first, a grade ahead of her. They were the seniors now, and those boys would either have jobs or get one soon.

Not a jock, they wouldn't go for her, no matter what sort of sex she offered. She scanned the pages. Not a geek boy. She couldn't stomach that. Someone somewhere in between. Smart but not popular. Shy but merely lacking confidence.

She turned page after page. The boys from Life Skills looked up at her and she dragged her fingernails across the picture to tear out their faces. Nasty punks.

Tina closed the yearbook. The search was pointless. Her rep at school was too bad, and anyone she might date would find out eventually.

She uncurled her legs in their purple and black striped leggings. Actually, she thought, looking down, she might want to rethink her wardrobe now. Clearly none of the boys her age were going to work. Even if she chose a different high school, she might pick another Arnie, or worse, get someone who would refuse to have anything to do with her or the baby. Or insist on an abortion. She shuddered.

No, what she really needed was a full-grown man. On the news all the time they showed men getting arrested for having sex with underage girls they'd found on the Internet.

Maybe it was her turn to find one of them.

3

IT'S RAINING MEN

Tina stared up at the church, the black steeple outlined against the red sky. Sunsets like that almost make her wish she didn't shoot solely in black and white. But an artist has to have a medium. Color was for the uninitiated, the digital techno-wowsers who oversaturated their pictures. Photoshopped them to death, until they had all the artistic merit of a kindergarten rainbow.

She was late for the meeting but not in any hurry. The big chick who ran the group, Stella, would probably be reading some inspirational passage again, and she didn't have the patience for that tripe. The only thing that inspired her at the moment was the idea of a man.

Tina yanked on the heavy door. The women were already seated inside in their circle. She noted the candles flickering in the background, the whiff of something weird, like those nasty deodorizer plug ins her mother placed all around the house.

"Come in, child," Stella said. "We're just gabbing."

Tina sprawled out in the chair, stretching her purple striped legs out in front of her. "What about?"

The fancy-dressed lawyer woman smiled at her. The one who'd been at the hospital, Melinda. "Doctors, mainly," she said. "And men."

Her favorite three-letter word. "I'm trying to find one of those myself."

Melinda raised a perfectly arched eyebrow. "A doctor or a man?"

Tina dug being shocking. "A man."

Everyone turned to look at her.

"Yeah. I figure my life got thrashed when I lost the baby. The good school—zapped. My parents want me to move back in. Arnie ditched me. I want all that back. Well, other than Arnie. He's a putz. I'm looking for an older man. One who can knock me up, get me back in my old school, and still help me with the baby."

The heater kicked on, a light roar that blasted a dry wave of hot air over their heads. Stella shifted in her chair. Melinda toyed with her sweater. A woman in a sweatsuit crossed her arms over her chest.

Ha, that got them. "You ladies got a problem with that?"

Stella held Tina's gaze firm and sure. "I think that if this is what you want, you should go for it. Do it wisely, and consider every possibility, but certainly follow your heart."

Well, that wasn't what she expected. "What, no lectures?"

"No lectures."

Tina pulled her striped knees up to her chest. "Cool."

Melinda leaned forward like she was going to say something, then sat back. Sweatsuit stared out over the church. They were riled, she could tell, but wouldn't show it. Just like her mother. What was with them? Afraid of their own opinions. She didn't have that problem.

Stella stared at each one of them like she was daring them to speak up. "I know you other ladies may not agree. But there is only one path we can follow and that is the one we ourselves choose. It doesn't matter if we're young or if others think we don't know what we're doing."

Sweatsuit woman coughed. "I hear that."

Stella nodded. "To do what anyone else thinks we should do is the big mistake. And in this group, well, sometimes we're the only ones who know where we've been and where we need to go. I will try to never disapprove. This is the one place where you're safe to speak your mind, no matter what's in it."

Stella picked up the book from the floor, and Tina groaned inwardly. She'd have to go into some inner brain chamber to suffer through the reading. But if she had to be somewhere, either here or some quack head shrink, here was better. These women didn't judge anybody for anything. And that wasn't so easy in life to find.

A father for her baby, that shouldn't be too hard either.

4

BLIND DATE

Tina parked outside the Ragin' Cajun and smoothed her black skirt. No tights today. She straightened the blue sweater and lifted a foot to adjust the strap of her heels. No pigtails either. She turned to the window of the car next to her and peered at her distorted reflection. Her black hair lay smooth and flat against her head. At least she didn't look like her mother.

As she walked to the entrance to the restaurant, she felt confident she'd pass for twenty-two, as she'd stated in her online profile on the dating site. The regular chat rooms had been full of gross men wanting to cyber-fuck. She'd decided to pony up the thirty bucks for a real shot at regular men. The online scene was chock full of prime candidates, men wanting to get married and have families. She'd been flooded with emails since she'd signed up and had her pick.

This one was thirty-three, never married, and an architectural preservationist, whatever that was, who made between fifty and seventy thousand dollars a year. His pictures weren't good quality, but he was cute enough, and she wanted a real smart one for the baby. He wrote her very nice emails, and they had talked on the phone twice.

She just had to keep her story straight.

When she opened the door, the smell of fried food accosted her, and the rumble of loud voices and clatter of dishes hit her like a blast. She glanced around the tables, mostly families before spread-out newspapers, tugging crawfish out of baskets and cracking open the small red bodies to access the meat. She turned away, repulsed.

"Tina?"

A blond man sat on a bench against the wall. He said she'd recognize him most by his height and when he stood, she knew it was certainly him. Six-five.

He towered over her, even in her heels.

"I'm Nate."

"Hi," she said, her belly suddenly fluttering. So much relied on this night. Her alternative school, her apartment, her happiness. She'd bought an ovulation kit and peed on the sticks religiously, reading everything she could on the mechanics of pregnancy. She'd seen her hormone surge the day before and knew that if things went right tonight, she could be having a positive pregnancy test within two weeks and could re-enroll in the alternative high school before the end of the term.

"You want to get something to eat?" he asked. "They have great etouffee here, or crawfish if you like that."

"Do you?"

He laughed. "Not at all. Makes me queasy just smelling it."

She released a breath. "I am so glad you said that. I can barely stand to look at the tables!"

"You want to go somewhere else, then?" He held her gaze, glasses glinting in the light. He had a tiny goatee, reddish blond and impeccably trimmed.

"Surely we can find a corner out of sight of the little red buggers," she said.

"Let's see what they've got then."

They ordered red beans and rice at the counter and settled on a table in the corner. Tina couldn't feel more pleased with how things were going. Nate was kind and courteous and smart—way more interesting than any of the high school boys she knew. He told her about his job and where he grew up, never talking too long without asking her polite questions.

"So what do you do?" he asked.

"Oh," Tina said, pausing to collect her thoughts. No mistakes. Say little and turn the conversation back to him. "I'm still in college. The five-year plan, you know." She laughed. "I hope to graduate before I'm thirty."

"I know how that is," he said. "I did two stints in grad school before I managed to finish."

Tina felt absolutely thrilled, the excitement flowing through her chest. Now she just had to get him interested in her, work him a little.

"So what part of town do you live in?" she asked, tucking her chin on her hands and looking up at him with big doe eyes, an expression she had practiced since she was twelve.

He didn't seem to react to that, but said, "Off Richmond. That string of apartment buildings just outside the loop."

"Oh! That's not far from here."

"Yeah. Very convenient to lots of bars and restaurants."

The word "bar" made her panic a little. She'd have to avoid any place where they might card her.

"I'm not much of a drinker," she said. "But I'd love to see your place. Does it have a pool?"

"Yes, it's really beautiful, set up like a waterfall."

She took his hand. "Oh please. I'd love to see it."

The light from the water spilled blue across the patterned tile of the pool. They sat at a table near the edge listening to the gurgle of the falls. Nate had been so darn courteous. He hadn't made a single move.

She'd have to speed things along.

She hugged herself tightly, faking a shiver. "It IS cold out here!" she said. "Is your apartment near here?"

"It's a bit of a walk, more toward the back," he said. His hair lit blue on one side. This really was a romantic spot. They ought to make use of it.

"We could walk there."

He smiled at her, so she slipped her arm around his waist and leaned into him. The top of her head barely met his chest. She'd never be able to kiss him without stairs.

"And I guess I'll keep you warm in the meantime," he said, reaching to cover her forearm with his free hand.

Much better.

They walked, her huddled against him, along a concrete sidewalk and then cut across a parking lot.

"You'll have to remind me where my car is later," she said. She'd had to sell an old necklace for gas money, but it had been worth it.

"You think you might forget?"

"You might make me forget."

He unlocked the door to his apartment. "It's a bachelor pad," he said. "I didn't clean ahead."

Tina held up both hands. "You should see my place," she said. "I can handle anything."

His cat met them as they walked in and rubbed against her legs. "Oh!" she said. "I love him! My parents never let me get a cat!"

Damn. She stroked the black cat and avoided looking at him. "As a kid, you know."

He didn't say anything, just sat down on a black futon.

She felt conspicuous, unsure. High school boys were always trying to jump on her. What should she do with this one?

She perched on the coffee table in front of him. The cat continued to weave between her ankles. Time for the hard press. Thank God she had some experience.

She leaned forward and laid her hands on his knees. He did not react, just watched her, mildly amused, his mouth almost smiling.

She slid her hands up his long thighs. He raised his eyebrows then and she held his gaze, unflinching.

He grasped her hands and pulled her over to him. She sat on his lap and finally, finally he kissed her. His goatee tickled her chin, but she stifled the giggle, intent on her purpose.

She opened her mouth and he responded, deepening the kiss. She resisted the urge to press, to get him inside her, to feel the pulse of his semen. She could picture it now, after viewing so many websites, the small white sperm wiggling its way up to her egg, fluffy and round.

She fixated a moment on the goal, the head penetrating the egg, beating out the thousands of other sperm surrounding the enormous fuzzy ball.

She reached for the waistband of his jeans, tugging at the snap. He pulled her closer and she pressed against him, her hand caught between their bodies. He was ready for her. She felt thrilled. It was going to happen!

She shifted over and straddled him. Damn clothes in the way. She pushed against him once or twice then slid away, reaching beneath her skirt to tug off her panties. She didn't really want to get all the way undressed, although she had prepared an explanation for her wrists.

"You sure about this?" Nate asked. His hands held her hips and his breathing came a little fast.

She smiled. "Absolutely." She tugged on his jeans.

"Let's go to the bedroom then," he said.

"Anything you want." She stood and let him lead her down the hall and into a darkened room.

She made out a bed in the dim light that penetrated the window blinds. She bent to slide the shoes off her feet.

Nate reached into a cabinet at the head of the bed.

"What are you doing?" Tina asked.

"Just getting something."

"Something?"

"Condoms, you know."

She washed cold. "What?"

He sat on the bed and drew her up next to him. "Change of heart? It's okay."

"I'm on the pill."

He let go of her and rested his hands on the bed. "I see."

"What, you don't want to now?"

"Tina, are you okay?" He pulled her down to him again and just held on, simply, lightly, without any undertone of sex.

"I don't like condoms—I'm allergic."

"Oh."

She pressed against him again. "See? It'll be fine."

He drew away slightly. "I can get the non-latex kind. For next time, you know. This was a little fast anyway."

"So you don't want to?" This could not be happening.

"I want to see you again," he said.

"But that will be too late!" She jumped from the bed, angry and disappointed.

This wasn't going to work. Nothing worked for her. She grabbed her shoes, running for the door.

He called out, "Tina, wait!" but she snatched her purse and hurtled away. The rough asphalt of the parking lot bit into her feet as she flew across the complex to her Jeep.

All this wasted time talking to this guy. She thought he'd be the one. "Damn it!" she called up into the sky. The egg. It wouldn't last. She'd just lost a whole month.

5

PREMATURITY

Tina sat on the bumper of her Jeep, waiting for the right moment.

The diner was a mile or so from her old school. She liked to immerse herself in old memories, and suddenly wanted to surround herself in the places where she'd been pregnant, accepted, and hanging out with other young women like herself—all jiggling kids or wolfing outrageous amounts of food. She and the other pregnant chicks had monopolized the milkshake fountain at Harry's Burger Barn.

She had hoped to run into someone, a sympathetic girl who would listen to her without the syrup her mother coated everything with, or the lessons of her father.

Finally, someone she knew trundled down the street, lugging a baby carrier. Tina dashed inside and ordered a cheeseburger, pretending not to notice Fiona struggle through the door. Tina couldn't see the baby inside, but it must be happy or sleeping, as it didn't make a sound.

After Fiona had ordered, she turned to pick up the carrier from where she'd plunked it on the floor and saw Tina.

"Oh my God, it's you!" She dashed over and bent over to hug Tina hard.

"God, I miss all you guys so much!" Tina peeked over at the blanket. "How is he doing? Carter, right? I think I watched him a time or two in the baby room."

Fiona sat on a chair and tugged the baby out of the seat. "He's doing great! He's six months old already and about to sit up!"

Tina's heart panged as Fiona lifted Carter up onto her shoulder. He tucked his cheek against her red sweater. Wisps of Fiona's white-blond hair crossed his nose and he sneezed.

"You look awful skinny already," Fiona said, shifting the baby to her lap. How is the baby doing? I heard he was born premature. Was it a boy or a girl? Is he still in the NICU? Amanda's baby was in NICU for two months. She said it was horrible and scary."

Tina gripped the table, trying to stay caught up with Fiona's startling chatter. Everyone thought her baby was still alive?

"Peanut is a boy," she said. "What all did you hear?"

"Oh, Ms. Rivers announced to the class a couple days after you left that you were in the hospital, and that your parents had said you'd gone into labor. We didn't know anything else. Several of us tried to call you at home, but no one got to talk to anybody. I hope you didn't think we gave up on you!"

"I was in the hospital a lot," Tina said. Her mind raced. If they thought her baby was still alive, could she go back to the school?

"Oh, I bet it was awful! Well, tell me what happened! Everyone's dying to know!"

Tina sat back and spun the tale as best she could. She'd gone into labor at twenty-three weeks, she said, figuring she'd better fudge to make it believable. Peanut weighed less than two pounds. He'd nearly died several times, but he was a fighter. His lungs had been much more developed than they thought.

"He weighs a little over two pounds now, finally, but I won't get to take him home until he's a least four, probably five."

Fiona gobbled her fries three at a time. "Ooohhhh, Tina. I'm so proud of you for holding up so well. I can't wait to tell everyone how you are!"

Tina stared at the baby's round head, throat tightening. This was not fair whatsoever. "I miss everybody."

"So when are you coming back?"

Tina gathered her trash onto her tray. She'd better go before she messed up and blew her chance. "I'm not sure. My parents are supposed to call the school, but they may not have yet. It's been pretty crazy with all the hospital stuff."

"I bet it has. Is there anything I can do?"

"That's really nice of you. If I think of something, I'll let you know."

Tina had to suppress the urge to skip as she headed back to her Jeep. This might work! And she could get pregnant again when she felt like it. As long as the school thought her baby was in NICU, she was safe. Then she could think of something else, maybe that her mom was keeping it, and she didn't want to take up a space at the school daycare.

She could download some NICU pictures on the Internet and pretend it was Peanut. This was totally going to work.

Tina had just coaxed the old Jeep to start when her cell phone rang. "Hey. It's Melinda."

"What's up?" Tina killed the engine and rested back against the seat.

"I was a little worried about your plan. Stella gave me your number. I had to coerce her."

Tina laughed. "I bet. I have unbelieveable news!"

"You find a man already?"

"Well, yeah, but that didn't work out. This is better. I ran into a girl from my old school and get this—they all think Peanut is still alive!"

The other end stayed silent, and Tina leaned her head on the steering wheel. "It's good news, really," she said.

"So what does this mean for you?"

"It means I can go back to the alternative school. As long as they don't figure it out."

"How long might that be?"

"Heck if I know! But I'm going to try and re-enroll tomorrow." Tina sat up again as someone walked by with a stroller, peering at her to see if she was familiar. Nope.

"Well, Tina, if that's what you're after, I hope it works for you. How much trouble can you get into if they find out?"

"I have no idea! But you're a lawyer right? You can bail me out of jail!"

Melinda laughed. "Sure, Tina. I can do that."

"But all is great! I'm great! So don't worry about me, okay?"

She could feel Melinda smile against the phone. "I'll try not to worry."

Tina hung up the phone and started the Jeep, backing out of the parking lot with a squeal of tires. This was a very good day indeed.

6

FORBIDDEN CORRIDORS

Tina straightened her shirt and checked herself in the window of her Jeep. She smoothed her spriggy ponytails and took a deep breath. Keep your story straight. Don't screw up.

She heaved her backpack on her shoulder. On the zipper pull, she'd added a photo keychain with a couple shots of a NICU baby she'd found on a website. Inside her binder, she placed a real photo of Peanut, the one without the wires.

She'd studied until late at night, memorizing things like Kangaroo Care and gavage feedings and I:E ratio. She could handle a quiz on her baby's progress.

If things went perfectly, she might not even need another baby. She could just stay in the school and graduate next year, get a scholarship far, far away and forget the whole thing.

But the cry of a baby the minute she yanked open the front door tightened her chest so hard she could scarcely catch her breath. Her baby was dead. Theirs weren't.

She sat on a bench by the baby room, listening. New moms had to come early and get their babies settled before going to class. The pregnant ones, sleepy or sick, would arrive just before the bell. Tina had come in the gap between, so the halls were still.

Mrs. Meachum's voice penetrated the din. "Little Angie's getting her first cereal today. Everyone come over and see how she takes it."

Tina's throat constricted. Peanut would never eat cereal, never get his first solids, in fact, he never got to eat at all. The ache in her chest grew monstrously large, her heart pounded, and the cuts on her wrists began to tingle, then burn.

This was where she wanted to be. The art teacher was amazing, so helpful and supportive. The classes were easy for her, based on real-life learning, with practical skills mixed in with the crap like history and algebra.

A laugh burst out from the room. "She hates it!" someone cried. More giggles.

The outside door swung open with a rush of cold air. Rosie hustled down the hall, her toddler on her hip. "Tina?" She slowed down. "Is that you?"

Tina waved lightly. Rosie was an artist too, like her. She'd come to the school as a freshman, so baby David would be three before she graduated.

Rosie sat on the bench next to her. "How is your baby? I heard you went into labor. You weren't due for a long time."

Tina stared at David, placidly sucking on a pacifier. The colorful bit of silicone bobbled in and out as he worked it. "It's touch and go."

Rosie's cheerful face collapsed into sorrow. "Oh my God. I'm so sorry. I will say prayers for him."

"Thanks."

"I'll be back in a minute." She stood up to take David into the day-care room.

Tina shuffled her feet on the floor. She no longer knew why she was there. These were nice people. She was going to lie to them all?

Mrs. Meachum poked her head out of the room. "Tina?"

Showtime. "Hey."

Mrs. Meachum took Rosie's spot on the bench, clasping Tina's hand in both of hers. Tina concentrated on the woman's rings, big bright gemstones on almost every finger. She never changed a diaper, obviously. That was the girls' job.

"I was awful sorry to hear about your baby," she said.

Tina's head snapped up. She knew.

"Did you come to pick up some things? I'm sure you weren't expecting to leave us so abruptly."

Shit. Tina nodded lamely.

"I'm sorry if the girls ask you about the baby. We decided not to announce it widely, for your privacy. Those who were close to you were told, of course."

Tina felt like she would throw up. She should have known they would find out. Her stupid mother probably called.

Mrs. Meachum squeezed her hand and suddenly this infuriated Tina. She yanked away and stood up, backing down the hall. She couldn't say anything, couldn't think of anything to say. Her throat burned like she'd drunk gasoline.

Rosie stepped out into corridor. "Tina? You okay?"

Tina shook her head. Some of the other girls popped out of the room, acting like they would come toward her, all of them holding babies in various stages of growth, like an army of mothers. She continued walking backward, faster now, until her hip bumped into the door.

"Tina, are you all right?" Mrs. Meachum also came forward. "I'm sure your friends would like to say goodbye."

Tina turned away and pushed through the door. Her head felt like it might explode. She ran, faster and faster, until she got to her Jeep. The key shook in her hand and she could barely get the stupid lock to open, but finally she was safely inside, turning on the engine, and pulling away, leaving the school behind. She couldn't go back there. She had nowhere to go. She had nothing. No baby, no boyfriend, no life, no future. Suddenly the razors beckoned again. A flash of metal in the sun roared into her eyes, like the reflection of her bathroom light on the blade. A marquee sign in front of a drug store hawked its sale: Gilette refills $6.99. Death was on her side.

7

BLADES, REVISITED

Tina didn't know who else to call. She'd tried Melinda but didn't get an answer. So she dialed the same number on the page from the hospital. She could picture the fat lady in her flowered dress.

"This is Stella."

"It's Tina. From the group."

"What's the matter, child?"

"I can't do it." Tina paced her apartment, occasionally checking on the boxes lined up along the edge of her sink. The plain white covers—six of them—all read "Single Edged Blades."

"Can't do what?"

"Keep on going."

"Sure you can."

Tina walked to the living room, pushing aside the curtain to stare at the main house. The shadow of her parents crossed the kitchen windows. They expected her for dinner. "There's no point."

"I can think of a few." Stella's voice was calm, utterly patient.

"Try me." Tina hoped the old woman could think of something, anything.

"Your next baby, for one."

Tina's legs collapsed, dumping her heavily on the floor. "It could die too."

"It could. Mine did."

"See?"

"I'm still here."

Tina laid her head on the sofa cushion. This pain was too much. "I've been cutting school."

"School isn't for everyone."

Tina loosed her grip on the phone. Who was this person? She wasn't like any grown-up she'd ever met. "You think I should quit."

"Nope."

"But you said it's not for everyone."

"Two separate things. It's not for everyone, but only you know if it's for you."

Tina closed her eyes. This was too complicated. "Everyone hates me there."

"Not true."

She sat up. "Is too. They call me 'baby killer.'"

Silence. She had the old lady by the balls.

"Everyone calls you that?"

Tina gripped the phone. "Practically."

"The teachers?"

"No, they just flunk me."

"Every person in the halls? Every single one?"

"No." Tina wanted to hang up now. She wanted sympathy, not an argument.

"Half?"

"No."

"Ten people? Have ten people said it?"

Damn it. "No."

"Let me tell you something. A certain percentage of the world are total schmucks. I mean worthless, hateful people. You can't live your life based on them."

Tina clenched her teeth. "But they're the only people I can see."

"Open your eyes; look around."

"What am I supposed to see if I do that?"

"A solution."

"What if I don't see one?"

"You can't see something you're not looking for."

Tina peeked out the curtain again. No shadows. Her parents had probably given up on her and sat down to eat. They really ought to walk over and insist. She'd go then, if they did.

"You still there, Tina?"

Tina sighed. "I don't even want to go back there."

"Then find a solution outside of school."

"I tried that!"

"Then try again."

"I'm sick of trying!"

"Then get sick!"

A hot bolt of anger shot through her, and Tina hung up the phone. This was pointless.

She crossed the apartment and went into the bathroom, staring at the boxes lined up like decks of cards. She swiped her arm across the lot of them, knocking them into the trash. Some missed, breaking open, spilling bright blades across the floor.

She snatched one up, laying the fine edge against her arm. It lined up neatly against the red welt of her healing scar. She closed her eyes, pressing the razor against her skin. She felt the prick but couldn't bring herself to make the cut.

"Chicken! Stupid crazy bitch!" Her voice rang against the mirror, bouncing off the white walls, echoing in the shower stall. She flung the razor across the room, bending over the sink. Open your eyes, Stella had said. Find a solution.

Arnie was out. Blind dating was out. Lying to get back into the school was out. In fact, the pregnant school was plain out.

She had nothing.

The blades winked at her like a promise. She whipped around and turned off the light.

The living room walls were still bare save for the print of Peanut she'd made at school. She stood on the sofa and pressed her nose to it. Could he see her? Did he know anything about his mother's pain?

A knock at the door startled her. The parents were actually going to assert themselves. What a lark.

She flung open the door. Her parents were there, but then so was someone else, a tall man in a uniform.

"Tina, this is Officer Kane," her mother said, her voice not quite steady.

"A cop?" Tina asked. She hadn't done anything illegal.

"Not quite," her father said. "He's in the truancy department of the school district." He handed her a printout with dates. "You have some explaining to do."

Tina backed away and sat on the sofa.

Her mom followed her inside. "This is it. We're closing up this apartment. You'll be back in the main house. You'll be going to school every day because I am going to drive you and pick you up."

Her father snatched her keys from the counter. "I'm taking everything but the main house key. No access to this apartment. No car. You got it?"

The truancy officer rocked on his heels, nodding. "We can probably get the fine removed if she attends every day over the next thirty."

Her mom seemed ten feet tall, towering over Tina. She'd folded herself up into the tiniest package imaginable on the sofa, like a kitten.

"Oh she will," her mother said. "If I have to go to school with her."

Guess they'd decided to be parents after all.

8

VIGILANTE JUSTICE

She needed longer hair.

During the breaks and lunch, she could get by blasting punk music in her ears to avoid hearing anything anyone said. But during class, the ear buds with their white wires were too obvious. Maybe a wig.

She sat under the oak tree, eyes focused on a blank page of her notebook, waiting out the lunch period. It was the worst half-hour of the day, but she'd endure. She was stuck.

The nasty blonde from Life Skills walked by with her insipid crew. Damn, she'd looked up. One of them pretended to trip on her backpack, spilling the contents on the grass and knocking over her coke. Her trig homework got soaked.

She lifted it, letting the liquid roll off. Endure. She could endure.

"Hey. You okay?"

The words kind of penetrated, but she kept her head down. She didn't care what anyone had to say.

A pair of the most nerdy argyle socks ever paused by her knees. The penny loafers were '80s Goodwill.

"You okay?" The question warbled through the crashing of drums. A butt joined the argyle socks. He'd sat down.

She looked up. It was the boy from the darkroom. Simon. She turned off the music.

"You're back at newspaper," he said. "And Life Skills. I'm in both of those."

Bitterness rose in her. "Yeah. I'm real popular there. You got something you want to call me? Baby Killer? Misfit? Goth Bitch?"

He stared up into the tree. "Actually, I reported the whole lot of them to the vice principal about an hour ago. Stole one of their little signs as proof. I'm a real nerdy narc that way. They're all getting a two-day suspension. They'll be called in after lunch. I might just go back and mention that little number they just did on your homework. See if we can go for three."

Tina pulled the earplugs out. "You'd do that?"

"Yeah. Assholes like that don't need to get off scot-free. I felt it was my civic duty." He held out his hand. "Does that make us friends, or do you not hang out with goody-goody types?"

She accepted his hand. "I can be persuaded as long as it doesn't damage my rep as a bad girl."

"No chance of that."

They held hands longer than necessary. He was a nerd, no doubt about it. Black glasses. Red plaid shirt. Narrow jeans and those weird loafers. All he was missing was the pocket protector.

He raised his arm and waved to another group of students sitting across the lawn.

They ambled up, a mix of nerd and alternative, skaters and hacker types.

"You're sort of a hero in our circles," Simon said. "We love anybody who draws the foul so we can bring down the enemy."

Tina glanced over the crowd, all seeming friendly even through carefully arranged pouts or scowls, mostly misfits.

"The enemy?" she asked.

An overweight girl with fake red hair stepped forward. "Oh yeah. Mean girls. Type A's. Alpha males. Jocks and their bitches."

"You're our poster child," said a boy in ripped jeans and a red mesh top.

"I think she's in," Simon said. "We'll cover every class, and anybody who messes with her will have to deal with us."

Tina closed her mouth, realizing her jaw had been hanging open. "What does that mean?"

The bell rang. Simon stood and took her hand to help her up. "It means if it's a teacher's pet nerd type like me who can take action, we get them suspended. If it takes breaking in and changing their schedule or grades, Slayer here will handle it." He pointed to the boy in the red shirt.

"I handle the fear tactics," said a red-haired girl, slamming a fist into her palm. "Bathrooms are my specialty."

Tina had to laugh. "You guys are great. What do I have to do?"

"Just be you," Simon said. "Stick close and draw the foul." He handed her the backpack and her soggy homework.

Tina fell in beside them as they walked toward the building. "I can do that."

The fat lady had been right all along.

PART FOUR: *Janet*

1

PROPOSALS

Janet peered at the digital clock that controlled the school's bell system. 2:30. Time to preside over the end of the school day. She liked to watch the parents motor through the circle drive to pick up their children, bright and cheerful, waving and happy. Kids came up for hugs, which often embarrassed her, but she accepted the sentiment. Children were emotional, affectionate, undiscerning. Thankfully she did not come off as imposing as she had in her corporate jobs. Being around kids was good for her, even if she was the principal and not a teacher.

She stood up from her desk and immediately felt a gush between her legs. Not again. After seven weeks of bleeding, she'd had a reprieve, enough to make her feel confident to go without protection. Mistake. Now she'd have to hurry to change and make the bell.

She slipped into her private bathroom and opened the drawer beneath the sink where she kept her pads. Empty. When had she used the last one?

She cleaned herself up, wondering if she should raid the nurse's station but decided she didn't have time. Instead, she folded a layer of paper towels in her underwear. Unease rose in her as she thought of the blood and the never-ending process of her miscarriage. Ridiculous that she ever got pregnant to begin with. She wasn't even married. Of course they would have done so, but still. A rushed wedding, a baby soon after.

It didn't matter. The baby had never grown. She never saw anything resembling a fetus on the ultrasound. Just a partial sac that still refused to pass.

Her heels clacked on the waxed floor of the halls. She smoothed her skirt, trying to regain her poise. Mitchell Arts Academy was a top-tier private school, and as their first black director, her job was to diversify the student population. She enjoyed, as she did each afternoon, peeking inside the classrooms to see the variety of children she'd managed to attract, now donning coats and backpacks. She crossed the foyer and pushed through the exterior door.

A rainstorm threatened, the air heavy and thick. Cars lined up beneath the covered driveway and stretched through the parking lot and out into the street. She'd be standing in her pumps and suit for a good half-hour before the last parent left.

Fat raindrops began to fall partway through the process. Janet crossed her arms over her waist, glad for the extended canopy that kept the kids and staff dry. The rain came with a cold front, and the temperature dropped ten degrees in half an hour. She trembled as she waved and walked inside uncharacteristically early with a dozen cars still waiting in line.

The shivers had brought on mild cramps and another quick trip to the bathroom showed the blood had turned thick and black. She really should stop at a drug store on the way home, but Marcus wanted to see her tonight, so she shouldn't run late. She could bring a few extras from home and replenish tomorrow. She hurried back to her office to collect her things so she could beat traffic home.

She turned onto her street. The black BMW sat waiting in front of her house. Marcus. Why was he here so early? She gripped the wheel a little tighter, then forced herself to loosen up, smile, and wave at him as she passed by and clicked open the garage.

"Hey, baby," he said as she stepped out of the car. "You're a sight for a starved man."

"Hello, Marcus." She turned to open the door, but he caught her arm.

"Can't I get a better greeting than that?"

She leaned into him, forcing down the recoil she'd begun to feel since the miscarriage. "Of course."

He kissed her, his warm lips pleasing and soft. He pulled her even closer, trapping her soft-sided briefcase between them. She did not resist. Eventually the bag bothered her, pressed into her ribs, and she pulled away.

"Am I allowed in?" he asked, threading his arm through hers and taking the briefcase.

"Of course."

"Are you okay?"

"I am."

He let it go, thankfully, and did not quiz her about how she felt or what was happening to her body. His questions oppressed her, sometimes squeezing what little control she had out of the seams of her well-stitched life.

She clicked on the kitchen lights. "Should I fix us some dinner tonight?" she asked. "We didn't really have plans."

"I have plans," he said. "And they should be starting any minute."

As if on cue, the doorbell rang. Marcus raced to the door, his lean body in perfect motion despite the pinstriped suit. She stood by the entry to the kitchen to watch.

"The first assault," he called out to her, then spoke with a delivery man. He returned with a large white bag. "Victuals, so my lady does not have to cook."

He spread out the containers—South American dishes from Churrasco's. Fried plantains and the various dipping sauces she loved. Twice-baked potatoes. Empanadas. It looked like every selection she'd ever ordered.

"You've quite a memory," she said as he pulled plates from her cabinets.

"For important things."

They sat at her table, and he lit the candelabra that she'd bought for decoration but never burned.

He waved the match to extinguish it. "I wanted to do things a little differently, but I got something today and I couldn't wait."

Janet propped her elbows on the table and rested her chin in her hands. Then she remembered the black bleeding. She had to take care of it before it leaked through her clothes.

She shoved her chair back to stand. "I need to—"

"You need to listen," he interrupted. "I've got something important to say."

She sat down again. "Okay."

"I know when you got pregnant we talked about getting married, and doing it quickly, so as not to raise a flag at your school." He leaned forward, snaking his hand beneath the table to find one of hers. "Then when the baby—when we learned you weren't pregnant anymore—you let it go. We never talked about it again."

Good Lord, he was going to propose. Janet felt sweat pop on the back of her neck where her suit chafed her. What would she say? They'd been dating two years, and when the accident had happened, the broken condom, they'd agreed marriage was prudent. But now? Why now?

He was still talking, and she'd missed a few sentences.

"Wait," she said. "I think I know where this is going."

Marcus jumped from his chair and rounded the table. "I'm not going to let you stop me." He tugged wildly inside his jacket pocket, trying to dislodge something—probably the ring box. Janet felt another prickle of heat. She wanted the moment to stop, to freeze, to go away. She wasn't up for this.

Marcus finally pulled his hand free and set the black box on the table.

"Please, Janet. You loved me enough when you were pregnant to think of marriage, and I am so in love with you. I want to marry you and let the babies come when they want to come. Please say you will marry me."

Concentrating to control every gesture, every breath, Janet reached for the box and popped it open. The ring sat nestled in velvet, an enormous princess-cut solitaire. She looked up at Marcus. She couldn't say anything. She flashed back to the anxious wait to test, the morning of the positive pregnancy stick. They had agreed, right away, to marry. Why couldn't she now?

"Marcus, I—"

He stopped her with a squeeze to her hand. "It's okay, Janet. Think it over. I won't press. I would never push."

A retreat. Relief coursed through her. "I know. And I'm so grateful."

He pulled her up to stand next to him. "I know we have all this wonderful food, but I just want to touch you."

He held her, and she looked over his shoulder. She could feel more blood coming out. He tried to kiss her but she stepped back, panicked he would try to get her into bed while she was such a mess.

"Marcus, let me … take care of something."

"What is it?"

"I just need to do something." Another pulse of something slid out. She couldn't bear it.

"Why are you pulling away? Are we ending?" His face expressed pain, so much pain. She couldn't manage it.

"No." She sounded harsher than she intended. "It's none of that."

"Then what?"

"I'm bleeding again. It's awful. Black."

"Still? Oh my God. Have you called the doctor?"

"Yes. They think it's normal. They still just recommend a D&C. I don't want that."

"I know you don't. But it's been a long time. You don't want to change your mind?"

"No. You should understand that. The body can handle these things. It should happen on its own."

"I'm just worried about you."

Janet felt the familiar hardening inside, the chill that flowed through her, first in trickles, then expanding until she grew totally cold. "Then let me go take care of this."

She turned away but he grabbed her hand.

"I don't know how you can be like this," he said. "I just don't get it. Our baby … our baby, and you just … you never even cried."

Janet looked at him, backlit by the candles, his face mostly in shadow. She could still make out the lines on his forehead, the tension around his eyes. The frown. She knew she disappointed him, sweet, sentimental Marcus. "I don't really … cry. You know this."

"But this is different. It's a baby. Our baby. Our life together."

"It was never a baby, Marcus. It was just an empty sac. It was never anything."

Marcus backed up to the dining room chair and sat down, snapping the ring box shut with a loud pop.

She couldn't stand the tension anymore, the spread of emotion fogging everything they said. She turned to hurry down the hall to the bathroom but still heard his mumbled words.

"It was to me."

2

FEAR

This bleeding had to be wrong.

Janet felt another gush as she radioed the head of maintenance to signal the all clear, then followed the animated students of her school back into the building. They were happy and buzzing after the fire drill, despite the chill outside. Spring couldn't come too soon, and neither could her recovery.

A D&C surgery seemed inevitable. She pictured herself, mask on her face, going under. Then the frantic commands of the doctor. Nurses rushing in a crash cart. The beep of a machine. A doctor shouting, "Clear!"

Janet gripped her clipboard. It was just anesthesia. People did it every day.

When the halls were quiet again, she entered her office, glancing around to make sure no one would disturb her in the next couple of minutes. With one eye on the window looking over the front desk, she quickly typed "excessive bleeding after miscarriage" into a search box.

The results lined up in bold on the page. Uterine perforation. Infection. Missed abortion.

This still wasn't telling her anything new. She'd read these topics before.

She typed in "prolonged bleeding after miscarriage."

The first links were all the same. She scanned page two and saw a new term. Hydatidiform mole.

She read quickly. Molar pregnancy. Regrowth of tissue. Potential to become invasive cancer.

Fear burgeoned in her belly. She glanced through the glass pane by her door again and then picked up her phone. Her doctor would have to listen to her. She dialed.

"Dr. Antone's office. This is Marge."

Great. Marge.

"Hello Marge. This is Janet Jones, a patient. I had a miscarriage two months ago. I would like to talk to Dr. Antone."

"What's it regarding?"

Janet gripped the edge of her desk to keep her composure. "I am still bleeding, and now I'm getting worried about a molar pregnancy. I think I have some of the signs."

"Oh. I see. Molar pregnancy is quite rare. Do you have grape-like clusters falling out of your vagina?"

Janet cleared her throat. "Well, no."

"Are you filling more than one pad every few hours?"

"No, not that either."

"Severe nausea and vomiting?"

"No."

Marge sighed. "Women search their computers and call thinking they have a molar or some other disaster. Miscarriages can take a long time to resolve."

"I'd still like to talk to Dr. Antone."

"I'll leave him a message."

"Thank you." She hadn't even finished before the woman hung up.

Janet reset the phone, heart burning with adrenaline and fear.

Her cell phone beeped. Marcus again. He'd left last night while she was in the bathroom, which had been quite a shock to her. He'd never been one for dramatic exits. He obviously felt bad about it today. She wasn't ready to talk to him, not yet. She wanted to figure out how to fix things, the spurned proposal, his upset over the loss, one she didn't quite share.

Marcus put so much stock in romance. She remembered the teddy bears on her bed, the flowers with baby themes. The food and the candles and the ring. It was not a good match. He should have someone sentimental. She suspected a good part of his attraction to her was the challenge of making her more warm-hearted.

The clock bleeped a warning. Fifteen minutes until the bell. Time to walk the halls before dismissal.

A pre-kindergarten class filed past, the four-year-olds jostling each other. The line wiggled out of order. "Sorry," the teacher said to Janet. "Come class, hold on to the rail! No pushing! Ms. Jones is watching!"

The teacher seemed nervous that she would disapprove of the rather minor disruption. They were small children. She understood. How cold did they think she was?

She missed a step and stumbled lightly. The jar of her body brought another gush of bleeding. Thick, she could tell. Probably sticky and black again.

Janet felt dizzy and grasped the rail as the children re-assembled against the wall. One small black boy had eyes like Marcus. Another little girl's cheekbones mirrored her own.

What would her baby have looked like? She tried to walk with poise, but each step felt like a stagger. She couldn't drag her gaze away from the children. One had her nose. Another the same texture as her hair. They could all be hers.

She stumbled to the end of the line, her purse dangling from her elbow. Her baby had never been a baby. She shouldn't think this way.

"You okay, Ms. Jones?"

Janet stared at the teacher, confused. "I'm fine," she mumbled and continued down the hall.

No child would ever look like her. She had turned away her fiancé; the bleeding would never stop. She'd never get married, never have children. She'd forever herd other people's progeny through the halls and send them home while she sat alone with a book each night.

She sat on a bench by the front door. She could picture the stream of blood coming out of her, viscous and black, down her body and into the ground, like an oil spill, choking out the grass, seeping below the surface, killing everything.

She leaned against the brick wall, hot and frightened at the wave of emotion. She gulped air, grasping an iron armrest, trying to regain her poise.

The hormones. It had to be hormones. She never thought this way, felt this way, and certainly didn't act this way. She'd been brought up to admire control, determination, and independence. Whatever was wrecking her now was outside the normal experience. She was not to blame for it, but she could fight it with knowledge and self-assurance.

She stood, returned her bag to its place on her shoulder, and pushed through the outer doors of the school. The cool air refreshed her and once again she completed the day as she always did, with competence and restraint.

3

MEETING

Janet shivered as she crossed the parking lot to the church. Easter had already passed. It should be warm already. She so hated being cold.

Inside, Stella and Raven sat near each other in the ring of chairs, talking in hushed tones. At her arrival, they moved apart. "Hello, Janet," Stella said.

"Everything okay?"

Stella shook her head. "Not in the least."

Janet lowered herself into a chair, smoothing her brown slacks. A nervous gesture. Her mother would be mortified. "What's happened?"

Stella threw up her hands. "Good God, you name it. Raven's having a hard time with the baby dance—"

"He can't get it up." Raven's eyes were surrounded in mottled mascara. "I told him it's because he hasn't dealt with the baby's death. And so he walked out."

Janet exhaled slowly. "How long as he had the problem?"

"Since I ovulated two weeks ago. I missed the meeting, but it was for nothing."

Stella pressed her hands against her temples. "Let's think about this."

"Think about what?" Melinda slipped into the ring of chairs and sat down.

"What might be causing Raven's husband to be impotent."

"He taking any medicines?" Melinda asked. "Because Jake took some antibiotic once, and he was totally shot until a couple days after he was done."

"Oh my God," Raven said. "He was taking something for a sinus infection. The package didn't mention it."

"Not a listed side effect," Melinda said. "We checked too."

"Boys don't report these things," Stella said. "Might cause them to admit something they'd rather ignore."

Raven jumped out of her chair. "I have to go call him! Now!" She bent down to give Melinda a quick hug. "Thank you."

Janet tugged at a small imperfection in her trouser crease. Such an easy fix for Raven. Her own problems loomed large and hideous. She shifted on the uncomfortable chair, and another small gush slid out of her. She sucked in a breath.

"You okay, Janet?" Stella asked.

She pressed her hand to her stomach, willing the bleeding to dry up and go away. "Still bleeding." With the admission, she gave up on her poise and bent forward in the chair. The pressure against her belly felt good.

Stella leaned toward her and let her glasses fall from her hand to swing on the gold chain.

Janet grasped the edge of the chair to steady herself. She'd never spoken up much before, but if Melinda could admit to throwing her baby in the trash, and Dot could talk about the placenta in her freezer, surely she could say this. "I keep looking at all the children in the school. I think of what it would be like if they were mine. I don't know where this is coming from. I didn't even want to get pregnant. I'm not even married. It must be the hormones."

"Lots of crazy things happen after a loss," Stella said. "And you never know what it's going to be."

"Like blood on the floor," Melinda said. "I think I finally kicked it."

The door opened, sending a rush of cold air through the group. Dot hurried in and sat on a chair. She had given up the sweats for jeans and a silky blouse. Her hair was curled and sprayed away from her face. She still wore the cross, but she wasn't bent over it.

"You look pretty, Dot," Janet said. Steering the conversation away was a relief. She'd said enough.

"What happened?" Stella asked. "It looks like something good."

Dot twirled a tiny gold ring on her finger. "I'm getting divorced good and proper, when I can afford the fees."

"That's a good thing?" Stella asked.

"Yeah, my husband ditched me. I got pregnant by someone else." Her voice faltered. Janet realized she wasn't the only one to get pregnant accidentally. Or to lose it.

"You haven't talked about it. Are you ready?" Stella asked.

Dot shrugged. "The baby didn't have a brain. I had to abort it or I could die, they said. I watched the screen as they did it. His heartbeat. I saw it stop."

The candles flickered. Janet's eyes burned. So much emotion.

"You doing okay?" Melinda asked.

"I plan on getting married again. When I'm free. Things will be better."

Melinda tugged a card out of her purse. "Call me tomorrow. We'll have it done in two months."

Dot took the card. "I can't save money too fast, even with Gary helping. But he'll help."

"Don't worry about it," Melinda said. "We'll get it square one way or another."

Dot stared at the card. "That's mighty fine of you." Her face contorted, like she would cry. "I reckon you all aren't religious types, being so educated and all, but I think God is maybe forgiving me finally."

"That's what He does," Melinda said.

Janet swallowed. Religion had never had much place in her own home, although growing up, they did go to Sunday school every week. It's like God began and ended at the church door.

Another gush pulsed out of her, and she hugged her belly. All the heat drained out of her face, and she knew she was growing pale. She wouldn't be able to hide it.

"Janet, I'm so worried about you," Stella said. "There's some hideous complications out there. This is going on too long."

Janet rocked in her chair. It embarrassed her, but she needed the soothing motion. "I know. I looked some things up. But my doctor put me off again."

Stella fiddled with her glasses chain. "Then it's time for a new one. Do either one of you have an ob/gyn you could recommend? Maybe Janet could start over with someone else."

"Oh, that's not necessary," Janet said. "Seems like a new doctor would be even less inclined to listen."

"Mine is wonderful," Melinda said. "He's very gentle and caring. I wished for him more than once when I went to the ER."

"Oh, don't ever go to the ER with a miscarriage if you can help it," Stella said. "You should hear some of the tales the women who've come through here have shared. They've done nasty things like throw babies right in the medical waste cans in front of the mothers, or keep parents there for hours before finally sending them on home with nothing done." Stella sat more stiffly in her chair and smoothed her paisley skirt. "That hospital stuff is just plain no good. I didn't go myself."

"Weren't you scared?" Janet asked.

"I was scared plenty, but I was more scared of the ER. I did the right thing, I think. I wouldn't change it."

Melinda handed Janet a phone number on a scrap of paper. "Is the baby's father helping at all?" she asked.

Janet shook her head. "I put him off. He was so…" What was he? "He handled the situation differently than I did."

Stella grasped her swinging glasses to hold them still. "Please listen here, Janet. This is nothing to trifle with. I don't want to scare you, but you can be putting your ability to have children in the future at risk. There's scar tissue. There's damage that could be getting done."

God. But her doctor had brushed aside her concerns. Actually, no, Marge had. She was the gatekeeper and a terrible one at that.

"Please, Janet, call someone new tomorrow," Stella said. "I'm going to check on you and make sure you did it."

"She's a pushy broad," Dot said. "You better do what she says."

Janet attempted a feeble smile. The very idea of starting over with another doctor's office exhausted her. But later, as they stood to adjourn the meeting, a wave of nausea coursed through her, and she decided she'd endured enough.

4

ER REVISITED

Janet sat in her car outside the church. The other women had driven away, but she waited, sticky with blood, remembering Stella's warning. She couldn't decide if she was overreacting or not. Certainly she could wait until morning and call Melinda's doctor. She didn't have to make a big deal out of this.

Except it was a big deal. Two months of thick black bleeding was not normal. She'd read books, searched the Internet, and listened to other stories in the pregnancy loss group. Nothing about her pregnancy and even her life had been normal since that damn fool condom broke.

She drove to a nearby drugstore to purchase another package of panty liners. She handed over the money absently and carted the bag to her car, sick of the pads, sick of the blood, sick of everything.

"Miss?"

A stooped man in grubby clothes and a ball cap leaned over a make-shift cane.

She glanced around the parking lot, fear coursing hot through her body. "Yes?"

"Can you spare some change? I got a bad knee, and I'm powerfully hungry."

Janet looked in the man's eyes, drawn and dark within the deep sockets. He had purple marks across his cheeks.

Her parents would have nodded politely then turned away. They believed every person should stand on their own without assistance from anybody else. Janet had paid her own way through college, found her first job, and bought her first home with only the quiet murmurs of approval on the other end of the phone line.

She reached into her purse and pulled out her entire stack of bills. "Here," she said, and shoved the wad into his hand. "It's enough for a hotel, even, if you want it, or new clothes," she hesitated. "Or several days of booze."

The man looked at the money and didn't speak. Janet sat in her car and closed the door behind her. She sensed the disapproving glance of her parents as she started the engine. She didn't have to be their model daughter all the time. Their model of a daughter. She had only just begun to realize they might have been wrong, raised her poorly. Cost her Marcus.

She intended to drive home, but when she saw the sign for the exit to the hospital, she took it. The warnings about the ER reverberated, but suddenly she'd chosen a path. She'd see it through.

She killed the car in the hospital parking lot and leaned her head on the steering wheel. Her future had been so structured for so long and now it unraveled, strand by strand. She thought of her parents up in Maine. She had never called them to let them know about the baby or her loss of it. They scarcely even knew Marcus' name, much less how close they'd come to getting married. They would not have understood how Janet could have gotten in such a mess.

When she first learned she was pregnant, Janet had planned to call them. Marcus had been so exuberant, showing up at six in the morning on the day she tested so he wouldn't miss it. He'd danced around the marble bathroom in complete disregard for their personal and professional debacle.

She and her parents were straightforward—smart and polite. Janet visited them every summer for a week as well as four days at Christmas. They spent long hours quietly talking about work and current events at the mosaic table on the back porch overlooking Sebago Lake.

She'd modeled herself after them, ambitious but not driven, proud but not haughty, compassionate but not emotional.

One evening a month after the test, she'd gone to the bathroom after having sex with Marcus—he'd been so overwrought and romantic, surrounding her with pink and blue bears—and saw blood when she wiped. At that moment she felt glad she hadn't called them. They would not have approved of any of it, and now they didn't have to know.

Marcus had blubbered like a fool at the sonogram a few days later when they found only an empty sac. Janet had lost patience with his constant need for comfort and to talk about what happened. She assumed life would go on as usual—work and dinners, quiet evenings and occasional sex. But Marcus had changed. Instead of the steady, mildly amusing man she'd begun dating over a year earlier, he became soft, introspective, moody, and emotional. Janet hoped he would self-correct, but the scene when he proposed obviously showed he hadn't.

Something brushed against the door of her car. She lifted her head. A man was carrying a young girl curled up high against his neck. Her face wasn't visible beneath his chin, but her hair spilled across his arm. The girl's legs dangled limply over his elbow. Just as Janet suppressed the urge to open the door and ask if they were okay, the girl popped her head up and grabbed the man's nose in a playful tweak. Janet relaxed against the seat and watched them cross the parking lot.

A memory surfaced, long lost. Her dad, laughing and tossing her in the air and holding her up high against his neck, her knees by his ear, feet dangling in black Mary Janes. He'd covered her cheek with kisses and nestled her under his chin.

"Daddy, you're prickly!" she'd said, laughing and pushing away.

But he held her in his strong arms, spinning in circles across the lawn of their house.

A cascade of images followed. Her mother's face, tight and grief stricken on Janet's first day of preschool.

Her small light coat was unbuttoned, and she skipped along the sidewalk, excited to join the dozens of other children playing on the jungle gym inside the courtyard. She pulled her mother along by the hand, impatient, then realized they had stopped. She turned. Mama was crying.

"Mama? Why are you sad?"

Her mother had knelt down and held on to her. "You're getting all grown up, Janet. You aren't my baby anymore."

"New baby," Janet said, and patted her mother's round belly. "I'm the big sister!"

But Mama had just cried harder and Janet hadn't known what to do—torn between the happy shrieks from the playground and her mother's tears.

"Let's go on now," Mama finally said, smoothing Janet's hair. "I know I have to let you go."

Janet had immediately begun to skip again.

Her mother had once been soft, and so had her father. Hugs and kisses, laughter and tears, curling up in the evenings and jumping on the bed. When had it changed?

The sick heat in her belly warned her before she consciously acknowledged the thought.

When Ethan died.

Her baby brother had died after surgery for a congenital heart condition. He never woke from the anesthesia and spent several days on a ventilator before her parents were willing to turn it off. He was four years old, Janet just eight.

What horror to face, to choose the moment of your child's death, to see the machines whir to a stop, the monitors to beep, the line of the heartbeat to go flat. No one really recovers from that. It must be easier to harden your heart, close the recesses of pain, and live life more simply and with calm deliberation.

She thought of Dot then, forced to terminate her pregnancy. She had also chosen the moment of her baby's death. Her hand automatically flew to her own belly. Had a baby ever been there? Did she really lose anything?

She remembered Ethan, his head of tight curls, his piggish nose, bright eyes. "Nanet" he'd called her. "Sissa Nanet." And now she cried, hot flowing tears, a shuddering of her entire body.

Her mother had sat on the edge of her bed after the funeral, stiff and expressionless, tugging her brother's stuffed animals away from Janet's arms.

"He's gone, and there's nothing we can do about it," she had said. "I'll put these away. Now go wash your face."

Janet had wanted to cry, but her mother's tone scared her. She ran through the house to her father, who sat in a ladder-back chair by a table spread with food.

She ran up to his knee and buried her head in his lap.

"This is quite a mess we have here," he said. "Up, up, now Janet. Let's get to cleaning. We're done with crying."

She'd looked up at his clenched jaw, the tightness around his eyes. He didn't look like her daddy.

He pushed her away and stood. "Your mother will appreciate it if we get a head start."

Unable to do anything else, with nowhere to turn, Janet had simply begun taking plates to the kitchen.

⤦⥱⤧

In the hospital parking lot, the car felt too confining, too warm, so she opened the door to gulp the cool evening air.

Her brother. Her baby. Her boyfriend. She'd lost so much. She wiped her face with her hands and cleaned them on her skirt. So there, Mother, she thought, imagining her horror at Janet's loss of composure.

A siren sounded in the distance and grew louder as it approached the hospital. Janet watched the colored lights as it flew into the drive and paramedics leapt out the back.

The girl on the gurney could be her—dark skinned, thin, tight hair. Her eyes were closed, but Janet could tell from the calm faces of the couple who also filed out of the ambulance that the problem wasn't serious. They walked in a measured pace, heads pressed close as they chatted with animated hand gestures.

She should go in. Whatever faced her next was inside those doors, and she was ready to tackle it.

The brightness of the ER blinded her after the dim light of the parking lot. She pressed her purse to her belly and walked up to the admitting nurse.

"I'm having a miscarriage," she told the registration attendant. "I need to see a doctor."

The woman passed her the forms, and she sat on a row of blue chairs. She started crying again, hot tears that caused her nose to run. She filled out the paper on the clipboard and stretched out on the chairs, feeling the occasional pulse of black blood flow out of her, knowing she looked unladylike and inappropriate on the awkward row of plastic, but not caring.

A nurse touched her arm. "Ms. Jones?"

Janet nodded.

"Come with me."

She explained her situation sketchily, not wanting to suggest what was wrong, but let them decide. A woman doctor arrived, performed a pelvic, and told the nurse to draw blood.

Janet lay on the paper-covered cushions, pressing the cotton ball against the crook of her arm, and thought of Marcus. Should she call him? She didn't want to be alone now.

Tears flowed out again, hot and wet. She'd blown that, she knew. He hadn't even tried calling since the day after the proposal. As good looking, successful, and romantic as he was, he probably had a number of women he could choose from. Certainly someone less stoic than her. Someone who could appreciate him.

The doctor returned, smoothing her sleek brown hair behind an ear. She sat on a stool near the end of the exam table.

"Ms. Jones. Your pregnancy hormone levels are very high—far too high for someone who miscarried months ago. I suspect you have retained tissue from the loss, but I also think we should consider, based on your symptoms—the tarry discharge especially—that we may have gestational trophoblastic disease.

"Molar pregnancy."

"Yes."

Janet sucked in a breath. "I suspected it."

"It's hard to diagnose. It's rare."

"My doctor wouldn't listen to me."

The woman pinched her lips into a firm line. "I hate that, but it happens. Like I said, it's rare. OBs deal with so many normal situations, sometimes an unusual one is hard to spot."

"Will it become cancer?"

"Not likely. It is very responsive to treatment. Even though your levels are high and we've waited a little long, a D&C will very likely take care of it. If it doesn't, a couple rounds of methotrexate should take care of it."

"Side effects?"

"With the low dose, there aren't many but you might feel some nausea or headache. But we'll cross that bridge if you have to take it. Are you planning to get pregnant again?"

"No."

"Okay, because that's important. You will need to be monitored for a year or so to make sure the trophoblasts do not return. It can potentially invade the lining and become cancer. We have to keep an eye on it."

"I'll be glad right now just to stop bleeding."

The doctor nodded. "Would you like to go to your regular OB for the D&C or have it performed here? I'd like to get this process going for you quickly."

"I think I just fired my OB," Janet said. "When could we do it here?"

"I'll send someone in to make an appointment."

"Can you do it?"

The doctor looked up from her file. "That can be arranged."

"Will you have to put me under?" She hesitated. "My brother died. Ethan. He was four. He never came out of the anesthesia."

"Was there an allergy? A reaction?"

"I don't think so, no. He had … a heart condition."

"You can be awake for the procedure if you prefer. It's done both ways—local or general."

Janet exhaled in a rush. "Thank you."

"I'll give you a list of ob/gyns for follow-up," the doctor said. "I'll check off the ones I know personally and might be a better fit for you. You'll be seeing them a lot. But I think I can get you started and on your way to recovery." She held out her hand.

Janet took it, grasping her fingers as though she were drowning. "Thank you."

The doctor nodded. "Of course. We'll be in touch. Let's get the D&C done within the week."

Janet dressed slowly. Her suit sleeves were soggy. Her pantyhose had runs in them. This seemed right. You don't lose a baby, end a relationship, and get diagnosed with a long-term disease without some messiness, some trauma. She bent to pull up her stockings then suddenly changed her mind and tossed them in the trash.

Maybe later she'd call Marcus. And her mom.

5

ANESTHESIA

Janet tapped her pencil absently on her desk. She had already told her secretary and the dean of curriculum that she would be out on Thursday for a minor procedure. But she had a problem. Someone had to drive her home.

"Can't I take a taxi?" she asked the man who had come into the ER to schedule her surgery.

"We don't prefer that," he said. "In case something happens on the way home."

Her position as a principal was not conducive to work friendships. And she'd found when she left her old company three years ago that those relationships had ended with the job. The small cadre of women she'd sometimes eaten lunch with had rarely gotten together after work, and only then for the rare happy hour.

Where did she have friends?

The flowered curtain on the window reminded her of Stella's dresses. Of course.

She tugged the pink half-sheet of the miscarriage group out from under a file in her drawer, relieved to see an email address as well as

Stella's number. A phone call seemed too personal still, even though what she was asking was extremely so. She typed out a light-hearted email thanking Stella for making her go to the doctor and mentioning the surgery. Was she available for a hand-hold?

She sent it, instantly regretting the last line, but unable to retrieve the message. Stella might not be able to get away from her shop anyway. If it didn't work, she could call Marcus. He wouldn't turn her down.

But she'd let him go. It was better to keep the break clean.

After lunch, she was relieved to see a reply. Stella would be delighted to come. She had some bead work that she couldn't finish at the store with all the commotion. Perfect work for sitting in a waiting room.

Janet collapsed her head into her hands with relief. She'd never reached out for help before, certainly not with someone she knew so little. But this was her new life.

Stella organized her beads on a little tray as they waited for Janet to be called back to be prepped for surgery.

"You anxious?" Stella asked. "You seem a little anxious."

Stella had no idea about her brother, or the anesthesia, or Janet's fears. "Not fond of doctors."

"No one is," Stella said. "Skipped the whole thing with my first loss. Wouldn't go to the hospital."

"I can understand that." Janet's hands were clammy, and goose bumps prickled across her arms. She kept picturing the IV, the mask on her face, the world going black. A crash cart, the beeping line of her heartbeat going flat. Her breathing accelerated until she started to hyperventilate.

Stella shoved the tray on a nearby chair and snatched at her hand. "Breathe, child, breathe. It's going to be okay."

Janet's lungs felt squeezed. Stella pushed on her back, forcing her to drop her face between her knees.

"Slow that breath down. I don't want to have to put a bag on your face."

Janet sputtered a laugh. "What?"

"That's better. A bag. So you will breathe again."

Janet managed to gulp a breath. She relaxed a bit and then it was over. She calmed and sat up.

"You're going to make it through this," Stella said.

Janet pressed her hand against her chest, grateful for each intake of air. "I'm glad you're here."

The nurse called her name. "Thank you," she said to Stella.

"Not a problem. This is a work day after all." Stella picked up her tray. "I'll be here."

The nurse led her back to a large room with ten empty beds. "This is the prep room. We'll get you dressed and ready for the procedure." She showed Janet the gown and blanket. "It's a little chilly in here."

Janet accepted the bag for her clothes. "And it's just a local, right. No general?"

The nurse checked the clipboard. "It is. Nothing to it. You'll be awake the whole time, but you will have an IV, and you will feel a little out of it, like it's not happening. Go ahead and hop on the bed when you're dressed. We'll be rolling you in and out of here."

She pulled a curtain around the bed and left Janet to change.

Janet stepped out of the practical clothes she'd bought just for this occasion—a velour sweat suit and plain white tennis shoes. Not quite jeans, but she'd work up to that. Now that she saw her life from the outside, she wondered how she'd ever captured Marcus at all. Everyone had to see what an uptight control freak she had been.

Just the thought of all that made the tears flow. Now she was the opposite extreme. She could only hope that getting the bad cells out of her body would help her find balance between her old self and the new.

She'd barely pulled the blanket over her cold legs when the nurse returned. "Tight schedule," the woman said, quickly fitting a monitor to Janet's finger and taping it down. "I'm going to go ahead and start the IV."

Janet didn't wince at the prick in her hand. She watched the clear saline flow down to her arm, dripping from the plastic bag. The nurse used a needle to shoot something into the injection port. "You're going to feel a little hazy soon," she said. "Just relax."

But Janet couldn't relax. As the drips continued, her panic rose. The heart rate on the monitor lurched. The nurse took her hand. "It will be fine. You're going to be fine."

She pictured Ethan in her place, his eyes drooping, seeing their mother and father for the last time. She hadn't been there, but the image was perfectly clear.

She wanted to jerk the IV out, to run. The nurse stroked her hand. "You're fine."

"My brother died after surgery. He was four."

"That's plenty reason to be nervous."

"He never woke up."

"I saw the note about it in your file. It's not going to happen to you."

Janet forced her shoulders to relax. What did it matter if it did? She wouldn't know. Ethan didn't know. He sank into oblivion painlessly, quietly.

She closed her eyes.

"That's better," the nurse said. "We're going to roll you down to surgery now."

Janet nodded. She'd be fine. Either way, she'd be fine.

6

RESOLUTION

Janet steered the rental car along the winding lane that led to her parents' lake house in Maine. Right after the D&C she decided to fly there and had arranged for a few days' leave from school. The only person she had told where she was going, actually, was Stella.

Janet had not grown up in this old-fashioned house on the shore of Sebago Lake. Shortly after Ethan died, they closed up the row house in the Back Cove section of Portland. Her family lived in a series of homes as Janet attended school and her father taught history at the University of Southern Maine campus nearby. They never left the vicinity of her Catholic school, but never remained in the same home for more than a few years, either.

"You uprooted me," Janet said to the windshield, which reflected the sun and shadows of the towering red maples and pine. "You never let me have a home."

Only when Janet left for college had her parents settled in the lake house, as if deeming it safe to get attached to a home again now that their daughter was gone.

More and more of her life was beginning to make sense now. The quiet pride. The abbreviated hugs. The simplicity in their relationship. They had no passion, no emotional attachment, no expectations or fear of disappointment. She could have been their distant cousin, or a colleague, or a stranger.

She pulled onto the leaf-strewn driveway alongside their white clapboard house. The wind blew high here, and Janet smoothed her hair self-consciously before walking around to the back porch where her parents undoubtedly sat in sweaters and drank hot tea from big blue mugs.

She heard the clink of ceramic on tile as she rounded the corner. Her father sat bent over a crossword, the fine burr of hair brushed with gray. The sun struck his straight nose, and she couldn't see his eyes as his glasses had slipped down. One hand still cupped the oversized mug.

Her mother had her back to Janet, and the stiff upright posture reminded her of home in all its formality and restraint.

The dry leaves crunched beneath her step and her father looked up, peering at her, then adjusting his glasses.

"Janet?"

Her mother turned, the blue flowers of her housecoat crinkling with the twist in her shoulders. Janet felt hyper-alert, sensitive, able to take in each detail.

"Yes, Father. I'm here."

"Well, I'll be," her mother said. "Is something the matter? Why didn't you call?"

"I wanted to surprise you," Janet said, feeling suddenly lightheaded. She sat down opposite them at the mosaic table, running her fingers along the cool smooth tiles fitted together to create a mural of the sea. Her parents had worked four years on it, nipping bits of color and placing each shard carefully into the scene according to a pattern they'd found in a book.

"Aren't you ... aren't you glad to see me?" Janet knew she could never maintain the poise she'd once had with them. Her hand trembled as it continued to glide across the table, following the indentions of grout and tile.

Her parents exchanged a glance. "Of course, Janet," her father said. "We're just surprised, is all, like you said. You wanted a surprise, and well, we're surprised."

Janet watched him from across the gleaming surface. He had lost his usual careful elocution and actually stuttered.

"We're delighted for the unexpected visit." Her mother glanced at the corner of the house as though she might peek into Janet's car. "Did you bring your things?"

"Actually, I traveled pretty light. I'll need to buy a toothbrush." The giddy feeling increased until she gripped the edge of the table. "Imagine, forgetting a toothbrush!"

Her parents glanced at each other again. "Janet, are you quite all right?" her father asked. "Are you in some sort of trouble?"

"No! Yes! I mean, I was, but I'm not now. I'm fine. Sort of fine." She stopped.

"Can you tell us what happened?" Her father removed his glasses, and his eyes were calm but concerned, his bushy gray brows drawn together.

Her mom had clasped her hands before her face as if in prayer. Her eyes were colder, steady, almost disdainful, as if she didn't want to hear what Janet might say.

"I met a man. I love him. His name is Marcus. We—we were going to get married, but I've put him off. I'm not sure why." She rubbed her fingers along the variants of blue and sea green chips, all flush and polished and perfectly inlaid.

"Are you looking for advice?" her father asked.

His eyebrows had relaxed. She'd said nothing too shocking. "Yes. No. Maybe." She tried to reign in her spiraling thoughts. What had she come here to say? To accuse them of?

"There's more. I'm … sick. I have something called gestational trophoblastic disease."

Her mother pressed her hand against her chest. "Is it serious?"

"A little. I had to have surgery last week. It went well. They are monitoring me now, to see what it does. It might grow again, or we might have gotten all the cells."

"Is it cancer?" Her mother's voice sounded small and tight.

"Not yet. Just a precancerous condition. It rarely becomes cancer. We're treating it, though. I'll start chemotherapy—a very light form—if the cells come back."

"You said gestational." Her father also moved his fingers across the tiles, as though reading the Braille Janet had already laid out.

She nodded. "It's a post-pregnancy condition."

"You were pregnant?" he asked.

"Yes."

"With this man who wants to marry you, I presume?" Her mother's voice had risen like a wave, dark and pitched, with a touch of menace.

"Yes. But naturally the baby wasn't viable, with my condition. I lost it. It died." Her fingers trembled visibly now, and she pulled away from the mosaic and gripped them under the table.

"Did your man—Marcus—did he not want to marry you after this?" her father asked.

"Yes, he did. He did. I just wasn't—I didn't. I didn't answer."

"You didn't answer his proposal."

"Correct."

"But you said you loved him."

Janet stared above her father's eyes at the gray fuzz of his hair. "I do. I really do."

"What is stopping you then?" Her mother still sat ramrod straight, her elbows hard against the table, her arms upright. Her nails were cut close and unpolished.

"I—I think it has to do with Ethan."

At his name, her mother's hands fluttered, then fell still, one fist tucked inside the palm of the other. "Whatever for?" she asked.

Janet clenched her jaw, drew a breath, and knew she had to begin. "Mother, Father. After Ethan died, you treated me differently. You weren't the same. You didn't love me like you had. You didn't laugh."

"Those were hard days, Janet," her father said.

"But you never changed back. You never let me cry. You never cried. No one played with me. No one seemed to care about me anymore. I was just another object in the room." Her voice was breaking, her face, she could feel, was contorted.

She couldn't bear to look at them, see if she hurt them or if her words bounced right off their steel facades.

"We did the best we could," her mother said. "The past is done."

"But it's not done! It's here, right now! Marcus told me I never cared about the baby, or about him. He said I didn't feel anything! I'm going to lose him because of how I was raised! How you raised me!"

186

Her last word rang against the table and faded into the trees. Gulls circled the shallow water and bleated their squawky bird-song. The wind picked up suddenly and shook the trees, leaves shivering and rustling in an elongated ripple.

Her mother stood and tugged open the screen door. The wood planks slammed against the frame from the tightness of the spring.

Her father reached across the table. "Give me your hand," he said.

She extended her arm, threading her way through the mugs and books and papers. He pressed his thumb into her palm and gripped her fingers.

"I never felt comfortable with the changes in our house after your brother's funeral. But when your life trajectory is irreparably altered, you often find you can't go back to the person you were. Your mother no longer had in her the innocent hope that had been the hallmark of her love. I could not break through to her, and so instead followed her lead. I failed you in this. And I am sorry."

"I was just a little girl."

"I know."

His hand felt warm and rough against the outdoor chill. Late afternoon was falling into evening, and the sky over the lake already shifted from white to yellow, tinged with a hint of orange.

He squeezed her fingers. "You know, I can already see that baby has changed you."

"Life does that," Janet whispered.

"I think you'll find your way. You won't make the mistakes we made."

"What do I do about Mother?"

"She'll come around."

A shadow filled the screen; then her mother opened the door with another squeak and a slam.

"I'm not much for this sort of conversation, but I can tell you what to do." She held out the phone.

Janet released her father's hand and took it. "Who am I supposed to call?"

"You know who to call. If he's half the man you deserve, he'll be here by the weekend. Tell him your parents would like to meet their future son."

Janet held the phone lightly in her palm. Her mother watched her, unsmiling, more determined than compassionate. Her father leaned against the table, brows raised high over animated eyes.

"You going to listen in?" Janet asked.

"To every word," he said.

She dialed the number. He might not even want to talk to her anymore.

The line connected. "Hello?" he said.

She felt paralyzed, her throat too tight and dry.

"Hello?"

He wouldn't recognize this number. She'd never called him from her parents' home.

"Marcus, it's Janet."

"Oh my God. Baby, are you okay?"

"I—I. No."

"Can I come over? Of course not. This area code is way long distance. Where are you?"

"My parents in Maine.

"Are they okay? Did something happen?"

Marcus, her Marcus. Always so quick to worry. "No, nothing like that. They … they want to meet you."

"I can be on a plane in an hour."

"Just like that?"

"You want me to come?"

"I do."

She could hear the smile in his voice. "Then yes, just like that."

Janet looked up at her parents, her mother standing behind her father, her hands curled around his shoulders. "He's coming," she said.

They nodded.

"Janet?" Marcus said.

"Yes."

"Will you marry me?"

"What?"

"Will you marry me?" he repeated.

"This weekend?"

"Maybe. But sometime. Will you?"

Janet choked, laughing and crying simultaneously. "Get here and I'll give you an answer."

"I'm walking out the door."

He hung up and she could picture him already, throwing things willy-nilly in a bag, and maybe, like her, abandoning the whole thing and just jumping in the car to get to the airport.

Her Marcus. He was on his way.

PART FIVE: *Stella*

1

JEWELS

Spermatozoa leapt onto the glass counter, lifting a paw to the rack of pale green necklaces winking in the late afternoon sun.

"Don't even think about it, you rat-tailed fur ball." Stella reached beneath the cash register for one of the seven water guns she stored around the shop precisely for moments like this.

The cat froze, nose to the air, and turned his eye to Stella as if to say, "What-freaking-ever."

"So that's the way it's going to be, eh?" She squinted an eye and aimed at the white star on his black chest.

He stretched his leg lazily and grazed the closest string of beads, setting the cluster to tinkling.

"That does it," Stella said, pulling back her trigger finger and spewing a stream of water across the shop.

The cat arched into the air, one leg missing the counter on the landing. He flipped off the end in a snarling hiss.

Stella gasped and rounded the counter, her hip grazing the metal corner and snagging her knit blouse. She spun, tugging on the fabric.

Her cat landed on the polished concrete floor and flashed between her ankles, knocking her off balance.

"Hiiiiyeee!" She flailed, reaching for the glass table top but grasping only air. The water gun clattered to the floor, and Stella landed unceremoniously on her ample backside. The jaw-snapping jar to her spine rumbled plumb up to her head.

Oh that damn cat! Stella slapped her hands on the floor.

She heaved herself on to her knees, feeling the extra pounds. She wasn't a young lithe thing anymore. She'd stopped watching her weight four years ago, a fortieth birthday present to herself.

The world was made of the skinny and the fat, she knew. She'd made the transition, and that suited her fine. Her husband Dane always grabbed her and laughed that she finally matched him. Now they could tumble together without any clashing of bones.

"Well, gosh!" The front door jingled and a stick-figure woman decked in gold lamé entered the store. "You all right, honey?"

"Oh! Hello!" She tucked her pale blue-veined calves beneath her skirt and grasped the edge of the glass case to help her stand up.

"Should I call someone?" the woman slid her sunglasses further up into her white-blond hair.

"Oh, I'm fine, just fine … just you know, checking the ol' stability of the display counters." Stella rapped her hand sharply against a metal leg.

The woman nodded, shooting her a disdainful look. "I'm sure it happens … all the time." She arched a carefully waxed brow. Stella noticed with pleasure that the woman's mascara had smudged beneath her eyes. She recognized her type. Rich, overdressed, undernourished.

The woman fingered some of the sale items on the rack. Stella sat behind the counter and busied herself with fine wire and loose beads, creating a multi-strand bracelet while she had an audience. Customers loved the idea that the work was done right there in the shop and often bought a piece straight off her worktable. She'd double the price, out of contempt.

"Um, hello there?" The woman was leaning over the counter, her tan bosom straining against the square décolletage.

Avert your eyes, Stella thought, glancing instead at the green plastic water gun still on the floor. Otherwise she might start using the cleavage for target practice. She forced a grin. "Can I assist you?"

"Is everything in the whole store green and purple?" the woman asked.
Stella smiled. "Yes. I only work with two gems. Amethyst and peridot."
"How odd."
Stella maintained her smile. "They are unusual choices I know."
"You do all this yourself, then? You're the artist and the clerk?"
Stella stretched her smile another inch. "Yes! You know, hard to get good help these days!"
"I see." The woman turned away and slowly walked the store again. Stella continued stringing the beads, slanting her eyes occasionally out across the shop. The woman had encased her nonexistent behind in a shiny skirt and tottered on black stilettos. Stella hoped she was hungry and in pain.
"Well, thank you! Ta ta!" The woman dislodged her sunglasses from her processed hair and slipped back outside.
Stella sighed. 5:04. Closing time.
She pushed herself up from the chair, bracing her palms against the table for leverage, feeling every pound. Don't waddle, old woman, she chastised as she crossed the room to lock the front door. Keep some dignity.
A young couple passed by as she switched the sign to "Closed." They moved together fluidly down the sidewalk, his hand tucked inside the back pocket of her jeans. Love made the world go 'round. She was lucky for Dane. She never doubted that for a moment.
But she wouldn't see him for a bit. Tonight was the miscarriage meeting.
She lifted a display case from the window to carry to the back. She didn't want to go. She couldn't pinpoint exactly when the change had begun, but the group was taking more out of her lately than she was able to put in.
It wasn't the current set of ladies. They were all doing well and not causing her any trouble. In fact, this batch seemed to have had the most dramatic recoveries from their losses than she'd seen in a while. Melinda was all empowered again, working a new part-time position as an attorney. Janet was getting married. Crazy. After making that poor man suffer so.
And Dot had ditched her husband. Took on a Greek god, according to her. She was a changed woman since that happened, no more cross clutching and hair in her eyes.

Then there was Tina. Ever since the phone call, Stella had worried. She'd never lost a member, although more than one had come in with suicidal thoughts. The thoughts, they were common. Most everyone had them pass through. It was the actions that were bad. Even planning it was bad. And here Tina'd gone and done it, then almost done it again. Stella was glad her teen years were long gone. Tough years. She ought to call and check on the girl.

Stella paused before a lighted cabinet near the door to the back. Inside were the first two pieces she had ever designed, both bracelets, carefully displayed in their own glass case. The first, all amethyst, was strung on a fine silver chain. The second, made of peridot, she had alternated with gold beads.

Stella opened the case and fingered the two bracelets. A small gold plate beneath each one bore a name and a date, touched so many times in the late hours after the shop closed that the engraving had almost worn smooth. Angelica. 1997. Buddy. 1998.

She closed the cabinet. No time to dawdle today. She still had to drop Spermatozoa by the house before heading on to the church. The women would be waiting, and only she had a key.

2

IDES OF MARCH

Two other cars pulled up as Stella unlocked the door to the chapel behind the United Methodist Church. She waited for the girls to get out, glad for the chill against her hot face. She'd really had to rush.

"Hello, Stella," Raven said. She hurried along the walkway, her red skirt fluttering behind her.

"In like a lion, out like a lamb," Janet called, slamming the door to her blue Mercedes. "I wonder who will get dredged up with all this crazy weather."

The three women rearranged the back line of padded wood chairs into a circle. The door opened with a whoosh and Dot hurried in. "Am I late?"

"Not yet," Stella said.

Dot immediately slowed her pace, breathing heavily. "I couldn't find anyone to close for me."

"It's okay. We haven't started." Stella lowered herself onto one of the small square seats. Her thighs, she noticed, extended well beyond the border of the chair. She might have to start keeping her weight in check now. No use adding diabetes to her list of ails.

They were all spreading, she noticed, watching the others settle into their places. Dot's children had probably each added five pounds.

Raven had confessed a compulsion to eat through her stress at her first meeting. The occasional glimpse of midriff Stella spotted beneath her sweater and the red skirt showed round rolls of fat. She seemed uncomfortable in her outfit today, constantly smoothing the fabric across her belly and tugging at her waistband. Recent gain. Outgrowing her fat clothes. Stella knew all about it.

Janet arranged herself primly on her chair, smoothing her beige suit. Not her, though, Stella thought. Skinny little thing yet. Stella would need to ask her about the return to school after her diagnosis and surgery. Can't be easy, surrounded by kids all the time.

"How have you been feeling, Janet?" Stella asked.

"Fine. Just knowing what it is has helped."

"When's your next checkup?

"I get a blood test every four weeks to make sure the levels stay down."

Stella nodded. She was so glad Janet had found a new doctor after all that suffering. One thing that had astounded her was how the women—smart, educated, strong women—never wanted to bother their caregivers. They silently suffered, trying to be low-maintenance patients despite their horrifying experiences.

"Well, let's get started. I have an inspirational reading to kick us off; then we'll check on how everyone is doing."

Stella slipped her reading glasses on, the gold chain cold against her cheeks. She glanced up to see if everyone was ready. Dot sat up straight in her chair, wearing a nice blouse and pants. The new man was a good thing.

Raven fiddled with the fabric of her skirt, adjusting its drape across her thighs. Her glossy black hair flowed down her back, but her face was quiet and alert. Stella wondered if she'd made up with her man after the bout of impotence. She'd have to ask about that too. No telling where Melinda and Tina were. Maybe they'd show up during the reading.

"This is from a book called *River Waters of the Heart*," Stella said. "I've recommended it before. Meditations mostly." She cleared her throat.

Wash yourselves clean, women, throw off the dirt of grief and the grime of regret. Plunge into the cold waters of the rivers' rapids, fast and white and breathtaking.

Stella droned on without paying attention to her own voice. She hated this crap, actually, but it killed time until everyone arrived. No use wasting good group talk if latecomers might miss something useful. Personally, she felt *River Waters* would come in handier if she used it to knock some of these women upside the head, but of course, she was the leader. She had to try and provide something for the bootstrap-challenged. She found herself at the end of the reading and closed the book.

"That was very beautiful," Raven said.

Janet nodded politely.

Stella stared at them all, her head empty of anything to say. Ten years of running the group, and it was coming to this. She wanted to make a break for the door, but instead, she asked, "Raven, is everything okay with your husband?"

The woman tugged at her skirt again. "He's back in the saddle, if you know what I mean. But my cycle seems off. Baby dust seems to be blowing elsewhere. I don't think we'll get it this month."

"I'm sure that's hard." Stella was glad the responses were so rote to her that she could come up with them without really thinking about it. She wondered who would take the group on if she left. Not too many women came through with her predicament, no kids, not ever, and willing to listen to stories over and over again without moving on.

"Every egg is a little death," Raven said, clutching handfuls of the red fabric in her hands. "Like another kid has died."

Stella could totally relate. "Wait until each egg has cost you ten grand," she said. "No baby and bankrupt to boot."

"Stella, I'm so sorry," Janet said. "I didn't realize."

"Didn't realize what?" Melinda sat among them, a waft of something expensive drifting across the room. Oh, to be rich. "Sorry I'm late."

"That I had to spend all my current and future money on in vitro procedures that didn't take," Stella said.

"Ouch," Melinda said.

"Ouch indeed." Stella glanced at the door, a portal from the stuffy room and into the cool outdoors. She shifted in her seat, trying to find a space where she didn't feel like her fat thighs were going to fall off the edge. She'd find that inner spot where the right answers flowed right on out, divert any conversation away from her own past, and just muck through the next hour.

3

CELEBRATION

The door jingled and Dane strode into the shop. Instantly Stella felt better, the dainty jewels throughout the store more delicate and pretty compared to the big mountain-man bulk of her husband. And she had news, big news.

She pinched closed the wire on the necklace in her hand so she could set it down. "I have been waiting for you to get here!"

"Well, aren't you all aglow! What's the big story, Stell?"

"I just made an astonishing sale. I mean huge." She stood from her work desk behind the counter and came around to Dane's side.

"Well, spill it, woman!"

"No, guess." She grabbed his meaty hand from the glass countertop and kissed it.

He rubbed his fingers against his chin, bristling the hair of his black and gray beard. "How many figures?"

"Five!"

"Whoop! That's a lot of numbers!" He scooped her up around her waist and twirled her.

Stella's head rushed with the wind, and she smacked him on the shoulder. "Put me down before we crack the floor by falling on it!" she said, laughing. "I ain't the skinny thing I once was."

He set her down and grabbed a handful of her backside. "That's right. Now you're a hot mama with lots more to love."

"Dane! A customer could walk in!" She pushed at his chest but didn't move his hand.

"So how much?"

"Eighteen thousand smackers. Isn't that crazy? That's almost half my stock! I'll have to work like mad to keep up!"

"Baby, I am so proud of you."

"I just can't believe it. Some outfit in Beverly Hills. They found that silly little website Kyle made for his high school computer project and wanted all the mid-range stuff I could send them."

"We'll have to thank our nephew! When will you get the money?"

"They are sending five grand next week for the first shipment. They want me to overnight what I have on hand as soon as I cash it."

"Whooeee, Stella! I knew you'd make it big. Your shop's always done all right, paying bills and all, but this is big time!"

"I know! Three month's sales in one phone call!"

"It's great. The first time we've been ahead since—"

Stella knew what he meant. "I know." She refused to let the thought of where their money had gone for all those years get her down. This was big.

"Let's celebrate." Dane grabbed her again.

"The store doesn't close until six! It's only two!"

Dane stode over to the door, flipped the lock and lowered the blinds. "It can be closed for an hour."

"Well, where shall we go? I already had lunch."

Dane grabbed her hand and led her to the back room. "Food wasn't my idea of celebrating."

Stella followed him to the back room. "Pooh Bear, you're something else."

"Yeah. And I got something else to show you."

She laughed and he shooed Spermatozoa off the chintz sofa in her office and dragged her down upon it.

"I really ought to go reopen the shop," Stella said a bit later, dragging a throw from the back of the sofa and covering them. The back office never had good heat and a cold front had blown through yesterday.

"In a minute. You're rich, remember?" Dane stroked her shoulder idly, his fringed lashes flat against his ruddy cheeks.

He really was so beautiful. Like a grizzly bear or something, so much hair everywhere. A thick crop of it on his head, no sign of thinning even though he'd hit fifty. Then the moustache and heavy beard.

Stella ran her hand down his chest. Hair galore. It might not be vogue, with men waxing right and left, but she loved it. Made her feel cushioned, surrounded, shrouded. She buried her nose in his neck. He gripped her more tightly in response.

"I love you, my Pell Mell Stell," he said.

She squeezed him this time, the familiar ache swelling out from her chest and thickening her throat. All this love they had and they couldn't share it with a family, couldn't pass it down.

Dane held on, surely knowing the way her thoughts had gone, as he always did. "So tell me about the group," he said. "Anything new?"

"Everything is new. Melinda's going to help Dot get divorced. Janet's getting married."

"What about that teenager?"

"She didn't come. I need to check on her."

"They all got good men?"

Stella punched his chest. "You shopping?"

"Nah. I know you worry about them."

"Tina's boyfriend took off, but the others seem all right. I keep thinking we should have a couples night or something, so I can show you off."

"They might carry me away if I'm such a catch."

Stella chuckled softly and they snuggled in, a progression of beeps from a delivery truck in reverse bleating outside the back door. "That yours?" Dane asked.

"Probably the deli next door."

"Mmmm. Deli."

"Hungry?" Stella propped herself up to look at him.

"Sex munchies."

Stella laughed. "Always with you. Food after sex."

"How you think I got so fat?" He pulled her down to him again.

He touched her hair, pushing it out of her face. "I know you ain't likely ever gonna get over our not having kids, Stell."

She rested her head back on his chest. She'd figured he'd get around to this. Every high in their life always seemed to be punctuated by this one low.

He cleared his throat, like he had a lump in it. "I'm gonna live my whole life rightful sorry for my part in all of it."

She sat up again and pushed her hand to his mouth. "Shush, Dane. One thing I've learned in all these years of running the group is that I'm damn lucky. Maybe I didn't get a family like we'd wanted, but I got you. And that's more than most people get."

He tucked her head down to him again and they lay a little longer, the rush of traffic seeping through the walls, doors slamming, people calling out, the world bustling outside their four walls.

4

SHOWERS

Stella patted her purse. She was well armed for the party. Fifth of vodka. She could spike most any drink with Smirnoff and not a soul would be the wiser. No way to get through a baby shower without it.

She rang the bell. Another newborn in the family. Each one felt like a fist in the gut. But she could handle it. Her loss in life was no reason to resent others who got what she had once longed for.

"Aunt Stella!" Kayleigh herself opened the door, her belly preceding her by at least three feet. Stella smiled and hugged the girl, all of twenty years old and already popping out puppies.

"You look mighty fine, little Kayleigh!"

"I'm so glad you're here!" She turned, no more than a mite with a basketball attached to her front, and announced. "Aunt Stell is here!"

Stella followed her into the room, where a dozen other women sat around on furniture and folding chairs. Her sister-in-law Patty, Kayleigh's mother, watched her through narrowed eyes.

She knows, Stella thought, once again touching her bag. She remembers.

She would not get drunk this time. Just a few nips to take the edge off. She normally didn't drink much at all, but this added to the glory of the alcohol in these moments. A cheap drunk! She stifled a giggle. Patty cleared her throat and Stella straightened her expression.

"I think everybody's here now!" Kaleigh chirped. An engagement ring on her hand flickered in the light from the sliding glass doors. Not quite going to make it to be legit. The party was actually a combination baby/wedding shower, but since the groom had a fully outfitted house, everyone had gone the baby direction.

Other than Stella. She laid her silver package amidst the pink bows and pastels. The crystal frames could be used for either purpose, she reasoned. But no need to step foot in one of those torturous baby superstores.

She lowered onto the overstuffed chambray sofa. The new room décor was so Patty, she thought. Shabby chic, trendy, but cheaply outfitted. Borderline tawdry, actually, with its fraying white lace cloths and bleached muslin drapery.

"Time for games," Kayleigh said, bouncing from chair to chair with a roll of toilet paper. "Mama isn't much for silliness, so I'm spearheading the fun at my own shower!"

Everyone glanced at Patty, who sat stiffly in an armchair, lips pursed. She nodded at the crowd and then waved her hand dismissively. "You guys go on and have your fun."

Kayleigh gestured to the roll in game-show-host style. "Okay, the object is to figure out how long a string of toilet paper it would take to go around my belly." Kayleigh turned, model-style, her hand on her hip, so everyone could assess her girth.

Stella sighed. She'd get through this one game and then steal away for her first bathroom break. She eyed the crystal bowl on the far table. Ah, good. Plain punch without any of that nasty sherbert inside. It would work quite well with vodka.

Kayleigh bounced from guest to guest, passing the Charmin. Stella recognized the quilting as she held the soft white roll in her hand. Stella stood, comparing her bulk to her niece. "Well, I think I might still have you beat for the time being," she said loudly, her voice echoing off the wood paneling. Too much, she thought. And she hadn't even started drinking.

She wrapped a length of tissue around her own belly, then tore off the strip. "I guess we'll find out for sure in a minute," she said, softening her tone. "It'll be a good laugh."

"Oh Aunt Stell, you're too much." Kayleigh tucked a stray lock of blond hair behind her ear and accepted the roll back.

Too much of many things, she thought as she plopped back on the sofa, compressing the cushions.

When everyone had taken a turn, other than Patty, who sat like she was impaled on a corn cob, Kayleigh danced around the room, allowing each woman to encircle her with their guess.

Titters rippled through the room at the outrageous length of tissue that wrapped the girl two times over. The next ended well before reaching all the way around.

Kayleigh paused before Stella. "Okay, Auntie Stell. Let's see how we compare."

Stella stood and pinned one end of her stream of toilet paper beneath Kayleigh's palm. She walked around the girl, tugging lightly on the strip to pull it taut without tearing the squares apart.

She made her way back to the front. The last square landed neatly with one inch of overlap on the end.

"Wow. Look at that! I think you are the closest!" Kayleigh dropped the tissue on the floor to wrap her arms around her.

Great. She and the pregnant girl had the same waistline.

"Get her prize!" Kayleigh said, waving at another young woman who stood by the food table drenched in pink cakes and strawberry tarts.

The girl presented her with a baby bottle festooned with Elmo. Stella placed it in the gift basket for Kayleigh, as was expected.

"Let's do the one-handed diaper race!" Kayleigh called, snatching a baby doll and a stack of Pampers.

Stella smoothed her dress. That was enough for her. She picked up her purse and stopped by the drink table, splashing a touch of punch into the tiny cup. Damn, they wouldn't have anything bigger.

She stepped into the kitchen, smiling and nodding over the bar as she flipped open her purse and pulled out the flask. Patty's back was to her, fortunately, or the old shrew might actually walk over and call her out. If so, she'd just go to the bathroom. But no use starting that number early in the party. She might need the escape later.

She filled the cup with vodka, drained it, and poured another half glass before replacing the flask and stepping back out. Another hefty splash of punch tinged the vodka pink enough to pass muster. She settled back on the sofa only after Grandmother Clarice was declared the winner of the diaper race.

"Who knew you still had that in you, Grandma!" Kayleigh said, her cheeks flushing red. "I know who to call in the dead of night!"

"Don't even try it!" Grandmother Clarice said.

Stella smiled at Clarice, Dane's stepmother. His real mom had died when he was twenty, but his dad had done right by the family by bringing on Clarice. Her feisty no-nonsense sensibility paired with to-the-bone compassion served them all well during those hard years with the infertility, and certainly the decade before, when all their troubles had surged with the miscarriage of baby Angelica.

Yep, she was a fine woman, and Stella was glad to have her around. Clarice glanced over at Stella, as if catching the direction of her thoughts, dropped her eyes to the drink, and winked.

Stella smiled at her. She'd been better than Stella's own mother, who'd spewed every trite expression ever taken down in Bartlett's little quote book. "It's God's will," was a favorite. So was "All good things come to those who wait."

Stella wanted to shove her basal thermometer up her mother's nose. They hadn't dropped ten grand per IVF round because she needed to cut back on her work, or stay home more, or just relax.

When Dane suggested they move to Texas to be near his family and put a little space between them and her mom, she'd agreed. Best decision they ever made. So much of their past had been tied up in Missouri, none of it good.

"Who's starving? I'm starving!" Kayleigh announced, bouncing back toward Stella. "I got to see if I can beat Aunt Stell's waistline before the baby comes!"

Stella crossed an arm over her stomach in the flowered tent-like dress and downed the rest of her drink. Good God, she loved that kid, but this was getting to be too much.

The women filed past the pink pastries. She'd skip the sweets in favor of liquor. She needed to get her buzz on to manage the ooohs and ahs of gift opening.

"So, Kayleigh," Clarice asked. "Did you ever decide on a name for the baby?"

Kayleigh swallowed a forkful of cake and said, "I think Paul and I finally agreed on one."

The murmuring in the room quieted down.

"Well, do tell us," Patty said, her frown deepening. She's irked, Stella thought. She wanted to be the first to know.

"Well," Kayleigh said, flushed with delight at the attention. "At first we thought something like Patricia, for mom," she gestured to her mother and smiled somewhat patronizingly. "Then we tried various combinations of Kayla and Kelly and Lee like mine." She glanced around the room, savoring the stillness, all eyes on her. "But we've decided on Angelica!"

Stella's stomach heaved, and she felt certain she'd throw up right there on the shabby-chic armrest. Her face burned, and what started as panic quickly sizzled into rage.

"How dare you!" She stood, sputtering, and her empty cup fell to the floor. "How could you do that?"

She looked around, but no one seemed to know what she was talking about.

"Oh do sit down, Stella. You're drinking again." Patty crossed her arms across her chest. "Don't wreck another family event."

Kayleigh's doe eyes filled with tears. "Aunt Stell, we worried you'd be mad. But we really loved the name. And it's not like you really got to use it."

Stella stumbled through the room, clutching her purse with one hand and the amethyst on her necklace in the other. Several of the women were mumbling to each other.

"What is she talking about?"

"What in the world?"

"It's the name."

"What's wrong with it?"

Grandmother Clarice stood, wavering over a cane. "Kayleigh meant no harm," she said. "We're dreadful sorry you're upset about it. Stella, we love you and recognize your distress. I think you naming your first lovely child when Kayleigh was small probably put some impression in her head and she just came to love the name without thinking about it."

Kayleigh bent over her belly, full on crying now.

Stella paused. "I trust your wisdom in this, Clarice," she said. "But that doesn't make it any easier, or any less wrong to me." She looked around the room, women all casting their eyes to the floor. "But none of you ever treated my babies like they were real or that I might consider myself a mother. And I done sat around and took it for ten years. But this here just beats all."

She opened the front door and stepped through.

The world spun in a whirl of blue sky and green grass. She couldn't drive. She knew this. She opened her car and sat, leaning her head on the steering wheel. Maybe she should call Dane to pick her up. She checked her watch. An hour until he got off shift. Damn.

Someone tapped on her window. She turned, bleary eyed, and peered out.

Grandmother Clarice. "Let me in, you twit!" she said, but her eyes were merry.

Stella couldn't roll down the window without putting the key in, so she opened the door.

"Scoot!"

Stella moved over on the broad front seat of her ancient Cadillac. The diminutive woman settled behind the wheel. "So this is what it feels like to drive a Caddy," she said. "Your father-in-law never gave me anything bigger than a Volkswagen." She held out her hands for the keys.

Stella raised her eyebrow. "I intended to sober up before the end of the party."

"I know. I've seen you do this a dozen times. Now give the keys to an old woman."

Stella passed her the metal ring. Clarice tossed her walking cane in the back and started the engine. "Nobody's going to say I'm too old!"

They rocketed across the street and Stella clutched the door, grabbing for the seatbelt. "I feel like a cheeseburger!" Clarice called over the roar of the radio. "They didn't have anything fit to eat at that lame party!"

"It was all pink!" Stella called back, finally snapping the belt into place and turning down the radio.

"Those girls get a theme and they run with it," Clarice said. "What is with all those worn out draperies?"

"Shabby chic." Stella stared out the window at the houses whizzing by. Clarice certainly knew how to punch the gas.

"Shabby crap. That son of mine sure did pick a doozy," she said. "Hopefully Kayleigh's not too late to save."

They rode on for a spell. Stella tried not to wince as Clarice slammed on the brakes for red lights and floored it on green. "Where we headed?" Stella asked.

"I already called that husband of yours."

"Oh?"

"He'll be out to meet us." Clarice glanced at Stella, then faced the road again. "You know, Kayleigh asked me if she should name the baby Angelica. She was pretty darn worried about it."

"Then why'd she do it?"

"She couldn't explain it. She just felt like it was special somehow, like the baby told her to call it that."

The light shone straight through the old woman's thinning hair and edged her in white. Stella could see every wrinkle, each smile line, deep creases thinning out until they disappeared into her pores. "I guess I'll have to live with it."

"That's what we do. For family anyway. Husbands we can do without. Totally ditchable if they're no good. But kids, aunts, nieces. They're keepers."

They pulled into the main parking lot of the refinery. Dane stood by the front entrance, leaning against a metal column.

"Isn't he the most beautiful thing?" Stella said. He walked toward them, a lanky off-centered stride, his black hair peppered with silver on his head and face.

"Yes, he is. I'm glad to call him a son of mine, even if I got him late. And I'm glad for you. You two would have made fine children." Clarice reached to clasp Stella's hand.

Dane dropped Clarice back off at the party, and they drove in silence. Stella stretched out on the flat broad seat, her head in his lap. He twirled her hair between his fingers.

"You gonna say what happened? Clarice just said she needed me."

"I'm sorry you had to take off."

"Larry went on shift early for me. He was already there."

Stella watched the minute tick by on the clock in the dash. Silly Caddy had an old-fashioned analog clock. It seemed out of place. She sighed. "Kayleigh is naming her baby Angelica."

"Whew."

"Yeah."

"Don't seem like too good an idea, naming your kid after a dead one."

"No, it doesn't."

"She sure about it?"

"Clarice said Kayleigh thought the baby was telling her to call it that."

"Good Lord."

Stella felt the muscle shift in his thigh as he pushed the accelerator. "It's been ten years since then. You think we're ever going to get over that?"

"Doesn't seem like it."

"Dane?"

"Yeah?"

"I want to go to the shop."

"What for?"

"I just need to."

He drifted across the lanes of the highway to exit early. The strip mall was deserted this early on a Sunday. Those that were open at all would do so at noon.

She opened the back door and headed straight for the cabinet where her children's bracelets lay. The worktables were strewn with amethyst and peridot in varying shapes. She'd packaged the first shipment on the big order but had many more pieces to make for the second.

She opened the little doors and slipped both bracelets on her wrist. They were tighter now, but still fit. Dane came up behind her, wrapping his arms around her waist. "What's up, Pell Mell Stell?"

"I don't know. I feel this unsettledness. This anxiety."

"The booze?"

"No." She pulled away and circled the tables, fingering random beads. "Maybe I'm worried I've crossed the line."

"What line?"

"With the babies. Maybe I shouldn't be exploiting them."

"How do you mean?"

Stella picked up two fists full of beads. "This! I started with each piece in memory of them. Every crystal was a moment of their lives, every finished piece a monument. I prayed over them, cried over them, set them aside with love and hope and some sort of belief that the women who bought them carried my babies around with them, that they had somehow got to meet other people, maybe even people they might have known if they had lived."

She sat on the work chair, letting the beads trickle wildly through her fingers, many rolling and dropping to the floor. "I would assess each person who bought something—maybe that would have been Angelica's kindergarten teacher, or this one was the lady who'd have cut her hair." She pushed beads into a pile.

"Now I'm doing it for money! Nothing but money! I've taken the very thing I once did out of love and turned it into profit! I've sold them out! I've sold their souls!"

She swept her arm along the table, knocking everything onto the floor. "Stella!"

"I'm awful! I used them! I used my babies!" She reached into the basket of finished pieces carefully packaged in plastic bags. "I can't believe it! I'm horrible! I'm awful! I didn't deserve them!" She tore at the bags, ripping them open and smashing the jewelry against the tables. Beads flew across the room, bits of silver and clasps disappearing into the dust in the corners.

Dane grabbed her arms and pressed them against her sides in a full body hug. "Stell! Stop! You didn't! It's not like that!"

"It is! It is! And now nobody cares enough about them any more to even leave their names alone!" She leaned over the table, forehead to the hard surface. Dane still held her, pulling her close to him.

"You loved them, Stell. You did. Nothing you do now can change that, and nobody can take that love away."

"Everybody else in that group is doing fine. They'll have their babies. They'll leave the group. And then it'll be new ones, and I'll patch them up and send them on, and they'll have their babies. I can't do it anymore. I don't want to. I have nothing. My babies are lost and gone and I can't even keep their memories pure."

She sobbed then, a rare thing, embarrassing and loud. He relaxed his grip and turned her to him, pressing her head into his chest. "It's okay, Stell. That group can go on without you if it needs to. And these bracelets are your love. This shop is your love. The babies gave you your start. And now maybe it's time to move on. Buy more colors. Be free of it."

Stella turned her head, looking across her shop. Every piece of jewelry was one of her babies, green and purple, August and February. She could not let that go. It was all she had.

5

ABANDONMENT

She was going to leave them. Maybe this would be the time to say it. It had certainly been that kind of day already.

Stella pushed the chairs together, like she had every two weeks for ten years. She'd never missed a meeting, she'd realized. In the early days, before she ran the group, she was still trying to get pregnant, and it was helpful to sit around the circle with other grieving women. Back then she still had hope in her heart that things would work out for her.

The money problem had finally gone away, well maybe, damn, had she really just wrecked a whole shipment? She moved the last chair into place and sat heavily upon it. No one had come early to help. In fact, everyone was late but her. Maybe this would be easy. The current crop of girls was doing pretty well. If they all moved on at the same time, she could close up without guilt. Just go down to the hospital and take all the fliers so they wouldn't pass any more out.

The heater kicked on, stirring the ceiling fans into a lazy circle and shifting the flames on the prayer candles that seemed eternally lit. Fire hazard, without a doubt. Stella moved her glasses to her nose and flipped through *River Waters of the Heart*. Oh hell, she was sick of that book. No use breaking it out anymore. She flung it under a side table.

What would she do next? The group didn't really take much of her time, but she could devote the two hours of each meeting to something new, something practical maybe. Like knitting. No, not that. Been there, failed that. Making pottery maybe. Add to her line at the shop. Or glass blowing, yes, that would be a good addition. Delicate ornaments and light catchers in green and violet.

The door shifted open and Melinda slipped inside. "I thought I was late!" she said, setting her purse on the floor and taking a seat.

"You are," Stella said. "I figured no one was coming."

Stella wished for the book back, something to do. The door swished open again and Dot and Janet came in.

"I hope this is the last cold front!" Janet said. "It's time for spring!"

"Says the spring bride," Stella said. "Happiness looks good on you."

And it did. Gone was the grim expression, the fear behind Janet's eyes. She had totally blossomed, as bright and shiny as the rock on her finger.

"That's some ring you got there," Dot said. "Probably worth more than my trailer."

Janet dropped her hand self-consciously.

She doesn't like money to show, Stella thought. Good breeding.

"No reading today?" Melinda asked.

Stella looked down at her empty lap. "No, no reading. Thought it was time for a change."

Melinda's gaze seemed to penetrate Stella's skull. She knew something was up. Hell, Stella never could hide anything. Might as well just say what she was thinking.

But the door opened again. Stella hoped it might be Tina, whom she still hadn't called, but a tiny woman flitted inside, as frightened and skittish as a sparrow.

Stella heaved herself to her feet. "Come on in, don't be shy."

The woman nodded and hurried to a chair. She could have practically sat on air, as wispy as she was. Not eighty pounds soaking wet, and the height of a child.

215

But when she turned to look at Stella, her eyes were so old, haunted and dark. She knew that look, knew it well from all the years of seeing newcomers arrive, with harrowing stories and disrupted lives.

"I'm Stella. I run this group. We're glad you found us."

The others murmured agreement. "What's your name?" Melinda asked.

"Camille." Her voice was like smoke, faint and wispy.

"Well, welcome, Camille," Stella said. "I guess we'll start with our introductions and updates." She didn't feel like going first. "Janet?"

Janet sat up in her chair, dressed more casually today in a corduroy trousers and a light blazer. "I am in recovery from a molar pregnancy. It's a precancerous condition where the baby doesn't grow, but instead trophoblastic cells. I won't be able to get pregnant again for at least a year."

"Oh my," Camille said. "I'm so sorry."

"It's okay," Janet said. "I'm fine." She turned to Dot.

"I'm Dot. My baby died a few months ago. Had a condition where he didn't have a brain. Had to go to an abortion clinic, sit amongst … sit amongst those people who didn't want their babies." She swallowed. "But life is good now. We'll have another, me and my new man."

Melinda waited to see if Dot was finished, then said, "I'm Melinda. I'm a lawyer."

She would say that first. Stella smiled to herself. The girl had made progress. They all had. As Melinda talked about the hallucinations and the baby she'd felt crazy going after, Stella remembered all the women who'd been through the doors. There had been some doozies. Some of them had flat-out lied, looking for attention. Stella knew enough about pregnancy to spot them, but she never let on in front of others. If they got too clingy or weird, she'd take them aside privately, reminding them that you can't see the baby's gender at ten weeks, or that you don't get pregnancy symptoms starting with the day you have unprotected sex.

One of the early fliers she'd made used the terms missed abortion and spontaneous abortion, as those were the medical ways of saying miscarriage. Some woman had gotten her panties in a wad, thinking the group was for people getting elective abortions and stormed in with her posse of pro-lifers, waving signs with fetus pictures. It took a good half hour to get it all straightened out.

Highs and lows. Melinda had stopped speaking. Camille sucked in a big breath. "I'm going to have to lie to my husband," she said.

Stella sat forward. "What about, child?"

"Birth control. He says we can't have any more children, and he didn't want this one. I think that's why it died. It knew it wasn't wanted."

Stella got this all the time. "Now, babies come along whether they are wanted or not. All these good ladies here desperately wanted their children and they died anyway."

Camille slapped her hand across her mouth. "I didn't mean it that way! Oh no, oh no! I ruin everything." She hopped up as if she'd run out, but Dot reached out an arm to stop her.

"Slow down, now," Dot said. "We don't judge anybody for anything here. You can talk all you want."

Camille sat back down. Stella admired Dot's presence. Just two meetings ago she wouldn't have looked out beyond her curtain of hair. "Thank you, Dot," she said. "You're all right, Camille. Just tell us what's going on."

"I can't go on unless I have another baby. I just can't."

Stella remembered Tina saying this too. She wished the girl was here. "What does your husband say, exactly?"

"That we can't afford the ones we got." Camille looked around. "We have three, and I love them. But I can't just stop now. I had this baby, and now there's this hole." She pushed her hand against her chest. "I can't live with this hole. So I poked one in my diaphragm."

Stella stifled her smile. That was one tactic that never worked. Taking sugar pills instead of your Ortho-Novums, now that'd do it. One former member had microwaved the condoms. "I understand how you're feeling. It's a hard thing to live with. You think he'll change his mind just because you trick him? Doesn't seem like the best plan, if he doesn't want a child."

"I don't care. He can't do anything once it's happened."

The heater clicked off, bathing the chapel in silence. Stella had run out of things to say.

"I think," Melinda said, "that maybe the problem isn't the baby, but the marriage."

Camille's hands fluttered to her neck. "Oh no! It can't be."

"I'm not saying you should do anything drastic," Melinda said. "But you probably need to work this difference out first before you can bring in another baby."

"I can't wait any longer! I'm already thirty-six!"

"You're a young pup yet," Dot said. "I don't think anybody here's much younger."

"I'm thirty-six as well," Melinda said. "And I don't have any children."

"I'm thirty-eight," Janet said. "I have to wait another year to try, with no guarantees."

"You are all plenty young," Stella said. "Why, even at forty-four, I might give it one more go if it weren't impossible for me."

"You never had any children?" Camille's voice was like a shriek caught in the wind.

"I did not." She wasn't up for going into this, not now. "But tell us about your three."

Camille smiled a sad smile. "Roosevelt is six, Eleanor is four, and little Teddy is two."

Stella pressed her lips together. "That sounds lovely."

"But I have to figure out what to do! I need a Franklin D!"

A kook. Another kook. Normally she wouldn't be so judgmental, but she felt done, so done. She couldn't stop herself. "It could be a girl."

"No, it won't be."

"Okay then." Stella sat up. "Let's get some updates. Janet, plans for your big day?"

"We're heading out as soon as school lets out," Janet said. "A destination wedding."

"Sounds lovely," Stella said. "Melinda, how goes court?"

"I'm doing backend work, mainly," she said. "Not up for litigation." She blushed, and Stella wondered if she was already pregnant again. Some women had all the easy eggs. "But Dot's case is going nicely." She smiled and reached out to squeeze Dot's arm.

"And I'll be getting hitched again soon after," Dot said. "Sounds like a lot of wedding bells will be a-ringin'."

"Weddings and babies," Stella said. "They go well together."

"Where's the teenager been?" asked Dot. "She doing all right?"

"I'm going to call her right after this," Stella said. "Check on her."

Camille sat rigidly in her chair. "I guess I'm the only one being told to stop having babies," she said.

"It happens from time to time," Stella said. "We've all got hard roads. Different roads, but all hard."

"No use trying to outdo each other," Dot said. "What's easy for one might break somebody else."

"I hear that," Stella said. She remembered the fire, the night sky, and letting Angelica go. How many people could do that? But of course, Melinda had thrown her baby in the trash. And Dot had walked in to a clinic, knowing she'd walk out without the baby.

Too many stories for anyone to bear.

After the meeting, Melinda hung around, waiting for her. "Can I interest you in coffee?" she asked.

Stella pushed the last chair back into its row. "That'd be all right."

They walked out together. "It's already warming up. I can feel the humidity," Stella said. "I'll be sweating by May."

"That's just a week away," Melinda said.

"You got a place in mind?" Stella asked.

"Starbucks is only a few blocks off."

Stella turned to lock the door to the chapel. "Works for me."

They ordered their lattes, and Stella idly sipped hers, wondering what Melinda wanted from her. "So what's on your mind, Ms. Attorney-at-Law?"

Melinda smiled. "Dot's case is going well. We'll get her extricated from that horrid husband and not let him take anything."

"Did he have money stashed?"

"Bound to. We're still looking, but Dot doesn't care. She just wants out."

"He going to fight over the kids?"

"Doesn't seem like it. Thankfully."

Stella settled back against the chair and leaned her head on the wall. "Yeah. She's not the first woman to get knocked up by a lover rather than a husband. Brings up all sorts of ill feelings when the baby dies. Sin. Punishment. Wrath of God is often involved. They'll do most anything as penance. I'm glad she's not staying with him out of misdirected guilt."

"So do you keep in touch with all these women you meet? It seems like most of us are pretty transitory."

"Yeah, the majority head out after three or four meetings. They get pregnant again, mostly, or tire of grieving and just move on. Often their partners aren't supportive of their sadness playing out too long. They guilt them into acting like they're better."

Melinda fell silent, staring out at the parking lot.

So she'd been mistreated too. Maybe that's what the meeting was about.

Stella tapped on the table. "So tell me about it."

Melinda pushed down on the plastic lid of her cup. "I don't know how to do it, how to be brave enough to get pregnant again."

"You started trying yet?"

"We have."

"Things going okay with the husband since you started working?"

"Oh, yes. I mean, as well as can be with Jake. He's not the patient sort." She swirled the cup in a lazy circle, then recognized the nervous habit and abruptly stopped. "A big-shot lawyer with the lack of compassion to show for it."

"Are you like him, as a lawyer, that is?"

She laughed nervously. "Not at his level. Not as a woman anyway. It's hard to move up. But I do okay."

"But he made you quit before. Will he again?"

"It's different this time. I have an easy job. No long hours like before."

"Is he gone a lot?"

"He has a lot of late nights, especially during litigation." Melinda set her cup down. "But I came here, actually, to talk about you."

Stella sat back in her chair. "Really?"

"You seem a little upset."

"There's good days and bad days." She wouldn't concede much more.

But Melinda seemed to sense this and switched tactics. "So, you do jewelry?"

Stella narrowed her eyes at the abrupt change of topic, but allowed it. "Yep, I've had my own shop for about five years now. Once we stopped dropping all our money into the infertility pit, I managed to open a little store front."

"You like it?"

Stella hesitated. She could still see the beads all over the floor. She hadn't opened today and wouldn't be able to open on time tomorrow. And the order, the big one. She'd destroyed all the merchandise.

"Stella?"

"It's good. It's fine."

"Spill."

"Nothing to spill."

Melinda leaned forward. "Who do you talk to about everything you deal with by running this group?"

"I have the greatest husband there ever was."

"That's good." Melinda tapped the side of cup. "But something happened today. You were not the same at all. If I didn't know better, I'd think you were ready to give up the group."

Stella kept her eyes on the table. Had she been obvious? Or was Melinda just that good? Maybe she could confess only part of it, to get her off her back. The best lie was a half-truth. "My niece is naming her baby what I chose for our first."

"Good Lord." Melinda exhaled in a long slow rush. "What made her think that was a good idea?"

Melinda's indignation helped. It seemed at the party everyone thought she was overreacting. She'd felt she'd underreacted, based on how strongly she felt like torching the place. "I don't know. Some say because I used the name when she was small. She claims her baby is asking to be called Angelica."

"Now that's a bit creepy."

"I agree. Like her kid has my kid's soul or something."

"You going to stand for it?"

"I don't see what I can do about it."

"You can insist. Make a scene. Taint the name for her."

For a high-society gal, she sure did act like a normal person. She must not have come from money. Stella instantly liked her better. "I already made a bit of a scene. Walked out of her party. Doesn't seem to matter that much. It's all bad blood."

"True." Melinda picked up the cup and swirled it again, caught herself, then shrugged and kept going. "Is your husband supportive? Was it your family or his?"

"His. And yes, he's amazing."

"What was his take on the baby shower?"

"He was angry too. He just didn't expect the aftermath."

"What happened?!"

Stella pressed her thumb against the plastic indentions in the top of her coffee cup. "I went a little loco, that's all. Smashed up some of my inventory. Felt like I was exploiting the kids." There, she'd said it.

"How on earth is your jewelry doing that?" Melinda leaned forward, her hands clutching the edge of the table.

"I just use amethyst and peridot in the designs, see. Their birthstones. It started out as an homage, but now it seems too ... commercial."

"Oh, Stella. Are you going to be able to fix it all? Do you plan to?"

"I still have a few weeks to get a big order in. But it's a lot of work, and my heart's not in it."

They sat there a while, not talking, people passing their table with fresh drinks, the smell of wet dirt from their shoes mingling with the roasted aroma of hot coffee.

"Are you going to quit the group?" Melinda asked.

"I don't know."

"But isn't it hard? All these stories?"

"Yes. And no. I always figured the time I spend with you all is like time with my kids. It's the only way they get to reach out and affect others."

Melinda smacked the table. "That's right. That's perfect. I don't know why I didn't think of that before."

"What?"

"That we can live out our children's lives in a way—do things on behalf of them. It gives them a chance to have an impact."

Melinda seemed all flushed suddenly. Stella liked it when that happened, when she could say something that gave the women their mojo back. Too bad nobody could help her find hers.

6

PILGRIMAGE

Stella pushed on the front door and it cracked open with a loud pop. Dane looked up from the sofa, where he sat watching television and drinking a beer.

"Hey, baby. How was the meeting? I've been worried about you."

"I figured." Stella dropped her bag and keys by the door and flopped beside him. "Swig?"

He passed her the bottle. "Must have been a rough one. You never ask for a drink."

"Outside of baby showers," she corrected. "Ugh. Piss water. I never want to drink this because it's piss water."

Dane laughed. "Beer snob."

"Alcoholic."

He pulled her head to his cheek, and they rocked together lightly. "Did you tell everyone what happened?"

"Not at the meeting. Didn't seem right."

"But what about you, baby? How many years you going to support other people before they help you?"

"I get my help by helping them. Besides," she punched him in the chest. "I got you."

"You do have that." He set the bottle on a side table. "Let me hang on to you a minute."

Stella felt her false brightness fall away as soon as he wrapped his arms around her. The sobs came again—damn—second time that day.

"Ah, Stell. Is it the jewelry still?"

"The babies seem so very far away."

"I think we need to make a pilgrimage."

Stella relaxed against him, the warmth of his skin seeping through the flannel shirt to her cheek. "Really? We haven't in a while."

"Yeah. Let's go."

They stood and held hands, heading to the back bedroom of the house, which they kept for storage. Dane flipped on the light, and they looked over the stacks of boxes.

"Geez, where is it?" he asked.

"It's in here somewhere." Stella waded through stacks of magazines and lifted a blanket. "Yeah, here it is."

"You got them both?"

Stella lifted a pink fabric-covered box. "Yes. The other is below it."

"Hand them over."

She passed the pink box, then a blue one over to his outstretched arms.

"Back in the living room?" he asked.

She nodded, already feeling the downward tug of emotion.

They walked through the hall. "Music too?" he asked.

She still could only nod.

He set the boxes on the coffee table and searched a moment through a case of CDs. Even though she sat on the sofa, out of view, she knew the one he was taking out. Country stuff. Reserved for this. Normally she couldn't stomach the sap.

The first notes came out the speaker, and she shifted down again. But the pilgrimage was purifying, reset them in a way.

"You ready, Pell?" Dane sat beside her, knees wide, hands clasped together.

"Yeah."

"How far back you want to go?"

"Just to Angelica."

"Okay." He slid the pink box nearer and lifted the lid.

The pregnancy stick lay on top. Stella reached for it and lifted it out.

She remembered ripping the protective plastic off and making Dane hold it between her legs as she peed.

"This is kind of kinky," he said, looking up at her with his crinkling eyes. He hadn't had a beard then, smooth faced, young, although hard then, already, with all he'd been through the last decade.

But they were together again and got married in a flash despite her family's uproar. Stella was 33, and they wanted to get on top of the baby plan after such a long wait, so she never even bothered with the Pill.

"This is it!" she said. "Pee a-comin'!"

The stream fell cleanly and hit the water. "I'm missing it!" he said, laughing. "How do you aim this thing!"

Her laughter made her pee jiggle, she could hear it splashing. "Keep trying or you'll have to fork over another ten bucks for a new one!"

"Ack! We're too poor for that!" He shifted his hand between her legs. "Got it!"

Her thighs had been so thin then, small and perfect even splayed out on the seat. She touched them self-consciously now, broad beneath her flowered dress, and passed the stick to Dane, who leaned against her on the sofa. "You peed on me!" he said.

"You loved it."

He kissed her forehead. "I did."

"God we were so happy when that line showed up."

"Look, it's still there." She tapped on the test stick.

"Yep. Some things are permanent."

Dane reached into the box. "Ah, your attempt at booties." He pulled out a tangle of pink yarn.

"Now now. I tried!" Stella examined the bungled knitting. She'd started the booties the same day, sitting with a how-to book and beginner needles.

Seven glorious weeks passed between when she took the home test and when they went to the doctor for her first checkup. Dane made enough money at the refinery to get by, and they had good insurance. She didn't mind her job as a clerk at a department store. They weren't rich or anything, but it would be okay. She was just glad he had a job, something the state had arranged.

The doctor didn't do a sonogram back then at the first visit, but he felt her belly, checked her urine, and said everything looked fine. They drew some blood to check her pregnancy hormone levels.

Two days later the bad part began.

"Your hCG level is a bit low," the nurse said on the phone. "It's not anything to worry about, as you may have just gotten your dates wrong. We'd like to check you again, today if possible."

She'd gone in and given more blood. She had no idea what they meant about her dates. Two days later, another phone call. They sent her to a radiologist for a sonogram.

Dane took off to go with her and held her hand as they watched the screen. No heartbeat. Baby measuring at six weeks instead of nine.

They had walked out in a daze. The world whizzed by in a blur of color and sound, but the two of them moved in slow motion.

"I don't want to go to work tomorrow," Dane said.

"I don't want to go home," she said. "All the things we've already done." She thought of the booties, the blanket, some stuffed animals they had already bought. Dane had come home every few days with something new.

"Let's just drive," she said. "See where we end up."

"You okay with that? Don't we need to see the doctor again?" He unlocked the car, but they stood outside it still.

"There will be time for doctors. Let's just take a trip together. You, me, and the baby. Before she's gone."

"She?"

"Yeah. She's a girl. I know this somehow."

They took off for the Ozarks near Eureka Springs, Arkansas, driving for hours, silently, before turning into Lake Leatherwood Park near dusk. The bumpy road jolted them as they peered out the dusty windows into the lines of trees. Only a swath of sky was visible above. Eventually they came to a clearing where empty RV hookups led to a circle drive, an office, and a dock with rental boats.

"We can just sleep in the car," Dane said.

"That's fine."

They paid $12 for a spot near the shore meant for tents. Stella felt the first cramps near dark.

"You okay, baby?" Dane came up behind her as she bent over. She felt like something was compressing her insides.

"No. I think something's happening. Maybe the baby is coming."

"Should we go to the hospital?"

"I don't want to. I don't want some strangers around me. I like it here. The sky. The lake. Trees."

"Well, here, sit on my shirt." Dane took off his flannel and spread it on the ground. Stella curled up on her side.

"Are you in pain, my poor Stell?"

"Not exactly." The cramps came in waves, but none of them were unmanageable. "I will bleed, though, I can feel it coming."

"You got anything?"

"No. I didn't think it would happen so quick."

"Maybe knowing about it somehow makes it happen. Like your brain admitting it to the body."

She began to cry then, tears spilling over her wrists. "I admit nothing."

Dane rummaged through the trunk and found a picnic blanket and a roll of shop towels.

"This might help." He knelt beside her and set the roll within easy reach. Night was rapidly falling. "I'm going to scavenge for firewood before it's too dark to see."

Stella was afraid to move. Each shift of her body brought her closer to some end. Dane returned with an armload of kindling, then crumpled some junk mail from the back seat to light.

He spread the blanket, and she crawled over to it. They lay together, her back curled into his chest. She felt safe then and fell asleep.

The crunch of logs dropping on the fire woke her. Dane had moved away from her to put more wood on.

"Sorry, Stell. I tried to be quiet."

She felt sore and stiff from sleeping on the hard ground. She moved to a sitting position. Immediately she felt a thickness pushing out.

"Oh God!" She stood and held her hand between her legs.

"What, baby!" Dane leapt over the fire to get to her.

She unfastened her jeans and yanked them down. "It's coming!"

He knelt before her as she pulled down her panties. "Is it there?" she asked.

"I think so." He helped her out of the clothes, carefully cradling the panties as she stepped out.

They held the underwear close to the fire, Dane's face tight and full of fear in the orange-red glow.

She reached behind her for the roll of shop towels and tore off a square. "Here, wrap her in this."

They separated the small ball from the underwear. "I can't make anything out," he said. "I don't know what I'm looking at."

"I don't know either."

Hysteria rose in her. Crickets chirped. The fire snapped and crackled. Everything was disjointed, a shattered puzzle. Blood flowed out of her and she just let it drop into the dirt as she squatted by Dane, who peered at the black mass in the blue towel.

He sobbed, a hard sound in the night. "What do I do with her? What is right to do?"

"Cover her," Stella said. "Wrap her up tight." Together they folded the corners of the square over baby.

"Should we bury her?"

"No! What if some animal digs her up?"

"Take her to the hospital? Shouldn't we go now?"

Stella let go of the bundle, and Dane pulled it to his chest. She tore off a section of the shop towels and stuffed them into the crotch of her jeans, then pulled them on.

"No. I don't want the hospital either." She sat on the blanket without fastening her pants. "Here, give her to me."

Dane moved close to her, resting against her side and shoulder. He passed her the bundle. She pressed it against her cheek. The towel was both soft and abrasive. It smelled of car oil and exhaust.

The weight of it comforted her. The baby had heft, thickness, and fit into her hand. "Ashes to ashes, dust to dust," she said. "I think we should send her into the sky."

Dane rested his head against her cheek. "Okay."

"Is the fire hot enough?"

"I think so. I got some pretty big logs."

"Let's just sit here a minute."

And they paused, holding the bundle, the firelight washing them orange. They heard the distant sound of geese and the occasional snap of some small animal scampering through the trees beyond the clearing.

A while later, when they felt ready, they crept over to the fire and set their baby in it. The sparks burst into heat, red and orange and white and bits of blue. The shop towel curled up and charred and dropped away. For a moment they heard a sizzle, then the flames calmed, settled back into the wood, and the night fell quiet and still.

Dane shifted on the sofa and took Stella's hand. "You still doing okay, Pell Mell Stell?"

She turned to him, holding a folded square of blue shop towel, another one from that same roll, and nodded. She couldn't talk just yet, not at this point of the pilgrimage.

"You sure you're up for both tonight?" He gathered her closer to him, and she leaned into his flannel, the smell of steel and dust on him still from the factory.

"I lost our babies for us," she croaked. "My body wouldn't hold them."

"Stell."

"It's true. And then they wouldn't come at all. After Buddy, they just didn't come at all. I was broken."

When Buddy failed to grow beyond six weeks, just died right there in her womb, the doctor had insisted on a D&C so they could test him. Turned out he was just fine, but her womb wasn't. They threw out terms like antiphospholipid antibodies and fetal blockers. They'd shipped blood to some special clinic. She'd had daily shots in her rear, and Dane had put more sperm in bottles than in her for a while.

But the in vitros didn't take, not even with three embryos inserted at a time. When no one could be sure if any of their solutions would do any good on another round, they opted to stop. They were broke.

"But Stella, if it weren't for me, we could have adopted." Dane squeezed her shoulder, his eyes hard and glittering. "You still could. If you'd just ditch me for some other man, some man without a history—"

"Stop it. Please. You're the only thing that's gotten me through this sorry life."

"If I could change things—"

"I know. Of course you would. I know."

"We could have started a family earlier, even, when you were younger, and maybe it would have been fine then. Maybe something out there's against us."

"I was happy to wait for you, Dane. You know that."

"I can't believe you waited all those years. I remember sitting there, alone in the cell, and wonder how I ever deserved you."

"We deserved each other."

They sat silently on the sofa for a moment, the soft flow of country music wrapping them in nostalgia.

"I remember the day I first saw you Stella. You were twenty-two with hair like an angel."

"A bleach job."

"Don't interrupt. And a body like a goddess."

"Now it's more like a Minotaur."

"Would you let a man tell a story about his love?" Dane tweaked her nose.

Stella sighed a big fake exhale, but she smiled. How she adored this man. "All right. Go on."

"And I was just working at a podunk Missouri filling station as a glorified gas pumper—"

"You were a mechanic."

"And your beat up little white Mustang was two quarts low."

"I think you drained it secretly."

"I would have if I thought of it."

"I never checked the dipstick."

"Ahh, dipping the stick."

"Yeah, we got around to that pretty fast!"

"And your mama was fit to be tied!"

"Ah, she just worried about me."

"I had a no-good reputation."

"You were sort of known around town as a bad boy."

"Stella, I should have been more grown. I should have held my temper."

They fell silent. Few nights change your life like that one had. She and Dane had gone to one of the two bars in town. She was barely legal but put on the booze when Dane was there to take care of her.

He'd probably gone over the top when he set her on the bar to dance, but she liked showing off for him. Someone had loaded up Eddie Rabbitt's "The Best Year of My Life" on the jukebox. Summer dictated a short white skirt and strappy sandals. She wore a pink halter that fell off one shoulder like in *Flashdance*.

But when the song ended and she reached for Dane to pull her down, Bobby Ray Wolf shoved him aside and grasped her hands, laughing.

Dane didn't hold to no antics and laid a meaty punch to Bobby Ray's gut and swung an uppercut into his jaw.

The brawl went on with the usual punches and smacking until Bobby Ray turned and grabbed a bar stool. Dane would have none of that and snatched it and cracked the wood seat up against the other man's face.

Bobby Ray stumbled, dazed, blood pouring out his nose, then his ears, and fell to the ground. He died two days later at County General and Dane, who hadn't even been talked to by the police up until then, was arrested.

They'd hoped for a light sentence, given the circumstances, but he'd been found guilty of voluntary manslaughter, a Class B Felony in Missouri, and had to complete 85 percent of his fifteen-year sentence.

Stella made the decision to wait for him although her Mama threw her out of the house. She was plenty grown and made her way by waitressing near the state penitentiary where Dane served his time. She saw him every Sunday for 149 weeks. The first one had been the worst.

Stella had arrived late, dashing in from her job, still wearing the little white apron splattered with grease.

The guard leered at her. Dane got angry right off, already frustrated and afraid she wouldn't show. He stood up suddenly, too menacing. The guard sounded the alarm and three men had hauled him off. She'd only been able to catch a glimpse of him.

After that he'd stayed calm, always calm. They slowly graduated from meetings with phones and tempered glass to sitting across a table where they could at least hold hands.

"My temper almost cost us everything," he said.

"Shhh." Stella stroked his wild hair. "You figured it out."

"There wasn't an adoption agency anywhere that would take us," he whispered. "No private families either. Maybe if I'd been a rich man, we could have bought somebody off. I don't know. Stell. I'm so sorry."

She ran her fingers through the soft bristles of his black beard, already shot through with hints of gray. No man she ever met was any better.

"It's all right, Dane. This is what life dealt us. All I can ever say when we talk about this is how much I love you, and I wouldn't change the part where I picked you."

7

YOUTH

Stella swept the last of the errant beads into the dust pan. She'd have to separate the gems from the dirt. Ugly work.

The shattered bracelets were beyond repair, the fine wire bent and twisted. She could salvage the clasps, but would need to restring it all. At least a month's worth of work was lost, and the order was due in a few days. She'd never sold to this company before. No telling how tolerant they might be.

She dumped the whole mess into a colander. Hopefully shaking the dirt out the bottom would make the job less hideous. The cat hair would be another matter. Spermatozoa threaded through her legs as if in apology.

"It's all right, cat. I should have kept it cleaner in here before going on a smash spree."

The door jingled in the main part of the shop, so Stella set the work aside and headed back to the front. Maybe she should close up for a few days until she got on top of this order.

Tina stood by the door, still wearing cutoffs and rainbow stockings, her hair sprigged out in ponytails shot through with streaks of pink.

Stella hurried toward her for an enveloping hug. "Look what the cat dragged in." She pulled away, the motherly rush thrumming through her. She'd never been so attached to a member of the group. "You got my call?"

"Thought I'd check out the shop."

"Aren't you supposed to be in school?"

Tina leaned against a counter. "Got accepted to the magnet."

"What? Really?"

"Yeah. A boy I know, Simon, he got in. Told me they were a little thin on photographers. Hooked me up with the counselor."

"But your record must have been shot."

"I only sent them the grades from the pregnant school. Perfect attendance and all A's and B's. They'll get the other stuff eventually, but by then I'll be in."

"I'm sure they'll see that if you can do good in one place, you'll do good in the other."

The girl wouldn't meet her eyes, watching the cat slink across the floor. Something was up.

"So. About the other day. When you called." Stella wasn't going to let it go. "Is it better now?"

"Oh yeah. It's all good. No more freak-outs."

"You sure?"

Tina met her eyes, briefly. "Yeah. Me and Simon, we'll probably hook up."

"But baby plans?"

"Nah. Simon wouldn't make a good dad. Not till he's thirty, at least. Besides, he's paranoid as all get-out. His mom threatened to cut off his nutsack if he knocked somebody up."

"His what?"

"His words, not his mom's."

The door jingled again. Stella's body tensed before her brain totally registered who it was. Kayleigh.

Tina turned, whistling lightly at the size of the other girl's belly. "Now that's a baby and a half in there. You got twins?"

Kayleigh frowned. "No."

Tina stared between them. She was curious, Stella could see, but held her tongue. "Did you want something from me?" Stella asked

Kayleigh, working hard to make it sound like a regular question, and not anything angry.

"I'm not going to name the baby Angelica." Fat tears were falling down her cheeks now. Such an emotional time, pregnancy. Hard to keep anything in check. Stella knew this.

"What made you change your mind?"

"How upset you were."

Stella exhaled in a gush. "Well, yes, I took it pretty hard."

"Mama said you were just drunk and all, but I knew."

Tina raised her eyebrows at that.

"I always drink at baby showers," Stella said.

"With cause," Tina said. "I mean, I would. If I were you. And legal."

Kayleigh turned to Tina. "Who are you anyway?"

Tina cocked her head. "A friend of Stella's. I used to be pregnant."

Kayleigh's face paled. "What happened?"

"He died."

"I'm sorry." More tears. Her little face was bright as a radish.

"Yeah, it sucked. When are you due?"

"About a month."

"I was due in May."

"So you're in Aunt Stella's group?"

"I was."

"Is," Stella said. "We're not letting you go that easy."

Tina shrugged. "I'm doing all right."

Stella watched the two of them, such young pups, talking like grown women. She'd spent those years kickin' it up, making trouble. Babies were the furthest thing from her mind. She'd taken real care about that. Maybe if she'd gotten lucky early on, let some boy plant a seed in her, she could have avoided everything that followed. Jealous Dane, knocking Bobby Ray upside the head with a stool. Those long, lonely years of waiting, working hard hours. And now this life, the one without kids of her own.

"You have a new name?" Stella asked.

Kayleigh shook her head. "Mama says it will just come to me, when I see her. I believe it."

"Peanut looked like a Peanut to me," Tina said.

"You're really lucky," Kayleigh said. "To have Aunt Stella take care of you when things go bad. I know she'd have been the first one I would have called."

"Is that so?" Stella's chest warmed a little. She'd always loved little Kayleigh. That's why the betrayal had shook her so hard.

"There ain't nobody that knows how to fix a broken heart like you, Aunt Stella. Everybody knows it. The way you stayed true to Uncle Dane. No telling what sort of hell his life would have been without you."

"She does got it going on," Tina said. "Bailed me out of a thing or two. With no preaching."

"Exactly," Kayleigh said.

Stella clamped her jaw to keep from getting all emotional. No time for having a meltdown. But these girls were the next round of women to try and start their families. Seemed like each generation got busier and busier, texting and cell phoning and searching on the Internet. Probably weren't used to someone with old-fashioned listening skills.

"I gotta go grab lunch," Tina said. "Then stopping by the new school for my books."

"I'm starving," Kayleigh said. "Can I come along?"

"Sure," Tina said. "Give me some good dirt on Aunt Stell. That might come in handy."

"You children get on out of here," Stella said, shooing them with her hands. "We old women have work to do."

The girls waved goodbye and headed out, Kayleigh with her third trimester waddle and Tina in a technicolor bounce. Spermatozoa hopped up onto the counter, spying the flash of light as the sun reflected from the glass door through the crystal beads in the display. He reached out his paw.

"Don't even think about it, you scar-faced cat-mongrel." Stella set him back on the floor. "You just don't learn. You and I just don't want to learn."

8

MAY DAY

"This was a good idea," Stella said, unpacking her cooler alongside Melinda in a neighborhood park not too far from the church where the women met. "The weather's finally turned fine." She glanced over at Dane, who was pounding a pole for horseshoes into the ground. Jake paced off the distance to set up the throw line. Melinda's stepkids had already dashed across the field to the playscape.

A huge gray van pulled up, sputtering and wheezing into the parking lot. Dot and her brood piled out like clowns in a miniature car.

"That's a lot of kids," Melinda said. "Somehow, when she said five, I just didn't visualize it."

Stella shielded her eyes from the sun. "Don't you got the sense God gave the man who invented birth control?" she called.

Dot smiled and passed a blond-headed girl to a husky man with merry blue eyes. "Nope. And probably ain't gonna stop here neither," she said.

"There'll be more if I have anything to say about it. Maybe not five more, but more." The man strode up to Stella with the toddler on his shoulders and held out his hand. "You must be Stella. I'm Gary."

"I am so very glad to meet you." Stella looked past Gary to Dot, who was pushing two tussling boys forward with a hand to each neck. "Dot, you were right. Greek God material all the way."

"Hey!" Dane said, coming up behind her and wrapping his arms around her waist. "I thought I was your young buck!"

"You're old news," Stella said. "I'm suddenly into wife swapping."

Dane turned her around and kissed her soundly. She could hear Gary's deep-throated laugh and the sounds of kids shouting.

"Jake!" Melinda called. "Bring those kids over! They can play with Dot's!"

Stella pulled away from Dane and clasped his jaw. "I love you, you know," she said.

He patted her rump. "I do know it."

Melinda touched her arm. "Is that Tina over there?" They peered across the park at a pack of approaching teenagers.

"Could be. She said she might stop by. With her posse, or something like that." Stella looked over the food Dot had brought over. Surely they had to start eating soon.

"Is Janet coming?" Dot asked. "I wanted to ask her about that gifted stuff. Sunny's been getting into all sorts of trouble at school, and her teacher says she's bored."

Stella slid onto the bench. "No, she ran off with that boyfriend of hers to get married. They should be back in a few weeks. Honeymoon in south of France or some such rich people's place. You'd have to ask Melinda about that. I've never been beyond the Bible belt."

"Good for Janet!" Melinda said. "Is she feeling better?"

"The D&C has worked so far, so she said." Stella popped open a bag of chips. "She has to be tested every few weeks."

"Hey." Tina stood, arms crossed, at the front of a mob of teenagers.

"That's quite a crew you've got there," Stella said. She twisted around painfully on the bench. Okay, no chips. She had to get this waistline under control. And thighs.

"This is Stella," Tina said to her friends, who stood awkwardly, toeing the dirt or glancing off into the sky. "And Melinda and Dot."

She pulled one of the boys to the front. He pushed up his black glasses with a finger to the bridge of his nose and nodded at them.

"And this is Simon. He's sort of my new boyfriend."

"Sort of?" Stella asked.

"Yeah. You'll know when he becomes full-fledged."

The boy's cheeks burst crimson. "Nice to meet you all," he said and backed into the rest of the group.

"We're just stopping by," Tina said, peering over the food. "We'll be around though."

"Well, here, at least take some drinks with you," Melinda said. "We got plenty."

The kids raided the ice chest and ambled off.

"I'm glad she's in with a crowd her age," Melinda said.

"Me too." Stella grabbed a handful of chips. Just one handful. To be social.

Dot scooted into the bench next to them. "Got the kids settled on the playscape. I should have five minutes before somebody hurts somebody else."

"Gary seems to have them well in hand," Melinda said. "Quite a looker, he is."

Dot smoothed her hair, tucking a stray wisp behind her ear. "Yeah, he is."

"How is that divorce coming?" Stella asked.

"Oh, well, Melinda here's helping me get it final."

"You're kinda busy for a gal who's a part-timer," Stella said.

Melinda smiled, "Well, when you meet women who are nothing but trouble, you stay busy."

"That's right, I like being trouble," Stella said.

The shouts of the children interrupted them. All of them had kids other than her, Stella realized, one way or another. Her chest tightened, and she reached for another handful of chips.

"We have surprises, ladies!" Dane and Jake came up from behind. Dane set a basket on the table. "Clear some space!"

They moved aside the chips and bowls and plates.

"First," Jake said. "We'll look at this." He spread a large rolled printout on the table.

"What is it?" Melinda asked.

"Stella's Courtyard," Dot read across the top.

"It's a memorial garden," Jake said. "I've already gotten the architect to draw up the plans."

"You're naming it for me?" She could scarcely get the words out.

"Of course!" Jake said. "Anybody who puts up with all these women deserves something named after her!"

"You deserve it, Pell-Mell," Dane said. "All those years of leading the group."

"Here's a small pond with a walkway that will be lined with stones. You can have the round stones alongside the pavement engraved with your baby's name."

"Is it only for miscarried babies?"

"We won't restrict it, I don't think," Jake said. "But the intent is that it is for babies who can't get buried or cremated traditionally, as the pregnancy wasn't far enough along to be legally recognized."

Dane opened the basket and set out four stones. "We've already done the first few."

Dot read them. "Angelica. Buddy. Peanut. Kelsey. That's mighty fine."

"Just tell us yours, and we'll get them done too."

"Bubba," Dot said. Jake jotted it down.

"When will it be built?" Melinda asked.

"We're still waiting on permits and approval by the city council," Jake said. "But we're making sure it passes."

"I don't even want to know how you're doing that!" Stella said. "Or maybe I do!"

Jake flashed a half smile that would melt sand into glass. "You know how it is—buy, beg, or bribe. It'll get done. Probably some time next year."

"Did you bring the other items?" Melinda asked Dane.

Stella eyed her husband. "You two in cahoots?"

"We are, and I did," he said. He reached beneath the bench and lifted one of Stella's work chests onto the table.

Jake rolled up the plans and stepped back.

What were they up to? "What's this?" Stella asked.

"Your broken bracelets," Dane said quietly. "Melinda asked if she and the others could help you fix them so you wouldn't lose your big sale."

"You think we all came just to sit in the sun and gab?" Dot reached over Stella to flip open the latch. "Give me some of those."

Dane began unpacking the tangle of beads and wire. "We figured we could at least undo the damage, and then you can tell us what we might be qualified to do to help fix them."

"Oh, it doesn't take any special skill," Stella said, pressing her hands to her hot cheeks. "Once you know how to string them and pinch the clasp."

"But your designs are uniquely yours," Melinda said. "Show us how you want them to look, and we'll make sure you don't lose all those orders. It's not too late, is it?"

"No. I mean, the order is late right now, but they haven't fussed about it."

"Then let's get busy," Melinda said.

"This is mighty nice of you all," Stella said.

"It's mighty nice for you to take care of all of us all these years," Dot said. "Think of all the mothers and babies who've been through your doors."

"It's been nothing, really," Stella said, sorting the loose green and purple beads into piles by size and cut. "Just something to pass the time. You ladies are the ones who need to get yourselves out and knocked up again, so you don't need to darken my door anymore."

Jake moved behind Melinda, putting his hands on her shoulders. Stella noted his protective stance and said, "Looks like you two already got something going."

Melinda smiled. "Yes, Stella. We're not really telling anyone yet, because, well, you know, it's so scary to think of going through it all again, but we are expecting."

"We just tested two days ago," Jake said.

"Good for you," Stella said, her throat constricting. "I can't wait for you to name that little one Stella Louise."

They all laughed.

"But I was going to name MY next one Stella Louise!" Dot said.

Melinda pulled a kinked-up wire free from a row of purple beads. "Stella knows she's secured her legacy. There are hundreds of women in this town who have been helped through dark days by her. We're very grateful."

Dot sat forward and tugged another handful of bracelets from the snarl. "Here's something I believe." She held up a green bracelet so that the sun shone clear through the colors on the beads. "I believe that when women like us meet, that our children in heaven also find their way to each other, on account of us all being in the same place and them watching over. So they're all together—Stella your pair, Melinda's, and mine. Right now, they're up there, singing maybe, or playing Red Rover, and probably laughing at us sitting around trying to fix a mess we ourselves made."

"That's beautiful," Melinda said, and they all looked through the bracelet and into the sky.

The sun burned fine and white overhead, and Stella raised a wire of amethyst gems to join Dot's peridot. The colors winked at her in the light of high noon. These were the birthstones of her children, the beginning and end of her motherhood.

She might have lost them, and not been able to be a mother proper to anyone, but she did have this, a good and strong purpose, a way to make a difference to people. And for that, she was definitely grateful. She wouldn't question it again.

The kids shouted nearby, a happy sound, and their fathers watched over them. Melinda and Dot admired the bracelets and how they were made, ready to help her. Stella looked at the women, remembering the faces of so many others who had passed through her life in their darkest days. Here today, in this green garden of sunshine and, eventually, a memorial site named for her, she was happy.

"I think we better get started," Melinda said. "Stella needs that order done."

Stella took one last glance at their uplifted bracelets. The bright flecks of green and purple sunlight rained down on her friends like the finest sparkle of dust.

AFTERWORD

Dozens of women provided the details that went into this book. Dot's surgery is set in the doctor's office where I was sent after a sonogram at twenty weeks revealed that my baby no longer had a heartbeat.

I was not warned ahead of time that the place where I would have my surgery was actually an abortion clinic. The glass bottles, the laughing gas, and the admonishment not to cry all happened to me.

Two details were not mine: another courageous mother shared having to watch the heartbeat go to zero after a fetal diagnosis meant the baby would die soon, and her own life was in danger. And another mom was told just before surgery that she needed to lose weight. I've since learned about a dozen more women who received callous comments about their weight during these already traumatic moments.

A piece of Melinda's tale comes from a mom who was on an out-of-state trip when she passed the sac and placenta of her miscarriage. She simply had to put everything in a garbage bag and leave it in a trash can, which haunted her a long time. Many mothers reported rocking baby blankets, dolls, or sonogram printouts after their loss, but Melinda's repeated retrieval of the baby from the freezer is purely fiction.

Accounts of managing stepchildren were generously detailed to me by those moms. Their insights were so helpful in shaping Melinda, especially stories of the ex-wives making the new wife into a villain even after a miscarriage. The story of one stepmother and stepdaughter finding a way to reconcile by making an angel scrapbook struck me so deeply that I included it in the novel.

Stella was shaped by several stories. One proud mama wears only jewelry made of peridot and amethyst for her baby's birthstones. Another mother had the experience of a close friend naming her baby the same name as her stillborn daughter because, "She hadn't really gotten to use the name." Another woman confessed to secretly drinking alcohol during baby showers. (I would too!)

The campfire scene really happened to one couple. The problem with how to handle a miscarried baby at home comes up often. Freezing the baby is one solution. Others bury them in the back yard. Sometimes the tissue is just flushed in the toilet. There is no easy way to do any of this. I encourage women to simply do what makes sense to you at the time. One of the brave mamas who gave details for this book kept the placenta to her baby in her freezer for two years just as Dot does.

One very common scene that did not make it into the novel, but one I've heard probably over one hundred times now, is hospital personnel in the ER dropping the miscarried babies into the hazardous waste containers while the mother is in the room. Stella makes reference to this. Really, this practice must stop.

The story is set in Houston, where I taught middle school. The High School for Pregnant Teens does not exist as depicted, although campuses like it opened across the country during the teen pregnancy boom in the 1990s. Houston ISD used to provide the "Kay Village," a program for pregnant girls. This school was rolled into a career center in 2006 and is scheduled for closure in 2011.

Title IX prevents pregnant girls from being forced to attend a separate school, but many districts provide this voluntary option. These schools' policies on what happens when the baby is miscarried or stillborn will vary. The miscarriage rate among teenagers is similar to the general population for first pregnancies—between ten and fifteen percent.

Many adults seem to assume that teenagers will be relieved to "get on with their lives" if their pregnancies end in miscarriage. I have learned from the teens who write me that this is not always the case, and a good number of them grieve and are completely unsupported in their grief.

Molar pregnancies like Janet's are indeed rare, but they do happen. Over the last decade, frustrated and worried women have emailed me, asking why their doctors won't pay attention to their symptoms, telling them to just "wait it out." I think this happens because obstetricians see so many situations, and most of the time, it works out the way they expect—the recovery may be short, medium, or long, but will not require intervention. But statistics like one in five hundred are meaningless if you are the *one*. I always tell women who can't get through to their doctors to start looking for one whose office responsiveness matches her needs. Not every doctor and every patient are going to be a good fit.

The women whose stories were included know who they are, as they were present for the blog posts and emails back in 2006 when *Baby Dust* began. Naturally, these situations happen over and over again, and I hope others take some comfort in knowing so many of us have walked the same path. We are survivors, and like Stella said, sometimes we don't have the luxury of acting like normal people. All anyone can expect is that we will do the best we can to recover and hold on to hope.

RESOURCES

Facts about Miscarriage
www.pregnancyloss.info
Deanna Roy created this web site in 1998 after the loss of Casey. It contains hundreds of pages of information on miscarriage, from symptoms to testing to recovery to trying again for another pregnancy. Visit our Facebook group by searching for "A Place for Our Angels."

Pregnancy and Infant Loss Remembrance Day
www.october15th.com
Robyn Bear worked tirelessly to have October 15 declared a national remembrance day in all fifty states. At 7 p.m. in your time zone, all over the world, grieving families light a candle for one hour to create a continuous wave of light in memory of our lost babies.

Faces of Loss, Faces of Hope
www.facesofloss.com
With the goal of making pregnancy loss as open a topic as breast cancer has become, the women of Faces of Loss post stories with the pictures of the mothers who have lost their babies as well as established local coffee groups of grieving moms throughout the US.

INCIID Infertility and Miscarriage Bulletin Board

http://www.inciid.org/

A lifesaving group of women and some of their spouses who will support you, tell you what to expect, and be a ready listener. They also have medical forums where doctors will answer your questions.

Mothers in Sympathy and Support

http://www.misschildren.org/

An extremely well done web site dealing with all aspects of miscarriage and its aftermath, including a pen pal system for bereaved mothers to contact other bereaved mothers.

Share

http://www.nationalshare.org/

A large, comprehensive miscarriage site with workshops, memorial gardens for baby dedications, and many poems and testimonials from bereaved parents.

HAND Support

http://www.handsupport.org/pregnancy-loss.html

HAND is a support group that has developed a very good fact sheet detailing what parents should do in the first hour, day, and weeks after a miscarriage.

The Compassionate Friends

http://www.compassionatefriends.org

A large organization focused on surviving the loss of a child of any age, with grief resources as well as their own remembrance day in December.

A Place to Remember

http://www.aplacetoremember.com/

An online memory garden with bookstores and other resources for memorializing babies, including funeral items.

In Memory of These Babies

Gabrielle Mary Johnson ~ 3-16-11

Lauren Elizabeth Corathers ~ 03-28-08

Peighton Larke ~ 2-09

Ryliegh Lianna Chalico ~ 05-17-11

Caleb Andrew Cordell ~ 11-06-03

Phillip Parker Cordell ~ 01-24-10

Lyndsee Paten Cordell ~ 06-15-11

Caleb Matthew Rowden ~ 6-10-11

Phillp Vincent ~ 10-30-07

Christopher Anthony ~ 1-15-98

Ti'Lynne Nicole ~ 7-6-02

Gabrielle Mary Johnson ~ 3-16-11

Bella Claire ~ 07-22-10

Ricardo Jr. ~ 02-18-11

Vincent Louis LeRoy ~ 1-16-04

Joy Noelle Cameron Delaney Bowers ~ 6-11-11

Baby Avitia ~ 8-22-10

Taylor Pentz ~ 11-05

Abigail Elizabeth Pentz ~ 7-9-06

Blake Thomas ~ 8-23-2010

Kinston Matthew McLendon ~ 3-30-11

Austen Leigh Hagenbuch ~ 7-11-10

Lauren Elizabeth Corathers ~ 3-28-08

Kaysen Phillips Damren ~ 01-05-11

Evan James Biffle ~ 6-2-11

Grady Leonard Bornhorst-Meade ~ 04-08-11

Oscar Young ~ 4-24-2011

Luis Álvarez-Morphy González ~ 12-15-10

Travis Dietrich ~ 9-27-07

Baby Boo ~ 4-3-04

Cameron Avery ~ 12-28-09

AA Lewis ~ 8-1997

Christian James Lewis ~ 8-6-04

MJ Lewis ~ 9-22-04

Melody Antonia ~ 11-14-1996

Joshua Antony ~ 10-16-05

Sophie Angharad ~ 04-17-06

Ashlee Elizabeth Phipps ~ 7-17-03

Christian Hinshaw ~ 1-29-04

Meredith Hinshaw ~ 3-7-05

Baby Thurston ~ 3-17-09

Taylor ~ 5-1-08

Taylor Sharitt ~ 9-16-09

Nolan Timothy Bernard ~ 2-19-11

Luke, Alanna & Noah Avallone ~ 11-4-08

Megan Mele ~ 9-25-04

Baby Boo Mele ~ 2-8-07

Little One Mele ~ 4-24-07

Samuel Mele ~ 8-7-07

Christina Mele ~ 3-7-08

Christopher Mele ~ 7-29-08

Pumpkin Mele ~ 1-23-09

Kaycee ~ 1-28-10

Kamrie Rose ~ 2-22-11

Leto Gumkowski ~ 12-19-08

Annalease Nichole Reed Lost ~ 2-17-11

Lucas Charles Wood (Luke) ~ 12-24-10

Gabriel Adam Townsend ~ 1-30-10

Bella Mae Martin ~ 2-11

Ayden Hebert ~ 10-14-09

Eseranza Gemini Olvera

& Carina Gemini Olvera ~ 1-14-10

Baby Olvera ~ 4-14-11

Isaiah Ray Vaughn ~ 07-1997

Faith Renae Vaughn ~ 04-1998

Noah Christopher ~ 4-27-11

Brianna Rena' ~ 4-26-11

Baby "Gregory" Albamonte ~ 9-28-09

Hadley Alice Miller ~ 9-24-10

Conley Andrew Miller ~ 7-6-10

R.W. Fletcher ~ 3-19-07

Eagan Nathaniel ~ 4-30-10

Baby Boo Traudt ~ 4-30-11

Brooklyn Rose Vaughn ~ 3-10-01

Calvin ~ 7-14-02

Angel ~ 5-10-05

"Cougar" ~ 11-28-11

Matthew Ellis ~ 5-29-09

Gummy Bear ~ 2-06

Emily and Amelia Brickley ~ 3-18-1995

Hannah Rose Brickley ~ 3-10-07

Nathaniel Brickley ~ 10-10-07

Renee

Joy

Adolph

Robin

Fran

Arlene

Lucy Barbour ~ 12-5-1998

Aleah ~ 9-29-10

Reilley Pugh ~ 6-23-08

Brierley Isabel Samul ~ 10-25-05

Henry Philip Samul ~ 7-5-06

RuthAnn Samul ~ 2-11-07

Olivia Grace Samul ~ 12-19-08

Baby Haggerty ~ 8-31-08

Macayla BriAnn Clanton ~ 12-21-06

James Michael Bargmann ~ 10-23-06

Veronica ~ 4-19-07

Baby M ~ 10-14-07

Baby Simpson ~ 6-18-10

Kennedy Kate Cedars ~ 10-22-09

Hayley Paige Brooks-Oakley ~ 7-21-02

Caspar joe Holt 4th-16th ~ 11-09

Evangeline Violet Edgeton ~ 8-7-07

Grace Loewen ~ 9-23-10

Hunter Louis Fratangeli ~ 2-5-09

Joshua Michael ~ 11-25-11

Marissa Leigh ~ 4-22-05

Gabriel Alexander ~ 1-3-11

Jessica Skye Sylvester ~ 8-8-10

Hunter Joshua Tyler Saurer ~ 8-24-10

Olivia Sue ~ 5-20-10

Abigail Facer ~ 1998

Cooper Christine Fresh ~ 4-5-11

Braydon John Kimbrough ~ 8-8-10

Connor Blaze Robinson ~ 5-9-07

April Serenity Rox ~ 4-10

Hannah Grace Henson ~ 5-12-09

Gabreal Rae Clark ~ 7-16-07

Colin Daniel Williams ~ 1-27-11

Zachary Alexander Evans-Connors ~ 1-3-11

Braden Thomas Barrett ~ 6-2-10

Tyler Eric Bruno 19w3d ~ 12-24-10

Ryan Angel Ogilvie ~ 4-7-11

Elaina Hope Fast ~ 3-8-11

Raphael Dubree Ramlall ~ 1-21-11

The Cloke Triplets ~ 1-7-11

Cadyn Joseph

Adalyn Grace

Mikayla Michelle

Asher Draven Fowler ~ 1-6-11

Jeffery Scott Kimbrough ~ 5-4-1990

Matilda Lamond ~ 12-11-10

Noah Mbangweta ~ 9-24-10

Jaydn ~ 8-3-05

Keagan James Niehaus ~ 3-18-10

Jacob, Jeremy and Justin ~ 9-24-99

Gabriella Reann Beasley ~ 7-11-10

Katarina Francesca Bianco ~ 8-25-06

Aaden Drew Stambaugh ~ 5-30-09

Sophie Clegg ~ 3-17-09

Gavin Christopher ~ 5-6-11

Avery Addison Winker ~ 12-5-11

Baby Kolm ~ 2-12-09

Luke Howard Pendleton ~ 7-6-10

Baby "Colt" ~ 5-18-11

Baby Lockard ~ 12-1-10

Catherine Rose BeDard ~ 5-23-1999

Jordan Lynn Schmid ~ 12-15-07

Natalie Grace ~ 5-14-00

Yuri Gold ~ 4-13-11

Baby Amelia ~ 5-9-11

Daniel ~ 6-16-05

Shaedia Elizabeth Hernandez ~ 1-5-11

Michail Lowell Myers ~ 6-24-1980

CaMya Jamise Terry ~ 9-22-03

Odhin John Keith Yates ~ 5-12-11

Daniel Joaquin Gonzales ~ 6-9-10

Jillian Paige Wiles ~ 6-8-03

Spring ~ 6-3-11

Dove ~ 6-10-11

Paygyn Hope Kitchen ~ 12-29-10

Baby Kozera ~ 5-11-11

Nathan Needham ~ 5-28-11

Kezia Nicole Bergquist ~ 6-18-11

Hope Rowland ~ 4-28-11

Coralee Grace Carroll

& Brayden Chance Carroll ~ 9-7-10

Caleb Sheldon Jenna Maggie ~ 7-4-04

Evan James Biffle ~ 6-2-2011

Nikki Perez ~ 1-19-06

Savannah Elaine Berumen-Owens ~ 5-24-11

Baby Angel ~ 6-13-11

Collins Randall Huffman ~ 5-18-11

Jared Everhardt ~ 5-18-11

Isla Gray ~ 2-25-11

Jackson David Frazee ~ 8-21-05

Kevin Charles Sorbin ~ 6-1-11

Evangeline Mariah ~ 2-27-1991

Lincoln Anthony Clason ~ 10-1-10

Amelia Hanna Williams ~ 06-21-11

Travis Dietrich ~ 9-27-07

William Alejandro Kramer ~ 8-23-10

Jose Antonio Febles ~ 4-24-11

Baby "Able" Hagerman ~ 7-1-11

Taylor ~ 11-05

Abigail Elizabeth ~ 7-9-06

Baby Jirovec ~ 07-19-2009

Autumn Katherine Sullivan ~ 12-4-04

Brook Marie Olson ~ 10-4-04

Connor Allen Olson ~ 07-28-06

Garson Lee Olson ~ 11-2-10

Jameson Manigo-Ritter ~ 5-30-11

Christian Lee Stamey ~ 8-27-10

Lauren Elizabeth Corathers ~ 3-28-08

Stella Grace Carland ~ 12-23-10

Sofia Rodrigues ~ 5-11-11

CPSIA information can be obtained at www.ICGtesting.com
Printed in the USA
LVOW101212260712

291674LV00001B/129/P

9 780984 187928